A BREWSKI FOR THE OLD MAN

A BREWSKI FOR THE OLD MAN

PHYLLIS SMALLMAN

Cheers!

Phyllis Smallman

McArthur & Company
Toronto

This edition published in Canada in 2010 by
McArthur & Company
322 King Street West, Suite 402
Toronto, Ontario
M5V 1J2
www.mcarthur-co.com

Library and Archives Canada Cataloguing in Publication

Smallman, Phyllis
A brewski for the old man / Phyllis Smallman.

(A Sherri Travis mystery)
ISBN 978-1-55278-836-3

I. Title. II. Series: Smallman, Phyllis. Sherri Travis mystery.

PS8637.M36B74 2010   C813'.6   C2009-907361-7

Cover and text design by Tania Craan
Printed in Canada by Webcom

The publisher would like to acknowledge the financial support
of the Government of Canada through the Canada Book Fund
and the Canada Council for our publishing activities. The publisher
further wishes to acknowledge the financial support of the Ontario
Arts Council and the OMDC for our publishing program.

10 9 8 7 6 5 4 3 2 1

For my children of the heart

Margaret Everett
&
Dominic Wild

CHAPTER 1

Brian Spears put his right hand up to his right cheek to cover his motioning left forefinger.

"Is that a transvestite?"

I looked down the bar to where he was pointing. "Either trannie or a regular guy who makes really bad clothing choices."

His voice rose with his eyebrows in outrage. "Do you allow them in here?"

"Honey, I allow you in here, which goes to show how broad-minded I am…broad-minded and broad-assed, although I don't think the two always go together."

Three stools away Peter raised his hand. He either wanted permission to leave the room or he was signaling for another drink. Since we were in the Sunset Bar and Grill down in Jacaranda, Florida, I was betting it was another Scotch he wanted and since I, Sherri Travis, was behind the bar, I went and got him a fresh drink.

Customers were really ticking me off that night. Normally I can put up with any damn thing, but at that moment I wished they'd all disappear, which of course would make me do the same. You see, I'd recently acquired the Sunset — or at least the bank and a silent partner, who had way too much to say, allowed me to work here about twelve or fourteen hours a day, seven days a week. Nice of them, wasn't it? Anyway, the whole world was bugging me that night.

"You're starting to sound just like Miss Emma," Brian told me when I came back to drop off his third and last drink of the night.

"Ah, so my surliness hasn't gone unnoticed."

"Not for a moment."

Memories of Miss Emma brought an answering smile to my face. "Miss Emma hired me when I left Jimmy and came back to Jacaranda to start over. She owned the Sunset then."

Brian said, "Wasn't she something?"

I shook my finger under his nose and did a bad imitation of a wonderful old broad. "Be careful, girl. Pay attention and don't believe everything you hear." I laughed. "You know how I make a decision these days?"

"I shudder to think," said Brian, sipping his Grey Goose with lime.

"I ask myself, what would Miss Emma do?"

"Well, that should give you lots of scope for mayhem."

"If you can't think for yourself, that's what happens. You turn into someone else." I glanced down the bar to where she had always perched on the stool farthest from the door, a living Buddha with piercing black eyes. "She could watch the whole room from there and sometimes, when I move quick, I think I catch a glimpse of her still watching the till like a hawk with his eye on a mouse."

"I thought it was the customers she had her eye on," Brian said.

"Oh, she watched the customers too, but it was the money

that really interested her. By the end of the night she'd know within a buck or two what should be in the till. It certainly discouraged sticky fingers, always a problem when cash is involved, and it's one of the reasons I slip behind the bar every night and mix a few drinks. Doesn't hurt to keep a real close eye on things and let the staff know you're there, just like Miss Emma did."

Brian added, "That woman knew everything about everyone, knew all their secrets and everything that went on in Jacaranda. She was a great big sponge, taking it all in and not giving anything back until you squeezed her real hard."

"And good luck to anyone trying that," I added. "She'd probably bite their arm off."

"Yeah," Brian's blue eyes sparkled. "Miss Emma could be a bit gruff."

"Gruff? Hell, she was downright caustic," I corrected. "Like the night a man sat down next to her and politely asked, 'Do you mind if I smoke?' Miss Emma gave a gigantic shrug and said, 'Smoke? I don't care if you burn up.'"

Brian wheezed with laughter, trying to get words out and pointing at me.

"If you're trying to tell me I'm beginning to act like her," I told him, "I already know it."

Brian nodded madly in agreement.

I sighed. "Yeah, these days I just don't care if you burn up."

"Well, it hasn't been a good year for you." Brian wiped his face with a pudgy hand. "First we get hit by Hurricane Myrna and then you get kidnapped by a psychopath — bound to take the shine off the apple."

The summer before, Hurricane Myrna had blown through Cypress Island and almost destroyed the Sunset. The previous owner, the guy who'd bought it from Miss Emma, was in financial trouble and couldn't find the money to rebuild. So, taking a nice little bit of insurance money I got when my god-awful husband was murdered, this fool rushed in where angels fear to tread and bought the Sunset. Unfortunately, the only thing I knew anything about was serving behind the bar. So there I was, up the yingyang in debt, learning on the job, and my partner…well, that's another story.

"How you doing, Sherri?" Brian asked and quickly raised his hand up to stop me from telling him I was just fine. "No, really, don't just make a joke. I want to know. Are you able to sleep again?"

"One good thing about the hours I keep, if I don't stay up worrying about the bailiff visiting, I'm unconscious when I hit the bed." I wasn't being entirely honest with Brian. The panic attacks were milder but ghosts and angst crowded the darkness. But the ghosts were my secret, no need to share them with Brian.

Miss Emma had known all about secrets. The day after I started work she knew about Jimmy, knew I'd left him to start a new life on my own and knew it was touch and go if I'd ever break free. Most of the story she got from me, not that she ever asked. Actually, she never showed much interest but I was compelled to tell her everything, just like her customers did.

It always amazes me what people will tell a complete stranger after a little alcohol. Worse than that, it's shocking what they'll tell the person behind the bar, someone who actually knows their name and someone they're going to have to face again. And after a night, or maybe an afternoon of standing with a foot on the brass rail, the next day they can't meet your eye and treat you with great circumspection. They only return to normal after you win them over, make them think you've forgotten everything they said and certainly don't hold any of it against them. You have to convince them it's all water down the drain — and it pretty much is.

I knew everyone in Jacaranda, although I didn't grow up there. We were too poor to live on Cypress Island. Even thirty years ago, working people had all been pushed back inland. I grew up just over the bridge on the mainland in a single wide trailer at the edge of a swamp. But every day, beginning in grade one, I came over the humpbacked bridge on a yellow schoolbus, with its roof painted white in an attempt to stop us kids from being fried by the sun, so I knew most of these people real well, except of course the tourists who swarmed down here like a cloud of locusts come November. In May they finally go North and leave us to ourselves again. Actually, they were the freest with secrets 'cause they'll never see you again. The things those people get up to. A drink or two and you hear it all. I wonder if psychiatrists have ever considered serving their patients booze? It would work for me. A little liquid truth serum and I turn into a real motor mouth, boring even myself.

But like I was saying, working behind the bar you hear all about people's secrets. You hear who's sleeping with whose wife; who's on the edge of bankruptcy; and know who has the door open and is peeking out of the closet.

"You listen with your deaf ear, you hear?" Miss Emma always advised.

I wish I'd learned to take Miss Emma's advice. Listening to other people's troubles and caring, thinking I can actually help, are big failings of mine. I didn't know it that night but other people's secrets were about to drag me under, about to put me in harm's way.

CHAPTER 2

It was September. I was hanging on to the Sunset by my gnawed-off fingernails until the tourists arrived near Christmas and made me rich. Yeah, right, like that was ever going to happen. I'd never be more than one mortgage payment away from bankruptcy, but a girl can dream. I was only starting to realize how hard it is to own a white elephant and drive a Porsche, but that's not what I want to tell you about. Let me tell you about collecting the rents.

The Sunset is on the second floor of an old hotel out on the beach. Being on the second floor we look over the Beach Road traffic and acres of sand, dotted with colorful umbrellas, to the azure blue Gulf of Mexico. That's what brings the money up the stairs or gets them into that tiny breathless elevator — an endless view of the gulf.

Down below the Sunset are two stores: Rowell's Books and News and the Beach Bag, owned by Rena Cagel, a store full of beach clothing, cheap boogie boards and gift items like pieces of driftwood painted with shore birds. After the hurricane ripped through Jacaranda I bought the building. The tenant for the clothing store didn't return after the hurricane so Rena took over the lease. She worked almost as many hours a week as I did and without her sixteen-year-old daughter Lacey's free labor it would have be impossible for her to keep going. On the misery-loves-company principle, the three of us became friends, Lacey, Rena and I. We shared stories and sympathy about living on the edge of financial disaster, but it was a limited friendship you understand, we never shared our pasts. There was enough in our present financial quicksand to fuel the discussion.

The day after my conversation with Brian, I stepped out of the Sunset into a wall of Florida heat blown up from South America. At ten in the morning, when I arrived to start the day's work, it was in the eighties. When I took the stairs down to the covered patio where the stucco walls were painted with beach scenes, herons, palms and umbrellas, the temperature had spiraled into the high nineties, but at least the gulf delivered a breeze to dry the sweat that popped out all over my body.

"Excuse me." A young woman in beach gear came towards me holding out a tiny camera. "Would you mind taking our picture?" She pointed out the right button to push and hurried to snuggle up against her two giggling friends who where already posing in front of a faux palm.

Taking someone's picture in front of the beach scene painted on the side of the building is a daily occurrence. This patio, where people waited for a table to come free upstairs, was an attraction all its own. It's strange to me how many people have their picture taken here against the fake beach backdrop when the real thing is right across the road, but I feel I'm connected forever to people from all over the country through those photographs in unknown albums.

I handed back the camera and stepped into the Beach Bag

where Lacey was ringing up a purchase. Lacey was beautiful. There was no other word for her flawless golden skin, light brown hair and big hazel eyes. She had it all and, at thirty-one, I was just starting to look at young beauties like her with a tiny worm of jealousy and regret for what I'd had and didn't realize. Then again, probably at sixty I'll look at forty-year-olds the same way. Like the song says, "You don't know what you've got 'til it's gone."

Lacey handed a shocking pink shopping bag to her customer and greeted me with a smile. "How's it going, Sherri?"

"Brilliant, I'm at least a hundred bucks away from disaster. And you?"

She gave a soft lift of a shoulder and a lonesome fractured smile. "Okay." She crossed her arms over her chest. "We're surviving." She was a kid who looked like she had everything, a terrific mom, looks, brains, but there was an air about her that said something was missing, a deep well of sadness I just couldn't figure. This aura of sadness called out to me, tugged at my heart and spoke to my soul, awakening a strange protective instinct in me, something I wasn't accustomed to feeling.

Sometimes I feared for Lacey, worried that the blackness would swamp her, sweeping her away from us. Dramatic I know, but that's how it seemed. She always made me want to start tap dancing or making funny faces, anything to put a smile on her face.

"Mom said to give you this." She opened the till and brought out an envelope. "Rent check."

"Thanks. I'm going to the bank. Want me to bring you back a burger from Fat Tony's?"

A faint smile teased her lips, the best I ever got from her. "Isaak will kill you if he finds you eating someone else's food."

"True. He goes crazy if I eat anywhere else. I've started sneaking around and lying about why I won't be eating in. Being unfaithful is a new experience for me. Who knew I'd be cheating on a food Nazi that I pay, but sometimes you just crave variety." Her smile grew. I felt like I'd just won a marathon.

"He's a great chef, an asset for the Sunset and I was happy to steal him from the Bath and Tennis Club, but he's killing me. I've gained ten pounds since he became chef. Want fries?"

"Yup," Lacey said.

"We'll go crazy. I'll hide out down here with you and eat it. Isaak need never know."

Someone pulled up in front of the store. She turned to look and the laughter went out of her face, replaced by pain. Her back stiffened and her features hardened.

"Lacey?"

I stepped sideways to look out the window, expecting to see someone her own age, to see normal teenage stuff, broken hearts and broken friendships, but that wasn't it. It was far worse than that — for both of us.

The worst part of my past stared back at me. Lacey and I had something in common, shared a horrible secret. I looked to Lacey and saw my younger self in her eyes. I wanted to reach out to that other me, to comfort her, to make it right and to correct things left undone and erase an open sore in myself I'd nurtured too long.

A ghost, no, more than a ghost, a nightmare lurked beyond the glass.

CHAPTER 3

A hulking big boss SUV, black and raised up high over the wheels, crouched in front of the store. Spotlights that were mounted up near the roof, as if they were used for hunting down prey at night, gave it a malevolent, dangerous look. The driver, wearing a taupe-colored uniform, sat in the driver's seat with both hands locked on the steering wheel and stared straight through us. He was thick-necked with a military-style haircut, the way he'd always worn it.

Next to him, Rena, Lacey's mother, bent towards him as she spoke, her body soft and yielding, cajoling him. It told everything about their relationship. She reached out a hand to him, touched his arm, her body language saying she was begging. He didn't respond.

"Oh my god," I said. The words slipped from me unheeded. This was the man Rena talked about in worshipful tones. This was RJ.

I'd seen this scene acted out before in another time and another place. Only then it had been my own mother begging and pleading for love. Memories full of cruel, torturous emotions swamped me. For years, not a day had gone by that I hadn't thought about him. Not a day I hadn't cringed in shame at his memory. Now my feelings had changed. I wasn't afraid or embarrassed or sad anymore. Now blind rage hurtled through my body like a runaway train.

"Who is that?" I asked, although I knew perfectly well.

"Ray John Leenders," Lacey hissed. If I hadn't already guessed, her tone would have told me all I needed to know about what the man behind the wheel had done to her. Bile rose in my throat. I covered my mouth with my hand.

Rena bent forward to gather up her purse, paused, then leaned over to kiss Ray John softly on the cheek, cupping his square jaw with her hand. He didn't unfreeze.

She hopped down from the vehicle and closed the door gently with both hands. Rena was barely clear of the door when the brutish dark vehicle slammed backwards. The sign on the door said *The Preserves, Security, R.J. Leenders*. The SUV shot forward, hesitating but not stopping at the exit to the parking lot, before it took off down Beach Road.

Rena, stepping delicately across the sidewalk in stiletto heels designed for sitting not walking, tip-toed to the shop. She was really quite young to have a sixteen-year-old daughter, only in her late thirties, and she worked hard to keep her figure and looks. A strawberry blonde, perhaps more blonde than she'd been born, she still had the unlined porcelain skin of redheads.

She stepped through the tinkling door. "Oh god, these shoes are killing me." She gave us a glorious smile and minced towards the counter. "Ray loves high, high heels on me but then he doesn't have to walk in them." Behind the counter she bent to change into sandals, her breasts falling forward from the low-necked skin-tight tee. Her outfit was years too young for her, but I'd always assumed she dressed like that because most of the people coming into the store were young. Now I remembered that Ray John had always insisted that my mother dress provocatively. You don't cover up a prize. The whole point is to show off a trophy and have it admired by other men.

"We went to Brandy's for lunch. I put on pounds." Her hands stopped digging through her purse. She looked up at us. "What's the matter?" she said looking from one of us to the other. Panic flooded her face. "What's happened?"

"Nothing, nothing," I blurted out in denial. "Gotta go," I said and fled the store.

Outside the sun was still shining. Seagulls circled and called out over the sand and the heat still pounded down, but I was cold. I stood with my arms wrapped around me, huddled against the building where no one could see me, trying to get it straight. Ray John left when I was barely thirteen but hardly a day went by when I didn't remember my two years of hell. My pain was fresh and raw again.

"Get it together. Nothing has changed," I told myself. "Just stay away from him. Go on with your life and forget about the past. Lacey and Rena's problems have nothing to do with you. There isn't room in your life for anyone else's problems." All good advice and I tried to pay attention, I really did.

CHAPTER 4

I slipped in past the customer leaving Peter Rowell's bookstore. "Sherri," he called in greeting. Peter and I had hit it off from the beginning. Not only did we share a love of books, we were both crazy about golf. But I couldn't share Peter's other big passion, cricket, a game he'd tried to explain to me but one I'd never been able to grasp. His love of the game was reflected all over the store with the names of book sections written on cricket bats. Pictures of great British cricketers hung above the racks devoted to newspapers and the world's biggest display of magazines.

"Good morning," he sang out cheerfully. His sparkling blue eyes and English accent always brightened my spirits, but not that day.

"Hi," I replied.

Peter's smile melted and his brow furrowed. "Not your normal sunny self today." He tilted his head to the side. "Are you all right? You look like you've seen a ghost."

A harsh bark of laughter exploded from me. I put my fingertips over my lips to stop the sound. "A ghost, yes, I've seen a ghost." I reached out and spun a carousel display of bookmarks without seeing them. "Do ghosts from your past ever haunt you?"

"All the time." His voice was soft. "Ghosts can stop the sun." His gentle smile was full of sympathy. "You can't run away from ghosts. They always know where to find you." He reached below the counter and brought out an envelope containing the rent check and slid it across the counter towards me. "You're working too hard — every hour god sends. You need to get away from here."

"No matter how many hours I work, there still aren't enough."

"You need a vacation. That will take care of the ghosts."

"And who will do the work?"

"Get more help. How long has it been since you played golf? Before you played every day, now…" He lifted his shoulders. "It isn't worth it, Sherri. Listen to a man who knows what he's talking about."

There was no use telling him I was barely breaking even financially and one more person on the payroll would tip me over into bankruptcy.

"Buy a good mystery and sit out on the beach for the afternoon."

"Ah, so now I see. You aren't interested in me; you're just trying to drum up business." I smiled to show him I didn't for a moment believe it.

"Business is important but life comes first."

"Did Clay put you up to this? It's exactly what he was telling me just before he left." Never mind that Clay had even more money in the Sunset than I did — the hours I'd been working were leading to arguments between us. Clay told me that if he'd known he was never going to see me he wouldn't have come into the Sunset with me. In frustration he'd left two days before to crew in a yacht race from Miami to Cuba.

"How is the race going?" Peter asked. "Have they left for Cuba yet?"

"Nope, still stuck in Miami while protesters block their boats and federal agents search them. Their plan was to be gone for ten days, two weeks at the most. I don't think they're going to make that schedule now." What I didn't tell Peter was that I was happy with this delay. It would buy me a little time. Clay had said things had better change when he got back, an ultimatum I hadn't decided how to handle.

"Well, if Clay and I are both telling you the same thing, it must be true."

"I'll think about it on the way to the bank," I promised. And I did. There were things I didn't want to face, didn't want to deal with. Running away and starting over suddenly seemed very attractive.

When I returned with Lacey's burger and fries, Rena was busy with a customer. Lacey and I went to a small curtained-off office space at the back of the store and huddled on two little stools with our knees nearly touching. Lacey was dressed in khaki cargo pants and an oversized long-sleeved shirt over a tee. Unlike her mother, she never dressed suggestively but seemed to hide inside her clothes.

I handed Lacey a paper sack and said, "I'm taking the night off. Want to come to my place for dinner and a movie?" Even as I was asking I was calling myself all kinds of fool. I didn't want to know what was going on because then I'd have to deal with it. Miss Emma always said, "Don't rake the coals, 'less you want to start a fire."

Surprise lit Lacey's face — and why not? While I'd always been friendly towards her we were really too different in age to hang out. Somehow, without out really articulating it to myself, I'd decided I had to tell her what Ray John had done to me, to warn her if it hadn't already happened to her and let her know she wasn't alone if he'd already messed with her. That was all I was prepared to do, that much and no more.

"Yeah," Lacey said, cautious and uncertain. "Yeah, that sounds good."

CHAPTER 5

Lacey stopped dead in her tracks. "Wow." She turned around in the circular marble foyer of Clay's penthouse. "Wow," she said again when she had completed the circle.

"That's what everyone says." I pushed past her and led the way into the body of the apartment. "I'm denim and flip-flops and this is definitely haute couture."

I gave her the tour of Clay's penthouse apartment. Oh, excuse me, Clay always corrects me here, our penthouse apartment. Very little, besides my clothes swimming in the walk-in closet of the master bedroom, belongs to me, and those few things I brought with me scream out for attention, they look so out of place.

"I've never seen anything like this," Lacey said.

"Neither had I until I moved in to the Tradewinds but it didn't take long to get used to."

"He must be really rich." Her face turned red. "Sorry," she mumbled.

I laughed. "Let's take our pizza out to the conservatory. It overlooks the gulf."

I threw the crust of my pizza back into the cardboard box. "I have to tell you something, Lacey."

Her forehead wrinkled and she became very still. She waited. The bad news instinct in this kid was on full alert.

"When I was eleven, almost twelve, Ray John Leenders moved in with my mother and me."

Storm clouds formed in her eyes. I hurried on. "Not long after, he started trapping me in the hall or in the kitchen, anywhere, and touching me. I couldn't tell my mother. She loved him. She was wrapped up in him just like Rena is besotted with him now. I didn't want to make Ruth Ann choose between us and I guess I was embarrassed. Besides, I didn't think she'd believe me. I tried to stay away from him. I stayed at friends', begged to stay over at Marley's, anything not to be around him. Mom was a waitress and worked long hours so she wasn't always there, but Ray John was. And if I stayed at someone else's house, he'd come looking for me. Everyone thought it was so nice that he looked after a kid that wasn't his own."

She dropped the pizza onto her plate and stared down at it, body drooping, while I rushed on. "Things got worse. One day he tried to rape me but I got away." I took a deep breath and let it out slowly. Walking down memory lane stunk. "This time I told my mother. She believed me all right. I don't know why I doubted her." I pulled my hair back from my face and let it flop down my back. "Anyway, she was waiting for him when he came home. She lit right into him, said she was going to turn him in."

"He beat her, punched her right in the face. I got out an old shotgun of my dad's and threatened to kill him if he didn't stop. The damn shotgun wasn't even loaded. Didn't find that out 'til later but Ray John didn't know it."

"The thing was, the neighbors heard the ruckus and called the sheriff. The sheriff came in and found me holding the shotgun and screaming at Ray John that I was going to kill him."

Lacey's hands were trapped between her knees, shoulders hunched and eyes on the floor.

"Long and short of it was the sheriff took him on out of there. No charges were filed. Thing was, Ray John was a deputy sheriff."

She shrank into herself, making herself as small and self-contained as possible. She wouldn't look at me, didn't acknowledge my words in any way as I blundered on. "That was fine with me. I didn't want anyone to know what he'd been doing to me. I just wanted him gone and now he was. We never saw him again. I always thought the sheriff made it pretty clear to Ray John what would happen to him if he ever bothered us again."

Lacey was staring at her lap, her hair falling in front of her face like a veil.

"I don't figure Ray John has changed his ways, Lace. For a long time I didn't realize that, didn't realize he'd likely go after some other young girl, thought I was the only one. But I wasn't, was I?"

She stayed silent. I waited. Finally she shook her head no.

"Shit," I said, then, "tell me."

She did. Tears and choking sounds jumbled the words but she finally got it all out. It had been a lot worse for Lacey.

"I'm so sorry this happened to you, Lacey. I feel responsible. If we'd charged him back then maybe he would have gone to jail or something. Maybe this wouldn't have happened to you."

"No," she said, shaking her head. "RJ is responsible for this, not my mom, not you…RJ."

"We need to call the police now."

"No, no." She shook her head wildly and threw herself forward, grabbing my wrist. "Don't do that."

"But you can't go back there."

"Can I stay here?" She was begging not just with words but with her whole being.

I wanted to say, "God no." My own problems were more than enough to keep me up nights and I was no one's idea of a substitute parent, plus I really didn't know her.

But just as quickly as that thought entered my head came the denial. I knew her. Lacey was one more ghost, the shadow of the girl I used to be and if I didn't help her I was as guilty of her abuse as Ray John. I was stuck in her life the minute I looked out that window but what in hell was I letting myself in for?

Lacey called her mother on the phone and told her I'd invited her to stay out on the beach with me until Clay returned. She told her mom about the lap pool and gym and the tenth-floor penthouse with its conservatory full of orchids and the view out over the Gulf of Mexico. Told her mother about the amazing sunset and how much she wanted to stay. Finally Rena gave in.

"All we ever do is fight," Lacey told me. Relief from the bickering was probably what finally convinced Rena to let her stay, no solution to the situation but a time out for everybody.

Clothes were the next problem. I drove Lacey off the island, over the humpbacked bridge to the mainland and the neat subdivision of small ranch houses from the sixties where Rena and Lacey lived with Ray John. As we drew near the house, my pulse rate increased and sweat gathered in my armpits and around my hairline despite the air conditioning going full blast.

"He won't be there," Lacey said, as if she'd read my thoughts.

The house had white aluminum siding with black shutters. Along the front were shrubs, trimmed in perfect geometric shapes, nature tortured into submission. Tidy, tidy, tidy. Ray John was raised and trained in the military. He was a fanatic about neatness and controlling his environment, everything just so.

The shiny black painted door opened as we approached. Lacey didn't say hello but just slipped in past her mom, saying, "Sherri will take me to school and I'll come to the store when I get out." Already halfway down the hall, she called back, "It will be great."

Rena crossed her arms over her chest. The apprehensive look on her face told me she regretted letting herself be talked into this and was having serious second thoughts. "I'm not sure about this," she began.

"Really, Rena, I'll enjoy having company."

"I've heard," she sucked her lips in-between her teeth and bit down on them. "Well, I've heard some things about you." Embarrassment made her add, "Really, Sherri, I think you're great. You've been really good to us with the store and everything, but I heard your husband was murdered." She lifted her shoulders in embarrassment. "People say things."

"Did they tell you that a man was sent to jail for that?" I was betting she didn't know how close I'd come to being arrested for Jimmy's murder.

"Yes." But still she frowned. "There was that thing last year, those other murders."

"Odd, isn't it? They're the only murders we're ever likely to have here on Cypress Island and I was touched by them all. But that's just because it's a small town. Everyone here could say the same thing. They knew the people who were murdered plus the murderer."

She nodded, taken in by my logic but still not convinced a murderer wasn't going to jump out of the bushes if I was around. For a while that was pretty much how everyone in town felt about me. No one wanted to get too close in case they became an accidental target, but time had mellowed their discomfort.

"I just don't want anything to happen to Lace."

"Of course not. Neither do I."

Lacey bolted out from behind Rena with a suitcase and a bookbag. The kid must have had the suitcase already packed to be back so quick. Lacey scooted past her without stopping to say goodbye, just calling, "See ya," over her shoulder as she bolted to the pickup. Rena watched Lacey flee, opened her mouth to say something and then closed it. She hugged herself tighter. "I guess it'll be all right."

The truck door slammed. "Really, it will be fine," I told her.

My mobile rang as I pulled out of the drive. "You're kidding," I said when I heard who was calling and what they wanted. Now for sure I wasn't going to be lonely and that was fine with me. I'd spent the two nights since Clay left with the lights on 'til morning. Company was just fine with me.

CHAPTER 6

When we got back to the Tradewinds, Marley was waiting for us with a suitcase in her hand. Her face said, "Do not ask questions and don't mess with me." I didn't. Having been friends with Marley Hemming since Kittridge Elementary School, I knew when to remain silent for the sake of my own wellbeing. Besides, I knew what was wrong.

But I couldn't keep from poking at the bear in the cage for long. "How's David?" I asked as the elevator slid open in front of us.

She growled like a mad dog and jerked her suitcase inside.

"Marley is engaged to David Halliday," I told Lacey. "He's way too good for her, a Baptist minister even. Saint David I like to call him. I don't know what Marley calls him…probably sir." I slid my plastic key into the slot. "Marley's reformed now. She's gone from a party girl to a minister's future wife. That's a long trip, like from here to the moon, and it isn't going so well. Trying to be a saint like David is weighing heavy on her and pissing off just about everybody else who comes in contact with Marley."

Lacey looked from Marley to me, eyes wide and waiting for the explosion.

Marley glared at me, her jaw jutting out and the corners of

her mouth turned down. Her fiery red curls and sapling thin body throbbed with energy and life and it was touch and go if she was going to turn nine again and swing for me with her suitcase. Even the freckles on her face looked like they were ready to hop off and do battle.

She turned back to stare at the door.

"Even getting things done yesterday isn't fast enough for Marley so sitting still with ankles crossed and a cup of tea in her hand is a form of torture she'd only submit to for the love of a good man. I've done my best to drag her back to her evil ways, smoking and drinking, but she's tougher than I'd ever have thought. Temptation isn't going to take her down without a fight. Maybe you can help me with this, Lacey. Try to get her cussing or spitting or something."

"You two are friends, aren't you?" Lacey said. Something in her voice, a longing, and a yearning so great it was painful to hear made both Marley and I turn to her.

"Don't you have friends, Lacey?" Marley asked.

Lacey shook her head and looked down at the floor.

Marley looked at me over Lacey's bent head and mouthed, "Asshole."

The elevator opened in front of the doors to Clay's apartment.

"Last stop, ladies." I led the way.

As we crossed the circular foyer of the apartment with the pale marble floors, I said, "All girls together, it's been a long long time since I had a slumber party."

"If we can stand it, so can you," Marley said, marching off with the suitcase rattling behind her.

"Are you running away from the ladies of the choir, hiding out from the bible class or some other little factions at the First Baptist Church of Fellowship?" I asked her back. She ignored me, charging for the guest room like a determined matron at a Macy's sale.

My friend was really unhappy. I was going to enjoy this new situation. I was usually the one in shit up to my eyeballs and Marley was the friend giving the good advice and telling me what I should have done. How lovely to be the one making superior pronouncements. Of course, this was only going to work until she asked how Clay and I were getting along. Then…well, then I'd be forced to lie, one of the few things on earth I truly excel at.

Behind me Lace moved cautiously through the door. "Are you sure it's all right?" she whispered, suddenly shy.

"Honey, if the place survived me, you won't be a shock." I took the handle of her trundle suitcase. "Just don't annoy Mrs. Whiting, the housekeeper. She's really in charge here and she's going to complain like hell if we move the slightest little thing. Every day when I come home she's hidden every tube of lipstick away, insists that the apartment look exactly like it did when that glossy magazine photographed it. This is a shrine and she is its keeper. We are the mere mortals she is forced to tolerate."

Marley had already parked her ass in a chair in the guestroom, denim-clad legs splayed and arms thrown out over the sides of a chair covered in moiré silk. She looked really unhappy. How delightful. "Do you intend to share?" I asked.

"No," was her gracious reply.

"Charming." I trundled the suitcase past the door. "Looks like it's the den for you, Lace."

She followed silently behind me, still shocked and over-whelmed by the eighteen-foot ceilings, marble and mahogany that stunned any newcomer to Clay's world. The overpowering wealth of the place had terrified me when I first met Clay, but now I hardly saw it. It's true that you can get used to just about anything, but I've decided, given a choice, I'd rather get accustomed to excess rather than the stripped-down poverty I'd spent my life in.

The apartment was done in what the *Florida Interiors* magazine called the Plantation style. Sounded silly to me. I didn't think the stone urns full of orchids out in the conservatory qualified as a plantation.

I switched on the light to brighten the den, a room decorated in willow green, straw and cream colors. A pretty room, it was less formal than the rooms in the rest of the penthouse, which made it my favorite room in the three-thousand-square-foot apartment. "The couch pulls out into a queen-sized bed, the bathroom is over there, the TV is in this armoire, okay?"

Lacey nodded and said, "It's lovely," but then she probably would be willing to sleep out on the beach to be safe from the hands of R.J. Leenders.

Never one to sulk for long, Marley came out of her bedroom as we made up the sofa bed.

"Okay, you two finish this," I said. "I'm off to call Clay. I need a little sweet talk." The one thing I wouldn't be talking about to Clay was Ray John. He was a secret I hadn't shared with Clay yet.

But Clay had too much on his mind to be worrying about me. "There are more police, Coast Guard, Customs agents, Florida Marine Patrol, you name it, there are more of them than there are boaters or anti-Cuba marchers. Our boat was searched again today."

"What were they looking for?"

"Beats me, but they found a pile of booze in Kevin's locker. I didn't know how much he drinks and no one but me seems concerned about it. It's all still in there; they weren't looking for booze but for something else."

"What?"

"Who the hell knows?

"They must have some reason for searching the boats although I thought they'd be more worried about things coming into the country than going out."

"I think everyone is overdosing on paranoia, but it looks like they're going to let us leave tomorrow." He fell silent before adding in rather a sheepish tone, "To tell the truth, I've been trying to talk the guys out of it. Just forget the whole damn thing and go home."

"Is it that dangerous? If there's any question in your mind if it's safe to sail to Havana just forget about it. Fly back and I can pick you up in an hour. Let them go on without you."

"Well, that's not really it," he said. "It's safe enough." His tone was tender and reluctant.

"Not safety? You don't think it's dangerous?"

"No, it's not safety that's the issue."

"Then what's worrying you?"

Big sigh. "I'm just missing you," hesitant and almost pained. "I guess that's what's worrying me. Man, when did I turn into such a wimp?"

"Oh, you miss your sugar. You need a little candy, a little

sweet, honey?" That's when the safe-sex part started, although this was just a little too safe for my liking. I could've handled something a little more high risk than phone sex.

When I went back to the den forty minutes later I found Marley and Lacey well into the bonding rituals of females on their own.

"I kid you not," Marley was telling Lacey, who was sitting cross-legged on the bed while Marley lounged across the bottom. "Tell her it's true," Marley ordered. "Tell her that everyone in your family is named after states or cities."

"Well, not everyone. But we have a few." I flopped down in a butter yellow leather chair and held up my hand and started ticking off the names. "There's Aunt Carolina, Aunt Virginia, Aunt Georgia and then Aunt Atlanta. I have an uncle named Dakota and one named Nevada."

Lacey put her hand over her mouth to hide her smile. "My family was so poor Grandma used a beat-up old atlas of the U.S. to name her eight children instead of a baby book. Or maybe she had wanderlust. I'm only sure she had an atlas and they were poor. Thank god she stopped having kids before she got to Poughkeepsie."

Lacey's hand couldn't quite hide her smile.

"My dad is named Tulsa."

"But it worked," Marley put in. "Your Aunt Virginia was well named, virgin by name and virgin by inclination. That woman is just too ugly and mean to ever find a man."

"And Aunt Georgia, she was well named," I pointed out. "She's sweet, a real peach."

"Yeah, fuzzy and round. I think her mustache may be her best feature. Hasn't that woman ever heard of depilatories? Of course, she'd have to bathe in it." Marley pointed a finger at me. "See where your genes are leading you?"

Lacey snorted with laughter, spraying soda over herself.

I'd known her for six months and never seen her laugh outright. It was a good feeling if only temporary but maybe even this would show her things could get better.

"Listen Saint Marley, don't go trashing my family. At least none of them spread manure from the church door to the altar."

"Oh, trust you to bring that up."

"That's why she's hanging out here," I explained. "The Baptist church elders are out to lynch her."

Lacey's smiled faded. She looked at Marley and then me. "Really?"

Before Marley could answer, I jumped in with the story. "It came with Marley's handling of the Christmas pageant. Marley took over the pageant, just as she takes over everything she's associated with, and decided that what they really needed was to have Mary ride into the church on a real donkey. That wasn't too bad, despite the little deposit the donkey left on the way up the center aisle; it was the loud fart in the middle of the prayers and the hysteria it caused among the junior choir that sent events spiraling downhill."

Lacey was laughing again and even Marley stopped looking like she had a bellyache. "The sheep and the cow were no better behaved and the smell of barnyard did nothing to improve the behavior of the choir, and what should have been a magical evening turned into Barnum & Bailey when one little angel stepped forward for her solo and joined the rest of the animals, peeing on the altar steps."

"That wasn't my fault," Marley protested. "I can't be held responsible for that kid's bladder control."

"Oh yeah? Didn't you fill them full of juice and cookies before the parade?"

Marley was never one to give up on a good idea. "The church was packed. They never had so many kids in the choir or so many bums in the pews. Wasn't that the point, to get people out for the Christmas Eve service and make it a real Christmas experience?"

"Perhaps it was just too real for the elders, all that poop and stuff."

"What did they get so bent out of shape about?" Marley asked. Her face held a look of utter amazement. "I got it all cleaned up."

"And I may be wrong, seeing how religion and I are barely on a first-name basis, but a Baptist minister would probably frown on his future wife telling the ladies at bible class last week that it was like trying to herd cats, getting them to do anything."

Marley stopped smiling and sat up. "Who told you that? Was it David?"

"Lauren Sales. She was the only one who thought it was funny."

"Well, those women just wanted to drink coffee and gossip. There was work to be done."

"Maybe you should take a course in people management."

"If I do, I know who's going with me," she said, wagging a finger at me. "I heard you and Miguel going at it last week."

"He can't fire a supplier, that's my job. He just takes on too much."

"You two have been friends for a long time, haven't you?" said Lacey.

"Does it show?"

"Yes." The frown was back. "I've never had that kind of friend."

"Lucky you," Marley told her. "Who needs a friend who tells you you're bossy?"

"Well, you are. She is!" I said to Lacey. "But if Marley was running for president I'd go out and vote for the first time in my life. She's right more times than she's wrong and her heart encompasses the whole world. Oh, don't let it go to your head, Hemming, you're still the bossiest person on the planet."

The phone rang and I reached over and picked it up, saying, "Girls Just Want to Have Fun Boarding House."

I sat up. "Hi, Rena." The laughter drained from Lacey's face.

I got to my feet and left the room, closing the door behind me.

CHAPTER 7

Rena was saying, "Ray John just called. I'm sorry but he doesn't want Lacey staying with you. It's nothing against you, Sherri; it's just that she needs her routine. He's afraid her schoolwork will suffer and…" She searched for words. I could guess just how upset Ray John would be at having his plaything removed, and from what Lacey had told me whatever he wanted, he pretty well got. Rena was desperately in love with him and would do anything to keep him.

"It's all right with me," Rena told me, "but he really wants us to be together. As a family."

"Look, it's late, leave Lacey here for tonight and we'll talk about it tomorrow when she's in school. One night can't hurt, can it?"

"No," she hesitated and then said, "no," again, sounding relieved. "I'm sure he won't mind that. He won't be home until after seven tomorrow morning and Lacey leaves for school at seven-thirty. He'd hardly see her. That will be fine."

Her words gave me a sick feeling. Just how far was she willing to go to keep this man? How much was she willing to give up for love?

Clay called at six-thirty in the morning. I groaned hello.

"You okay?" Clay asked.

"Sure. You?"

"Almost. I never knew how much Kevin drank. Now I know why there were ten bottles of vodka in his locker. Was he always this way or is it because Ann left him? Last night he didn't come back to the boat. Graham went looking for him about one and dragged him back. He was on one of the other boats, dead drunk and in the bed of a Scandinavian blonde." I grunted in response, not caring a whole lot about Kevin's sex life.

"We finally got permission to sail and he's in the bag. Anyway, we've already sailed."

"Rah, rah," I said and dropped the phone onto the cradle, sympathizing with Kevin and wishing I hadn't finished the second bottle of wine Marley had opened.

Mornings are definitely not my time of day but I was a responsible adult now so I stumbled through a shower and out to the kitchen. I opened the polished aluminum sliding doors hiding the toaster and knocked over the orange juice. Then I poured water all over the counter trying to fill the water reserve on the coffee maker. When I picked up a serrated knife and the bag of bagels I'd taken out of the freezer the night before, Marley stepped in. "I'll drive Lace to school. You go back to bed before you hurt yourself," she said, taking the knife from my hand.

"What, you don't like my sweet morning face?"

"It'll sour the milk. Go."

I leaned against the counter, one bare foot resting on the other. "Thanks, Marley."

"Thank you. I'm more than happy to eat your bagels." She turned to look at me, then dropped the knife on the counter and whispered, "What's going on?" She jerked her head in the direction of the den, leaving no doubt what she was talking about. "What's up?"

My voice was as soft as I could make it. "Ray John Leenders is back in town." Her eyes got round.

"He lives with Rena and Lacey."

"Shit."

I grinned at her fall from grace. Any crack in her Mother Superior act always pleased me.

"Sorry to dump on you last night when you've got this," Marley whispered. While Lacey did homework I'd heard all about the rocky road to sainthood and her split from David as I finished the wine.

"It's all right. Your hurt is new, mine's old."

"No," she shook her head in disagreement. "I just don't think that's true." Her face wrinkled in thought. "Your hurt never stopped."

In a way it was true. Ray John's abuse was like a scar on my soul and on my memory. I turned away from Marley. "I've been working out just how I'm going to handle the meeting I intend to have with Ray John."

Marley said, "Leave it until tonight and I'll go with you. I can't get away this morning. I'm booked solid." Marley is a dental hygienist in a busy dental practice, often working long hours and a half-day on Saturdays to keep up. "I'll be done about six, I'll go with you."

"Nope. I'm going to see him this morning. Alone."

"Don't be silly. You can't go alone."

But I wouldn't be alone. I was taking an old friend, but not one I could tell Marley about. "I want to do this my way," I said.

Marley started to argue but Lacey came out of the den,

dressed in jeans and a long-sleeved tee-shirt and carrying her backpack, ready for school.

I waited until I knew Rena had opened the store and then I put on a fanny pack, wearing the pouch at the front where it would be nice and handy and where the replacement for my daddy's sixteenth birthday present, my special friend, a nice little Beretta, resided. Just to be sure Ray John would be alone, I swung by the store and saw Rena's beige sedan in the parking lot. Then I went to the neat little ranch house on Blossom Avenue.

Florida in September is pretty much like living in a sauna. At ten-thirty in the morning the day was already blistering hot. The humidity was way up there but I had the air conditioning cranked up so the sweat trickling down my side was from fear, not the weather. With each block my anger and conviction was seeping away like a spilled drink, to be replaced by gut-wrenching dread. I didn't want to do this. Should I wait for Marley? But I was afraid by six-thirty, even with Marley holding my hand, I'd probably find it impossible. Besides, I didn't want witnesses. Marley was way over on the sensible side of the upright-citizen path and what I had in mind wasn't even in the same county. Ray John needed to be spoken to in a language he understood.

The lift bridge was up, waiting for a yacht to clear. A line of cars piled up behind me, boxing me in so I couldn't change my mind and turn around and run back to the Sunset. Panic was squeezing the air out of me. I took deep breaths and waited. The idea of facing this man again set my heart pounding in my chest until I was afraid I would have a heart attack.

Could you die from anxiety? I had no idea. The bridge slowly went down. I could go.

The big ass SUV, with the oversized tires, was in the driveway. I pulled in behind it, trying to regulate my breathing to slow my racing heart and trying to find my courage. I left the keys in the ignition and the door open so I could leave fast. My right hand went to the comforting bulk at my waist as I climbed the steps like a snail. I wiped my sweaty palms on the ass of my jeans and then pressed the doorbell. While I waited I unzipped the pouch.

Nothing happened, at least not fast enough to suit me. I wanted him to get his ass out there so I could get it over with and be gone. I started kicking the black door, taking pleasure in the marks I was leaving on the fresh paint. Between the bell and my shoe, the racket got his attention. The door exploded open. I jumped away from his body towering over me, the iron railing biting into my butt as I stared up at Ray John. Leaning over me, inches from my nose, he shouted down into my face, "What? What the hell do you want?"

At five-foot-seven I was dwarfed by Ray John who stood a good seven inches above me. Barefoot and naked except for boxers, he must have been sleeping but the close-cropped fair hair was never going to give it away by being rumpled. When I'd known him he'd been big and fit, but now he was something else, almost grotesque with muscle definition. His neck had all but disappeared into ridges of muscle sloping down to his shoulders, making his head look undersized for his body. His arms, blown up with muscle, angled out from his body rather than hanging down as they would on a normal-sized man. It wasn't natural…but then nothing about this animal had ever been natural.

His iron-grey eyes drilled into me and his square jaw was clenched in anger; I had a strong sense it was taking a huge effort of will on his part not to pound me into the concrete.

"Do you know who I am?" I asked.

"You're the woman who's about to get her ass kicked back to the curb."

"I'm Ruth Ann Jenkins' daughter, Sherri, the woman who regrets not blowing your brains out when I had the chance." My right hand was wrapped around the cool metal in the pouch, giving me courage. "I'm the woman who's still tempted to rid the earth of your sorry ass."

Something registered in his eyes. He stood straighter, pulling himself away from me. "Who are you?"

"My name is Sherri Travis now. I'm the one Lacey is staying with. I know about you, know what you did to her and if you touch her again I'll have the police on you."

"You're full of shit."

"Am I? Just try coming near her again and I'll lay charges against you for what you did to me when I was a kid."

"Whose going to pay any attention to you?" he sneered, looking me up and down. "A slut like your mother."

"Stay away from Lacey or I'll see you in jail. I bet there's lots of others who'd come forward if this hits the papers." There was a darkening of his eyes, a wariness that told me it was true. I hadn't been the first one or the last one he'd abused. This knowledge weakened my legs and had me sagging down against the railing with the horror of it.

Wariness took over but the violence didn't leave him. He was still angry, still wanting to use his fists on me but he was more cautious now, another confirmation of his crimes.

I pressed my advantage. "Can you afford to get your name in the papers?" Another weird memory about Ray John came back, his overwhelming desire for respect. "And I'll make sure every one of your neighbors knows about it, make sure they all know what a pervert you are."

His eyes flicked sideways.

"I'll make sure they put Lacey somewhere safe where you'll never see her again." I slid sideways along the rail, slipping past him. "So you tell Rena you think Lacey should stay with me for now." I ran down the concrete steps.

I didn't look back, didn't even look in the rearview as I drove away. Trembling, every muscle in my body overloaded with adrenalin and fear, I could barely hold it together enough to drive — to get away from him. Two blocks down Blossom Avenue, I pulled over to the curb, opened the door and threw up.

I pulled a handful of tissues from the box under the dash and was still wiping my mouth when he hit me from behind.

CHAPTER 8

The impact threw me forward against the wheel and then jerked me back. No seatbelt, I'd just wanted to get away. I scrambled for it now.

Another hit but not as hard this time. In the rearview, I saw him getting out of his truck. I grabbed the door and slammed it shut, hitting the lock.

The pickup squealed forward as Ray John's hand reached for the door handle. "Oh god, oh god," I wailed, hanging on to the wheel and watching in the mirror as Ray John ran back to his SUV.

That's why I didn't see the guy backing out on the street in front of me. The old fool was just there, taking up two-thirds of the road, but then who expects a madwoman to be doing fifty in a subdivision. I only missed the Nissan by jolting over the curb, churning up someone's lawn and then rocketing back onto the road.

Ray John followed my path.

There was a stop sign ahead, one I had to obey at a four-lane street full of traffic. "Oh god, oh god," I wailed again. If I stopped for traffic would Ray John smash out a window and drag me out of the truck? But I had to stop. There was no way I could shoot into the traffic without stopping and waiting for a break in traffic. Both moves seemed equally dangerous.

I stopped. Watching to my left and watching for danger behind me in equal measure.

Ray John got out of the SUV. I slipped out the Beretta, clutching it in both hands like my daddy taught me and turned to the back window, holding the gun up nice and high so Ray John could see it.

Ray John saw my friend. He raised his head like a bull that scents something strange. Big but not stupid, his forward charge stopped. This wasn't supposed to happen to him. He was supposed to be in charge. I smiled in triumph before I turned away and slipped out into traffic, cutting off a van and pissing off yet another person.

I felt victorious for about a nanosecond. A normal guy would've backed off right there but Ray John wasn't done yet. He zigged and zagged through traffic and was on my tail again within a block. He stayed there all the way down Tamiami Trail, dangerously close, changing lanes when I did, running a red light to shadow me while horns blared and curses were shouted out windows.

Surely someone would call the cops.

Then I made a near fatal mistake. I headed over the south bridge and back onto Cypress Island and home…to safety. But not this time. There was no safe harbor for me.

CHAPTER 9

Warning alarms sounded as we approached the bridge. I watched the slowly descending arm, trying to judge. Could I beat it? I pressed the gas, hoping to slip under at the last possible second.

I was too far away — I hadn't a chance. I jolted to a stop as the candy-striped arm of the bridge shuttered into place three feet beyond my front bumper. And then the swing bridge began to open at an infuriating creep. That's where things went really wrong.

Ray John was right behind me. In front of me only the wooden barrier and twenty feet of pavement stood between me and a forty-foot drop into dark waters. I was trapped.

I felt his bumper butt up against Jimmy's little pickup.

"No, no." I straightlegged the brake, trying to keep the truck in place but even with the brakes locked the light pick- up was no match for the massive hunk of steel pushing it forward. Sweat rolled down my face, stinging my eyes, but no way was I going to take my hand off the wheel to wipe it away.

Ray John backed away and then hit me again.

The pickup jerked forward into the barrier.

"You son of a bitch, you aren't going to do this." I slammed the gearshift into park. I grabbed the Beretta and swung around to face him. "I am not going to die."

He saw the gun and ducked beneath the dash.

I waited. Sweat slid down my face, itched under my tee-shirt and trickled down my spine. Slowly his head came back up.

"Bastard," I mouthed at him.

He grinned at me, daring me to shoot him. The pickup rocked forward as he gunned the SUV.

I saw the attendant coming out of his kiosk to tear a strip off two reckless people he thought were playing games.

I took the safety off the gun and took aim on Ray John's chest. I thought I'd convinced him when he backed off. But it was only so he could take another run at me. The force of the hit drove the pickup forward and broke the barrier.

Behind the SUV the attendant saw my gun. The shock registered on his face before he fled back to the safety of his kiosk.

"God, let him call the cops," I prayed. For once in my mis-spent life I would be glad to see them.

Ray John's grin told me he was becoming more confident, less convinced I'd shoot him.

"I'll do it, I'll do it," I screamed even though he couldn't hear me. "I won't die alone."

Still up against the bumper, he revved his motor but he didn't slam into me again. Even this crazy bastard knew how far he could go. Even he could see the determination in me, the conviction that he would be killing two people.

We stared at each other, waiting for the next move.

Time slowed down and my pulse speeded up. Sweat dripped and my mouth grew dry. My hands began to shake. How could I make this right?

When the water traffic cleared, the wise attendant decided

his own personal safety lay in getting rid of the problem instead of keeping us trapped there waiting for the cops. The siren sounded the all clear, signaling that the bridge had swung closed.

I put my foot on the brake, trying to still keep Ray John covered with the gun, while I jammed the transmission into drive and then I shot forward, driving for my life.

The narrow twisting beach road wasn't meant for speed. Driving like maniacs, taking the sharp turns too fast, with palm fronds raking against the sides of our vehicles, we raced towards Jac. God help anyone coming south towards us.

There was no safe place to pass, not that that wouldn't have mattered to Ray John, but I stayed well over the middle line, forcing him to keep behind me. If he wanted to overtake me and cut me off he had to drive through the edge of palmetto and risk slamming into a palm tree, never mind oncoming traffic.

Twice our bumpers clashed on the four-mile race to Cypress. Once, an oncoming car was forced into the palmettos to avoid a head-on collision. I didn't look back.

Still going too fast, I pulled up into the parking lot of the town plaza with the cop shop. The black monster pulled in behind me but kept on going through the parking lot when I shot into a slot in front of the police office.

I couldn't go on, couldn't even get out of the truck and go for help. Shaking and trembling, I leaned forward, putting my head on the steering wheel, limp beyond bearing and asking unanswerable questions. Why had I let myself get involved? How had I let this happen? What had I unleashed and how could I end it? I knew our dance of fear had just begun. It wouldn't end until one of us was dead or in prison. I had to stop the terror.

With hands still trembling with fear, I called Detective Styles on my cell. I met Styles when Jimmy was murdered and Styles thought I was the most likely candidate for the electric chair. Go figure. But he was a good guy to have on your side and I needed him there now.

"Sherri, what's happening?" No hello. The man never changed. Small talk just wasn't the way he operated.

"I need to talk. Got any time?"

"For you, yes. Want to meet for coffee?"

"This needs privacy."

"I'll come to you at the Sunset."

"Perfect. I'm on my way there now."

That turned out not to be true. It took time to get the courage to leave the safety of my spot in front of the police station, while checking the mirror and waiting for Ray John to come back.

At the Sunset I fended off the staff with their lists of shift changes and complaints and went to the restaurant's ladies room. Sweat glued the drenched tee to my body, limp hair stuck to my face. It didn't matter. Nothing mattered but the fact I was alive. But how long could I stay alive? I leaned over a sink and sobbed.

Gwen Morrison, our glamorous blonde hostess who had been at the Sunset as long as I had, came through the door. I hid my face from her but she wasn't fooled. "What's up?" she said, full of concern.

The problem with confusing staff with family is they start thinking they own you, think they have a right to all of your life. "I just need a moment, Gwen. Can't you just leave me alone?"

"Well, excuse me," she said and left.

"Shit," I swore into the mirror.

The good thing about Gwen, her annoyance wouldn't last to the front desk and she always forgave my bitchiness.

I pulled off my tee before I splashed cold water on my face. I used paper towels to wash and dry my upper body. The shaking was easing as I pulled my hair back into a ponytail. There was a clean blouse in my office but I hadn't thought to bring it with me. I didn't care. I walked out of the washroom in my bra and unlocked my office door, the only place on the planet which was truly my own.

When I'd rebuilt the Sunset after Hurricane Myrna, I'd indulged myself. What did a few thousand more dollars' worth of debt matter with the shitload I was carrying? Now two walls of the office were covered in a cream-colored paper that looked like nubby raw linen while the other two were covered, floor to ceiling, with bookshelves that held every book I'd ever owned or Jimmy had ever stolen. Jimmy had played on the pro golf circuit all over the South and had this really bad habit of stopping at every library he came across and walking out with a few books for me, often very big glossy coffee-table books. Those were the presents he brought home from the tour. I think the thefts gave him a rush and Jimmy was all about putting a little excitement into his life with risky behavior, only one of the many reasons I'd left him.

No matter how I yelled at him about robbing libraries, he never stopped and I'd never gotten rid of the books. So now my shelves held books with the stamps from a multitude of libraries all over the South, my secret reward for another's crime.

Books give me comfort; like old friends they make me feel calm. When the bookshelves were first built, they were neat and tidy, but the contents seemed to migrate on their own. Here and there books had been slipped in on top of the stacks. In some spots books had gone missing while in others they now lay piled on their sides. Today I didn't even look at them.

My desk sat in front of the bookshelves, facing into the room. There was a second desk shoved against the opposite wall where Mary Harley sat a few hours a week inputting data and doing bookwork. She came in early and our days only overlapped for about a half-hour where we caught up on details. The desk chairs were both brown leather wingbacks. When Mary wasn't there, her chair was used by visitors and slid easily over the dark walnut floors to face my desk.

With trembling hands I pulled on the white blouse. A knock came at the door. Couldn't they get by for ten minutes without me? "What?" I yelled.

"It's me, Styles."

I threw open the door, so glad to see him I could have kissed him but that would have crossed a line we'd never even tip-toed close to.

I thought of Styles as the beige man and as usual he was wearing a beige suit and tie. Even his green eyes were pale, weird and slightly hypnotic. Only the white shirt and highly polished brown brogues relieved the eye. Everything about

Styles said safety and dependability, two things I had great need of at the moment.

Words tumbled out of my mouth. He already knew the beginnings of the story, how I'd once held a shotgun on Ray John and threatened to kill him. It was a story the sheriff had never forgotten, so when Styles investigated Jimmy's death Sheriff Disson was quick to bring him up to scratch on the back story and, given my history of violence, Styles had thought I just might be capable of blowing up Jimmy's boat with Jimmy on it.

Now he followed me into the room, listening to my disjointed account of Ray John's return, pulling Mary's chair around as I sank into the chair behind my desk while I told him that Lacey and Rena were now living with the man who had tried to rape me.

"Do you want to charge him?" Styles asked. "If you charge him with sex abuse, I can arrest him."

And it would all be out in the open, the ugly facts of my life and my mother's, exposed for everyone to see. I looked away. "Not yet."

"Is he abusing Lacey?"

Lacey had sworn me to secrecy but I needed to help her. I did up my remaining buttons and muttered. "Probably."

"You should have come right into the office and filed a report when you found out he was abusing his stepdaughter."

"I don't think they're married."

He raised his voice. "It doesn't matter." He was angry with me, which made two of us. "You have to stop it."

"How did this get to be my responsibility?"

"If you don't do something he'll go on molesting that girl."

"You think I don't know that? Lacey refuses to file a complaint. If you approach her about being sexually abused by Ray John she'll deny it, her word against mine. And I don't think Rena will help; something tells me Rena will deny it too. To be fair she might not even know."

"How old are you?" Styles asked

"None of your business," I shot back.

He grinned. "No, it's just that if you are seven years over the age of consent, if you are twenty-five and haven't charged him, Florida law says the statute of limitations has run out."

"So it's no longer a crime? Isn't that a kick in the head?"

"You can still charge him in civil court for what he did to you, but we can't bring him up on criminal charges."

"That would be great, wouldn't it? People are just starting to accept I'm not a complete wacko involved in every crime on the island, finally comfortable coming to the restaurant, and not afraid someone's going to burst in with a machine gun and blast away."

"You're exaggerating."

"And you don't know your ass from a hole in the ground about dealing with the public. The point is, I can't afford the scandal. I'm drowning in debt, mired in a quicksand of bills — the restaurant is barely making it. I need people to come through the door, any drop-off in customers will finish me. I've got to hold on 'til tourist season. Two more months, that's all I need." Bring on the tourists was my new mantra. "That will save me. No, I can't do this right now. I need people to forget my past, not rake it all up again. More scandal will keep them away." I was talking, talking, talking to convince both of us. "You can't expect me to destroy myself by charging Ray John."

"And maybe there's something else stopping you. Maybe you need Clay to forget your past as well."

I jerked up straight. "What's that supposed to mean?"

He lifted a shoulder. "You tell me. Seems to me you're always worrying about what he thinks. Like you're not good enough for him just the way you are."

"Clay has a lot of money in the Sunset. I don't want to lose his money." I rapped my knuckles on the desk to emphasize my words. "If I don't make it, if the Sunset can't turn a profit the way it is, Clay will have the building knocked down and then he will put up more condos. That was the condition he came into it with me. He's already told me this isn't a charity." I rubbed a tiny ache beginning to nibble away at my brain. "It's a sore point between Clay and me, me wanting to keep every-thing the way it is and Clay wanting to make several more fortunes. The two aren't compatible." Some days I didn't think we were either.

"Have you told Clay what Ray John did to you?"

"Shit, no."

"Maybe you should."

"No."

"Why?"

Now there was a question. The big one.

"Tell him," Styles urged.

"He doesn't need to know."

"You can't charge Ray John and not tell Clay. That's why you aren't charging Leenders, isn't it?"

Clay knew most of the baggage I carried around but just when he thought he'd heard it all, and he'd come to terms with it, there's one more secret to tell, one more ghost to exorcize, one more confession. How much could I tell him before he'd heard enough? My life before him, my ragtag upbringing, was chaotic and nothing like his clean, well-organized, controlled life. I was embarrassed by my past, ashamed of my family and of my own mistakes. There was already enough stuff driving us apart, leaving our relationship teetering on the edge of oblivion, without adding to the pile. How much more shit would it take to push it over? I didn't want him to walk out on me, didn't want to lose him, never mind that if he left so would my investment and even my home. But most of all I didn't want to lose Clay.

"This is about Rena and Lacey, not Clay and me."

"Isn't it?" He leaned towards me, elbows planted on knees and said, "I know how hard you want to fit in, to be part of his world."

"What are you talking about?"

"Oh, you mean to tell me the differences between you don't matter? You're the one always pointing them out."

"Well, Clay comes from an old Florida family while I come from an old trailer park. My former mother-in-law so charmingly calls me trash. She has a lot of descriptive adjectives to go along with that but it gives me indigestion to think about them."

"Do you really think it matters to Clay?"

"It matters to me."

"Why?"

"Clay is part of the establishment. I wait on them, wait on the social register, with a tray in my hand. It matters."

Styles added, "Not to mention he's a lot older than you."

"Only about twelve years older." I was guessing at the number because he kept all his documents well away from my greedy little eyes. Even the filing drawers in his den were locked, I know 'cause I'd tried them all, so you see our relationship had a few cracks in the wall of love.

"Not the best arrangement, is it?" Styles asked.

"Why don't we talk about you for a while?"

"Because I'm trying to make you see sense."

I threw the pen I'd been twirling between my fingers at the desk. It hit the wooden surface and then bounced off onto the floor. "Oh, is that what you're doing?"

"You have to stop Leenders."

"Ray John has caused me enough trouble. I won't let him ruin the one good thing in my life."

"How good is it if you're hiding things?"

I'd had enough. "I should have shot the son of a bitch at thirteen when I had the chance."

"I thought you were sixteen."

"That's what my mother told the sheriff."

"Why?" He seemed really curious about this, as though he really couldn't see what difference my age might make.

"She thought the cops might take me away or something if I was really young."

"Oh, yes," he said with a nod, "I remember your family's feelings about us."

"The point is, if I'd shot Ray John back then it would be all over by now, and it would have saved others a lot of pain." I pushed away from the desk. "I couldn't sleep last night wondering how many other kids he has done this to. I always thought it was only me, don't know why, but I did. It wasn't just me, was it?"

Styles leaned sideways to pick up the pen. "I'm pretty sure there will be a lot more out there." He set the pen down carefully on the desk. "I'll starting looking for them."

"Can you find them?" I leaned forward both hands flat on the desk. "Maybe one of them will charge him."

"You mean maybe someone else will do what you haven't got the guts to do?"

"Thanks for your understanding."

"My job isn't to make you feel good."

"No, that's what friends are for." He got to his feet. The visit was over and maybe something else too.

"Good bye, Ms. Travis." He closed the door softly behind him while I slumped down at the desk and buried my head in my folded arms. I just couldn't turn my life upside-down again. In the last two years I'd been accused of murder and I'd been kidnapped by a psychopath, which had nearly destroyed my sanity. After I was freed I spent months running from shadows. And I still woke screaming from nightmares and needing Clay to hold me in his arms until the shaking stopped. This was the first time he'd left me alone since Gina's murder. Part of his going away was to prove to me I didn't need him there every hour of the day, to prove I could stay alone at night, could sleep in the dark, could forget.

No one understood I still had serious issues and no one

knew how close I still was to a breakdown. Clay kept telling me I was stronger than I knew but he was wrong. He and Styles were both wrong. I was nowhere near being the brassy, gutsy girl I pretended to be. Inside was a shivering, quivering wreck. Each day, I secretly promised myself if it became too much to handle I'd just check myself into a really good rest home and go ahead and break down, let it all hang out, get it off my chest and purge myself, give in to all the terror and the fears and surrender to my dark side. Tomorrow, I promised myself, I'd do it tomorrow. Every day I told myself I'd give up tomorrow. I'd just get through the next twenty-four hours and the nice crackup I'd been promising myself was mine. I'd never been closer to throwing myself wholeheartedly into insanity than I was when Styles walked out of my office. He was right; I didn't have the guts to shoot Ray John — or to charge him.

Now there was one more thing to worry about besides shadows and financial ruin...Ray John. I hadn't told Styles that Ray John had tried to kill me. Hadn't told Styles that I'd held Ray John off with an unregistered Beretta.

The phone rang. I wiped my nose with a knuckle and picked up the phone. A supplier told me my bill was sixty days past due and if I didn't show up with a check immediately the meat order for that night wouldn't be delivered. I begged him to make the normal delivery, promised to have a check for him in the kitchen. He agreed but told me from now on his deliveries were strictly C.O.D.

CHAPTER 10

Rena was busy with customers but she gave me a "Hi" and a bright smile. She was wearing a silk spaghetti-strapped top with sequins in a vee down the front and tight jeans with embroidery along the outside of the legs. She looked terrific. Not a care in the world.

The store was busy for an out-of-season weekday. I checked out her new stock. Thong bikinis were given a big display area at the front of the store. Quite a few of them were being displayed on the beach as well, shocking our older tourists and a few of us natives. Beach Road ran right along the sand, sixty yards from the Gulf of Mexico, and traffic screeched to a halt every time a driver spotted a bare ass. Heads swiveled and fingers were pointed. On Sunday mornings, more than one sermon was directed to this abomination.

I held a raspberry pink thong swimming suit up and considered it but at $79.95 for about six square inches of material, I felt cheated. I'm the kind of customer who expects a whole outfit for that price, including shoes and bag. Thank heavens I wasn't the average consumer. Not everyone was as tight with their money as me; shoppers were keeping both Rena and I afloat. The rent from the two stores was a godsend for me and I needed it desperately to meet the mortgage payments.

I was on to the surfer shorts when Rena came to join me.

"For you I have a special discount," Rena told me, pulling out a pair of shorts in a black-and-white floral Hawaiian print.

"That's good to know." I looked at the other customers. "The store seems busy."

"I've passed my target for September already and there's still ten days to go." She clenched her fist and gave a little jab in triumph.

"You and Lacey have worked hard."

"I couldn't have done it, couldn't have even started this store without RJ's help. He put a lot of money into it. I want to make it work for him."

Crazy was looking more and more attractive now that my own success depended on the investment of my abuser, the man who was also abusing Lacey. Maybe I should just go check into some nice nuthouse and give it all up. Admitting defeat and rolling up like a fetus with my thumb in my mouth was becoming my primary goal in life.

"I don't know what I did to deserve a man like him." Rena's whole being shone with happiness when she talked about Ray John. "I sure hope he doesn't find out that he can do a whole lot better." Rena gave a nervous little giggle but it wasn't a joke. She really was scared to death he'd leave her, terrified he'd find someone new. The dread was there in the green eyes. She was begging to have her fears denied while I wanted to tell her it was the best thing that could happen to her and her daughter.

"I saw him this morning," I told her. "I went over to Blossom Avenue to talk to him."

"What?" Confusion and then anger showed on her face. "RJ? Did you wake him? You shouldn't have done that. He works shifts, you know. Works all the time, like fourteen hours a day, he's so devoted to his job. Those people out there don't know what they've got."

Yeah, a child abuser and woman basher...lucky them. Maybe I should tell them. It was a thought and one I'd be sure and share with Ray John if I ran into him again.

"You shouldn't have woken him." She started to wring her hands in apprehension, drifting sideways towards the phone. She stopped and said, "He needs his sleep," but still her eyes were on the phone sitting on the counter wanting to reassure him that she had nothing to do with me waking him and yet scared of doing the wrong thing. I read the story all too clearly, had seen Ruth Ann do the same things, protecting her new man and doing everything she could to keep him happy even at the expense of her own feelings.

"It's all right," I reassured her. "He's fine. And fine with Lacey staying with me for a while. I hate to be alone and she's good company, like a younger sister really, and she'll have fun on the beach and in the pool. There's a gym too." I almost threw in a facial and a body wrap, a true spa experience, to encourage Rena to agree.

Her face softened. "Lacey's been going through a bad time. The teenage years are hard."

"I remember. When did RJ move in?"

"Four years ago. Lacey was twelve."

"How did Lacey take to that?"

"She was fine at first but then...well, you know kids, she went right off him and started acting up. Wanted to go live with her dad in Alabama. No way I was going to let her live with that deadbeat; besides, he really doesn't want her although I wasn't going to tell Lacey that."

"Well, this will be a good time-out for everyone. And then later," I hunted for tact, not something I had in abundance. "Well, is there anyone else she could stay with, grandparents perhaps?

"Why?" She was too polite to tell me to mind my own business, but indignation at my suggestion pinched her features. "She doesn't need to stay with anyone. She's just being silly and after RJ has been so good to her. He's teaching her to drive and even paid for the Driver's Ed course." She paused. "Besides, even if there was a reason, we haven't any family."

How now brown cow?

At two-thirty I headed to the concrete bunker where I'd gone to high school to pick Lacey up. It looked like a factory, a factory where they manufactured flawed adults. It brought back a flood of memories. Unlike most people, I wanted to be in school. You'll never catch me whining about how horrible it was, the bad stuff happened when I wasn't at school. School was a safe place for me.

I was worried about finding Lacey in the crush of kids coming out of the building but it wasn't hard to spot Lace. She walked all alone, head down, bookbag clutched to her chest, her body language saying stay away from me. I got out of the pickup to go and meet her.

"Lacey," RJ roared behind me. I swung to face him. He didn't even know I was there, his eyes were fixed on Lacey. "Get over here," he ordered. He was parked two cars behind me, standing up in the open driver's door with his thick arms folded on the roof. It had the effect of making him look even larger and more powerful, looming over his boss truck at her. How could you refuse a man that could overshadow that piece of machinery?

Lacey froze. I jolted into action, racing forward and grabbing her by the forearm. "Come on. Let's get out of here." Pulling her along, I added, "You don't have to go with him."

RJ jumped down from his perch and exploded forward. Big but fast, he was between us and my little red pickup. Red veins in his neck bulged; his face pulsed with blood as if his head was about to explode.

"You don't have to go with him," I repeated, holding on tightly to her.

Lacey was making a low keening distress sound and pulling back from me to get away from Ray John. I tried to pull her to the right to step around him but he moved to cut us off. He smiled, evil and smarmy, and leaned his huge bulk against the passenger door of the red pickup.

"Get away from the door, Ray John," I hissed. "Lacey isn't going anywhere with you unless you want the biggest scene you've ever seen in your life." Lacey slid behind me, tight to my body.

He pointed a forefinger at my fanny pack with the Beretta. "You think a little pea shooter is going to save your ass, bitch?"

"It sure made you back off this morning. Now, get out of my way or I'll tell every one of these kids what you are — besides being an asshole. Someone will call the cops for sure. Besides, I have Rena's permission to take Lacey with me."

Anger contorted his face, his lips pursed and chewed as if there was something he couldn't swallow and wanted to hawk and spit. He didn't move from the truck.

"I've already told the police about you, told them what you did to me and if you try and take Lacey I'll call them again and have you arrested for kidnapping. Move!"

His fists clenched. He glared down at me, trying to decide if he could bully me aside.

"Go away." My voice was loud. With keen spectator instincts of someone else's disaster, a crowd was starting to form, making us the center of attention.

Ray John looked around, trying to judge if he could take Lacey away without interference.

"If you don't back off right now, I'll go to Rena and tell her the whole truth."

This got his attention. He was afraid of losing his soft landing. He pointed at me. "It's not over, not by a long shot." He swung away and stalked back to his truck.

"Get in the truck," I pushed Lacey forward and ran around to the driver's side. My hands were shaking so hard it took two tries to fit the key in the ignition. "It's all right, it's all right," I said over and over, trying to reassure myself as much as Lacey. I jerked away from the curb without checking my mirror. A horn blared and a car swerved around us.

Lacey turned and watched out the back window. "He's following us."

"Let him." But I reached up and adjusted the rearview. He was only inches off our bumper. "He can't do anything."

Intimidating us with size and closeness, he shadowed us. I

punched in Styles' number. He was at the police station so I told him what was happening and that's where I headed.

"He'll never let me go." Lacey's voice spoke of defeat and resignation.

I stopped for a red light. "You're not alone in this. Remember that." The hulking piece of steel hit our bumper, rocking the truck but not pushing us forward.

"Oh," Lacey said, startled, "sorry."

"Why?" I looked over at her. Tears were running down her cheeks. "Why are you sorry, you're not the idiot that's causing all this, you haven't hurt anyone."

"Have you really got a gun?" She pointed at the pouch.

"Yeah, but we don't need it."

"Good," she said. "Good." She gave a determined nod of her head and stared straight ahead. "I'm glad you've got a gun in your pouch."

I thought maybe she was hoping I'd shoot Ray John and get it over with. The truth was much worse.

CHAPTER 11

Styles was waiting in the parking lot as I pulled in. He came out to stand beside the driver's door, not looking at me but behind us at the SUV shadowing us. Styles started towards it but Ray John pulled out around us and took off.

I rolled down the window. "Thanks," I breathed.

Styles put both hands on the lowered window. He looked from Lacey to me before he asked, "What happened?"

I raised my shaking hand to the hair fallen from its elastic and brushed it back behind my ear. He reached out for my left hand on the steering wheel and squeezed it. "Take it easy."

I nodded and combed my hair back from my face with my fingers and redid the elastic. "This is Lacey Cagel."

He leaned around me. "Hi, Lacey."

Lacey ignored us. She was gripping the door handle, ready to bolt.

"Detective Styles is a friend of mine, a good guy."

"I don't want the police," she whispered.

"You don't have to do anything but talk to him. We just want you to be safe."

She swung to face me. "But I can go back to your place, right? I don't have to go back there."

I'd already assured her of this at least three times in the eight blocks between the high school and here but I did it again.

"Look, let's just go across to Fat Tony's and get a soda," Styles put in. "We'll just talk. No one is going to make you do anything you don't want to do."

And talk he did, softly and sweetly and with a kindness that would have melted most reluctant hearts — but not Lacey's. She just sat with the soda between her hands, looking down at it and shaking her head no, and then she excused herself and went to the ladies.

Styles watched her go and then looked into my eyes. "We had a report from the bridge keeper about a black muscle SUV and a red pickup earlier today. Want to tell me about it?"

"It was nothing."

"Without a complaint I can't have him brought in."

I shook my head.

Styles sighed. "My wife and I have just separated." It was the first personal thing Styles ever told me about himself; he wasn't the kind of guy who shared his life or his emotions. In fact I wasn't sure he had either. Locked down, solid and in control left no room for warm fuzzy confidences. "I've got a nine-year-old daughter," he said. "How do I stop this from happening to her?"

I gave it some thought. "Well maybe I'm not the best person to offer advice but I think you should tell your wife what happened to me. And tell your daughter, talk to her and let her know there are evil people out there who will try and take advantage of her. Only people who are ignorant can be preyed upon. Tell her she can come to you with anything, you won't get mad and you won't judge her." I thought about it. "Kids need to trust people before they can talk to them."

"Why didn't you tell your dad?"

That gave me a laugh. "He's a different sort of parent. Grandma said he went to 'Nam crazy and came back worse and he hasn't improved with age. I never knew what he'd do or how he'd react. No telling what rocket he'd go off on if I told him this. Someone would have died for certain."

"Are you sure?"

"Pretty much." I rubbed a bite of pain in my forehead. "I spent my childhood worrying about the adults around me, adults who acted more like kids than I did. One time, when I was about seven or eight, Daddy came out late at night and started shooting a gun off outside our trailer. Dead drunk, of course — he mostly was back then — he kept calling for the new man in my mom's life to come out.

"It was dark, probably after midnight. I remember waking up and thinking this was it, this time he was going to kill us all. It always seemed a possibility with my dad. I hid in my closet, pulling clothes over me and hoping he wouldn't find me. That's where my mother, Ruth Ann, unearthed me, still curled up in a ball afraid to come out.

"The new guy sharing her bed had already taken off, didn't even stop to pack. I heard his car leaving as Ruth Ann carried me back to her bed. You see what I mean? If I'd told my dad he would have killed Ray John. For sure. Maybe it would have been a good thing. Back then it didn't seem such a good idea. I didn't want Daddy to go to jail, although it wouldn't have been a new experience for him, that's for sure."

"And your mother didn't tell your father you'd been abused?"

"Nope, no way Ruth Ann was going to give Tully Jenkins

anything to get excited about. She knew even better than I did what a powder keg he was."

"A kid shouldn't have to think about things like that, shouldn't have to worry about what their parents are capable of…shouldn't know the wickedness of men like Leenders."

"Yeah, well life isn't perfect." I was starting to worry about the amount of time Lacey had been gone. Teenage girls like mirrors but this was getting silly.

"There's no record of sexual abuse on Ray John's file. Your mother should have told the police when they came."

"Remember I come from people who aren't real comfortable telling the police anything. Ruth Ann was afraid that social services would get involved and take me away. We would have been worked over twice, once by Ray John and then by the authorities. Better to look after things ourselves."

Styles' eyes slipped to the door of the john; he was getting antsy too. "Those days are gone, Sherri. Now you have to let the law handle it." He tilted his head towards the ladies room. "Think she's all right?"

"I'll check," I said and started to slide out of the booth.

Styles' hand on my arm stopped me. He picked up his glass and dragged on the watery dregs as Lacey slid back in beside me.

She seemed remarkably better, more composed, calm almost. Now call me suspicious, call me a worrier, but I've seen too much trouble not to know something else was going on here.

I was about to find out there was one more problem to deal with…a great big ugly one.

CHAPTER 12

Styles followed us back to the condo. He didn't need to suggest we stay in the ultra-secure building for the night, I'd already decided on that. We weren't even going for a walk on the beach. The sand would burn your feet anyway. It had been another scorching day and I'd seen enough fireworks for one day. I just wanted to chill, didn't even want to talk about what had happened. Lacey had enough pain without me prodding the wound. "Let's have a swim," I said. The private pool down on the beach was surrounded by an eight-foot-high spiked wrought-iron fence that kept everyone but the residents of the Tradewinds out. Safe.

"No, thanks."

"It will make you feel better."

"I've got this sore arm," she said, rubbing her arm just above the elbow. Lacey always, even in the hottest weather, wore long-sleeved blouses. Her eyes were deeking and diving, her shoulders were hunched.

I grabbed her arm and pushed up the sleeve of her oversized shirt. A new bandage sat among thin white lines of other cuts.

"You've been hurting yourself." Bright, aren't I? Like I was telling her something she didn't know. She pulled away from me and I let her go.

"This has to stop, Lace. My god, if you need to hurt someone, make it Ray John, not yourself." Another stupid thing to say, and one I soon regretted, but tactful and intelligent words aren't the first to jump to my lips. God would have done us all a favor if he'd just made me mute.

She ran into the den and shut the door. I followed her to the closed door. Sounds from the TV seeped out. I called the Sunset and told them I wouldn't be back in. Then I went to the kitchen and started cooking up a storm, my new way of dealing with stress.

By the time Marley arrived with chocolate cheesecake, I had steaks marinating, potatoes baking, shrimp boiled and on ice and two veggies ready to cook. Food may not solve problems but it makes them a whole lot easier to bear and it only makes you fat, unlike the nasty dangerous things I've done in the past to feel better.

I whispered the highlights of the day to Marley. "Shit," she said. "What are you going to do?"

"Not sure. Any ideas?

"You mean besides sticking to her like honey on bread? I'm there for that. If you're not around, I will be."

"But we can't be on top of her every minute."

"We can try," she said, opening the wonking great fridge and taking out a bottle of wine.

"Should we be doing that?" I asked, pointing at the bottle.
"What?"

"Drinking in front of the kid."

"Oh, you mean in case we add alcoholism to her list of problems."

"Yeah, something like that."

She filled a glass and handed to me. "I just escaped from a crowd of people who never let alcohol pass their lips. Even the blood of Christ was grape juice. Didn't stop them from having all the same troubles as Lacey; in fact, looking at them, pale and pudgy and all those upturned noses, I'd say incest was a real big problem."

"Oh, you've turned nasty and bitter, Sister Marley."

She described something impossible, but colorful, that I could do to myself as Lace came out of the den. Lacey grinned.

"You weren't supposed to hear that," Marley told her.

"I've just been telling Marley I don't think she's going to be a good influence on you and I was right. Just try to ignore everything she says."

"I will." Lacey slipped onto a black leather chair at the granite bar. "Can I have some of that?" She pointed at my glass of wine.

"Certainly not."

"Why not?"

"If you try all the vices now, what will be left for you when you're all grown up like us?"

She smiled.

"Have a soda instead. Dinner is about ready, just have to grill the steaks." I lifted the shrimp on their bed of crushed ice to the upper bar and sat the nippy horseradish sauce beside them. "Nosh on these to start, but watch Marley doesn't knock you off your stool to get to them."

"Har, har," Marley yodeled, sliding onto the stool next to Lacey. "Let me tell you about Sherri, the giant of the food world, Travis, who is known across the state for the prodigious amount of food she can eat."

"Pro-whatis? Where you getting all these big words from, girl?"

"And she's ignorant too," Marley added, wiping a gob of sauce off her chin with the back of her hand.

In the middle of disaster came a little core of sanity and delight. When Clay called, he could hear the laughter in the background. "Hey, don't do too well without me," he said.

"As if I could. Where are you?"

"The Dry Tortugas." The Dry Tortugas are a group of islands seventy miles west of Key West. There is no freshwater on the islands, but there are lots of turtles and an old Civil War fort, plus some of the best snorkeling you'll ever see. "We have to stay here for another day while we wait for the weather to clear."

"Whose stupid idea was it to hold a race before hurricane season was over?"

"We should be all right, nothing major out there. They're just being careful. As soon as the forecast clears, the race begins again. I'll be glad when this trip is over with. You get a whole different view of people when you live on a thirty-foot yacht with them. One's a control freak who has us polishing teak every spare second, and the other one turns out to be a secret drinker. It starts before lunch and goes on all day. By eight he's passed out somewhere on deck."

"You miss me, don't ya?"

"You don't know how much, which is a good thing. If you knew how much I missed you…well, my life would be hell."

"Oh, Clay, you are so wrong," I protested in my best little girl voice. "I'd never take advantage."

He laughed. "Already my life's not my own. Neither is my soul. I'm just trying to hold on to a little dignity here."

Would he come home if I asked him to? Likely, if he was able to find a way off those islands, but it wouldn't solve my problem. I needed to do that all on my own, needed the space to make a decision. Most of all I had to find the courage to throw my biggest secret out there for everyone to see.

"You just be careful. And win that damn race."

The phone rang. The red dial said two-thirty. Panic. No good news comes at that hour of the night. "Hello, hello," I shouted.

"Bitch. You're so going to regret this."

I slammed the phone down. How had he gotten the unlisted number? Rena, it had to be.

I was still awake when it rang at three-thirty. This time when I lifted the receiver I heard another phone pick up. I hadn't turned off the ringer of the phone in the den. I hit the Off button while the voice on the phone was still spewing obscenities and threats.

CHAPTER 13

"Don't tell anyone," Lacey said. We were in the truck and I was delivering her to school.

I took my eyes off the rearview. "What exactly aren't I supposed to tell? Things are piling up and I'm getting confused."

"About my arms." She sat hunched up in the corner as far away from me as she could get.

I turned left on Banyan and braked for a jogger darting across in front of me. "Can't promise that."

"Just for a little bit?"

"This is too big to hide. You need help."

"Even if I promise not to do it anymore?"

"Nope. I'm not your guardian, or warden or whatever. I'm not checking you out for fresh cuts, and I can't make sure you don't do it again."

"I wouldn't lie to you."

"Still nope." I parked in front of the school. "Have a good day." Silly words.

She pushed open the door. Reluctant and beaten, she dragged her backpack behind her.

I kept one eye peeled for Ray John and one eye on Lacey to make sure she didn't bolt. Lacey dragged herself into the building, not acknowledging the other kids, alone in a sea of humanity.

I went to see Rena. The store didn't open until ten but I knew she'd be there, tidying up, unpacking stock and doing the books.

Rena didn't look well. Her hair looked faded and dull, her normally impeccable makeup looked smudged over a bruise showing beneath the heavy foundation high on her left cheek. The love of her life seemed to be back to his old tricks.

Rena and I pretended she wasn't wearing the evidence of his cruelty, pretended life was just as it had been a day ago.

When the small talk ended, her shock began. "Did you know Lacey has been cutting herself?" I asked.

"What?" She backed away from me, her horror real. Denial quickly followed. "You're crazy."

"Nope. I've seen the scars."

"Lacey hasn't any scars."

"She has, Rena. And she admitted cutting herself, tried to make me promise not to tell you."

She covered her mouth with her hand, slowly shaking her head in denial before asking, "Why?"

Before I could reply, a fresh resolve gripped her. "She has to come home."

"What will that solve? She was cutting herself at home."

"I don't believe it."

"But it's true. We've got to get help for her."

Her face pulled into worried lines. "My insurance won't cover this and I can't afford it."

"Don't worry, I'll pay for now." Good going girl, let's just hope psychiatrists take store coupons. "The most important thing is that we get her some help."

"How could she do this to me?"

So stunning, it took my breath away. Maybe she didn't mean to be that selfish. Maybe like most of us she was just at the end of her rope and was coping with all she could handle before this.

I wanted to tell her about what Ray John was doing to her child. It was a great big lump in my throat, waiting to vomit out, but I'd promised Lacey, promised that I'd never tell her secret unless she gave me permission. I couldn't violate that. Well, not yet anyway.

"You try and find her some help and I'll keep a real close eye on her," I vowed.

It turned out to be one of many promises I couldn't keep in my life. But I started out with really good intentions.

Skip Nayato, the bartender already down from Vermont for the season, was working in the stockroom, setting up the bar for the day and ordering new stock. The resort in the North where he worked in the summer had closed after Labor Day and, like lots of people in the service industry, he had made his way south. That's how it is; lots of maids, gardeners and wait staff work the summers up in New England and Upper New York State and then come to Florida for the winter. It was early in the season to take on wait staff. I really didn't need any more bodies until November when the first snowbirds would trickle in, but Skip and I had worked together before and I knew he was too good to pass up.

Hurricane Myrna had not only wreaked havoc on the land-scape the winter before, it had kept the tourists away. People saw the pictures of the destruction on television and didn't realize Jacaranda was open for business. Many businesses that survived the hurricane failed in the tourist season that fol-lowed, including the place where Skip had worked. I was sure hoping the tourists would forget about hurricanes and come back in droves for the winter to save my ass.

Given the situation with Lacey, I was glad that I'd taken Skip on so early. I asked him to work extra hours and cover for me. Hee Haw, bring on the debt.

I checked the receipts from the night before. Not bad. I was mildly optimistic about my ability to stay afloat, and then I got on the phone and called Cordelia Grant, my friend who was a grief counselor. She'd know what to do for Lacey.

"She needs a child psychiatrist but I have to tell you there is a real shortage of them in this area. It may take months to get an appointment."

"I don't know why I say this, but I don't think she's got months. Lacey needs help now."

"Then call the family doctor. He may be able to treat her with antidepressants until she can get real help. You'll need to talk to him anyway, so that's a good place to start."

I called Rena. The phone rang in the store but no one answered.

There was nothing more to be done for Lacey; it was time to look after my own business. At the Stop and Shop, I went inside to pay for the gas. The clerk asked, "Will there be any-thing else?"

A six pack of Coors landed on the counter beside my hand. "And a brewski for the old man," a baritone voice said behind me.

CHAPTER 14

I turned around to face my father, Tully Jenkins.

"And a brewski for the old man," I told the clerk.

"How you doin', Sherri?"

"Not bad."

My cautious reply didn't change his grin.

"You?" I asked just to be polite.

He gave me a ragged charming smile, "What can I say? I'm old, ugly and mean, but still able to get out of bed come morning."

He looked better than his assessment. Tully has every bad habit a man can have, some of which he's taken to an art form, but he's been strangely unaffected by them. When I looked at him for signs of change there were very few. He'd looked much the same throughout my whole life, a few more wrinkles from the sun and the cigarette that always hung from the corner of his mouth, but that's about all. Sometimes I felt that one day I'd pass him in aging and while I grew old, he'd do a Dorian Gray and stand still. Only now was grey beginning to show in his dark hair.

Still dressed head to toe in denim and still wearing a black straw cowboy hat pushed back on his head, he was still handsome. No denying it. A parade of women had been taken in by his chiseled features and laughing black eyes. He'd never worried much about those women wising up and moving on, knowing there was another one in the next bar, truck stop or marina. Ruth Ann was the only one he couldn't seem to get over. In the past he'd gone to great lengths to get her back, even stopped drinking and catting around for a while. Then he'd get back to his old ways and Ruth Ann would throw him out again. Very entertaining, although ultimately tiring, but even that seemed to have died down.

He had turned sixty the summer before but was still all bone and sinew. His dark skin stayed the same color no matter what the time of year, but then he was outside all year round, seldom making any concession to the weather except to pull on a jean jacket if the temperature dipped below fifty. He was as dark and mean as the feral pigs he loved to hunt illegally in the scrub brush out around the state park east of Sarasota. Every Thanksgiving and again in March he'd have a pork barbecue. The pigs went on a spit over a hardwood fire early in the morning and cooked all day. People started dropping in around three, the women bringing potato salads and desserts, the men carrying twelve packs of beer and some lawn chairs. They'd sit themselves down and drink and laugh and make a little music while they watched the spit turn. When Tully decided the pigs were done, two men would lift the spit onto a scrubbed picnic table and they'd begin carving them up. Served on a fresh bun with some brown mustard, it's as sweet and tender a meal as you'll ever get.

I gave Tully a thin cautious smile and said, "That's good, glad to hear you're doing fine." I turned back to the clerk, holding out my hand for the change and grabbing my bottle of water, anxious to get away from Tully. I shoved the change in the pocket of my jeans as Tully reached out and picked up the beer.

"Well, see ya," I said and walked.

Tully beat me to the door. "Sherri, how's 'bout we get a little bite?"

I looked at him, trying to guess what he wanted, to judge if he was about to tell me some real bad news or if it was just a friendly offer. Yeah, right — as if. I knew it wasn't going to be the last option. I could only hope for a moderately bad crisis, if such a thing existed.

"Okay," I agreed cautiously, looking for the open pit about to swallow me.

"I'll drive." He pointed to the edge of the lot. "Park Jimmy's truck over there."

"It's my truck," I snapped. It had been Jimmy's until he died but it was mine now. Silly, but Clay always called it Jimmy's truck, making a big deal of it and always wanting me to get something different. Another little sliver of annoyance in our splintery lives together, and I'd grown stubborn about getting rid of it, not that I had any deep attachment to it and certainly not to Jimmy, like Marley keeps insisting. I just don't like being told what to do. Giving in just isn't my style.

Tully raised an eyebrow and said, "Fine, your truck."

I parked the truck and walked over to where he stood waiting for me, watching to make sure I really was coming and wasn't going to slip away at the last second — such a close and trusting family.

Tully also drove a pickup but it wasn't a pretty little red one like Jimmy's. Tully's was held together by rust and dirt. The back bumper was wired to the body to keep it off the pavement and there was a big dent in the tailgate.

The back of the truck was full of diving gear. People or jobs — sticking to things was not a talent Tully ever had. Only the Gulf of Mexico held his imagination and his faithfulness. A Peter Pan sort of person, the old coot still followed his holy grail, his dream of finding buried treasure. When he wasn't driving long-haul trucks or working shrimpers he was out diving to wrecks off the west coast of Florida, searching the aquamarine waters for Spanish bullion or Confederate ships that had sunk while loaded with money to buy arms in Europe. He had a hundred stories to justify his hope, plausible and exciting. I'd believed them all when he'd first told them to me, his eyes shining and his voice full of conviction.

I squawked the door of the truck open. The ripped upholstery, spewing stuffing, was covered with the rubbish; empty food containers, beer cans, tools and papers. He used his forearm to sweep it all to the floor. "Get in," he ordered, dropping the beer on top of the mess on the floor.

I set my bag on the seat and looked for a safe place to put my feet. Sticking out of the chaos under the Coors was one of those pamphlets you see in doctor's offices. This one was on angina. That's serious stuff, right? I looked at Tully. Was this what I was about to hear?

Ruth Ann had moved up to Carolina to be with my two half-sisters and their children. Tully was the only relative I had left. Suddenly I didn't want to be left alone. Even this old fart, who I avoided like a communicable disease, was better than nothing.

He had the truck started, coughing and shaking, and was fiddling with the radio. "Get in," he repeated.

I got in.

Tully drove east, past Tamiami Trail, past the I-75, towards farm country where palms and manicured lawns gave way to slash pines and palmettos. "You didn't tell me I'd need to pack a lunch just to get to the food."

He stayed silent, didn't seem in the mood to fight, which took away a lot of the fun of being with him. Fighting was generally what passed for quality time between Tully and me. He drove with the window rolled down and a hand resting out on the side mirror, heading towards where the sun rose, while the Dixie Chicks kept us company. A mile past Hobo Joe's Fireworks I was about to protest about the odyssey when he pulled in to the shell parking lot of an old roadhouse called The Dog Trot, or rather, The Dog rot. The *T* was long gone and *rot* better described what was happening to the place. Long and low, with a door in the middle and three narrow windows on either side filled with neon beer signs, decay was eating the ramshackle structure from the ground up. It was visibly gnawing away at the bottom of the grungy, grey-board siding to reveal black tarpaper beneath.

"They should change the name," I said staring out the window at the ruin of a building. "No way would the humane society let a dog in there."

"We just came to eat, not to do a house beautiful tour." His door screeched open so I made mine make that nice sound as well.

Inside things did not get better. The smell — stale beer, sweat and last week's fries — suited a room so dark you couldn't move from the door until your eyes adjusted to the gloom. It was silent, except for the scrape of a barstool on a plywood floor, as if the place were taking our measure, waiting to see if we might be dangerous.

The return of vision didn't change my first impression. Across from the door, a narrow bar ran most of the length of the back wall. Along the wall where we stood was a line of small scarred tables.

Business seemed slow. The only customer was a man at the bar studying the bottom of his beer glass. He didn't look up.

"Hi, Tully," the bartender called out. A big man, he leaned on the bar with both tattooed arms, looking like he was hoping someone would come along and try to give him lip. I couldn't imagine anyone crazy enough, or drunk enough, to do it, but the big guy would sure enjoy it if they did.

Dad grunted in reply and turned right, going to the last table and sat with his back to the end wall. I followed his lead and pulled out the chair against the side wall. With our backs protected from whatever might come, I was still regretting leaving my Beretta in the glove compartment. It seemed likely I'd have a use for it in a place like this.

"I'm not the delicate sort, really," I informed Tully, "but my stomach is saying don't even think of eating here."

"Hasn't killed me, has it?"

I kept any further opinions to myself and picked up the greasy card with the menu printed on it. "Going on the theory that it's always good to order something hot enough to kill germs and too hot to be touched by human hands, I'll have a grilled cheese."

"You'll be missing some of the best pulled pork you ever tasted."

"Sad, but then life is full of tough choices."

He grinned at me. I don't know why but he suddenly looked as delighted as I'd ever seen him. Maybe he knew something evil about the cheese in the place. He got up and went to the bar, putting in our orders and returning with two long necks.

Our past history was a battle zone of broken promises, wrecked intentions and shattered dreams, so we concentrated on our beers, trying to find conversation that was safe and not leading to war. I worked on the label while I tried to put words together. Finally I asked outright. "So, how sick are you?"

"What?"

"There was a pamphlet in the truck on angina."

"Naw, just indigestion."

"Don't shit a shitter, Daddy."

"I'm telling you it was nothing. Have to stop eating raw onions and chili, that's all." He winked at me and said, "It'll still take three good men to lick me."

I nodded. "Yeah, but it won't take 'em long." A strip of label came off in one satisfying full width.

I looked up at Tully. "I have to tell you something."

He had the bottle halfway to his mouth and he paused there, waiting. Just like me, Daddy could hear bad news coming miles away.

CHAPTER 15

"Now, don't blow your top until I've said it all." Yeah, right, as if that was ever going to happen.

He took a deep pull at the bottle. Lowering it, he said, "Okay."

I told him about Ray John.

Somehow he kept quiet through my long confession and in the end he said, "You should have shot the bastard. Better still," he stuck a forefinger in my face, "you should have told me and let me kill him."

This was going well. He was mad but not crazy. Not yet.

"Which is exactly why I didn't tell you."

He glared at me.

"I'm only telling you now so you won't be blindsided when it hits the papers." Not that Tully ever wasted time with the news, treating it with equal parts of disgust and scorn, but surely he had to have one friend or acquaintance who could read.

A man came through the door, looked around, saw us and said, "Hey, Tully." He started towards us.

"Bugger off," Daddy snarled.

It was fun to watch. The guy's eyes got wide, he leaned away from us at the same time as he executed a perfect pirouette, one leg bending up behind the other, and with his arms out for balance before both feet hit the floor, headed for the opposite end of the room.

Tully didn't seem to be impressed. Guess he was just used to people buggering off when he told them to, a trick I was seriously envious of.

"This guy Leenders going to give you any problem, I mean is he stalking you or something?"

"No. Anyway I live in the most secure building in the world and Clay's there. Well, normally he's there. He and another couple of guys have entered their sloop in a yacht race. He'll be back next week."

It occurred to me that I hadn't told my father I was living with Clay, and had never introduced them, but Tully was focused on the bad news.

"You want me to stay with you 'til he gets back?" The shock must have shown on my face because he added, "I'll do it if you want me to. Or you can come out and stay with me." Now, the inside of Tully's house looked like he was getting ready for a giant jumble sale, with diving gear, fishing tackle and tools piled on the chairs and the tables or on the floor, left just where he'd dropped them after last using them. But still he'd asked.

"No need for that," I assured him.

"Still you need someone there. You don't want to be alone while this is going on."

What comes after shock?

Tully nodded, deciding his idea was a good one. "I better come over."

"Why?"

"Hey, I'm your dad.

"Yeah, I remember." I smiled at him. "Marley's staying with me. And Lacey, Ray John's stepdaughter, a houseful, but thanks anyway."

He still wasn't convinced. "Seems some muscle might be needed."

"I'll call if I need you."

"Or call if you change your mind and want me to just shoot the son of a bitch. Save you all that court time."

"Naw, I'll give that a pass."

He nodded, slowly, watching me. "You really made something of yourself, a restaurant and all."

"Yeah, it's a real glamorous life. This morning my cleaner didn't show up so I ended up cleaning the toilets and running the vacuum around myself. Then the chicken supplier, I'm supposed to be there now by the way, refused to deliver any more chicken 'cause his bill is past sixty days. I'm on my way out there now to deliver a check that may even clear the bank, given a good night, and pick up about a hundred pounds of chicken. Meanwhile, the chef is trying to kill the sous-chef because he used the wrong marinade. Yup, I'm all about glamour."

He was smiling. Hot dog, the man was actually finding me amusing.

"By the way, do you think Ruth Ann is ever coming back?" I asked, pushing my luck now that I had him in a good mood.

"Nope."

"How do you feel about that?"

"Seems all right. It's just you and me now, kid."

All rightie then, that took care of that subject.

His smile was making me feel reckless and I was about to ask if there was anyone special in his life when the food arrived and saved me from that gross stupidity.

Halfway through the grilled cheese, the door opened and six raucous bikers flowed in, and then someone started up the music and Toby Keith started singing about how he loved this bar.

"This place isn't much different from the first bar I worked in," I told Tully. "When Jimmy went off to college on that golf scholarship and I followed him, he started doing some really heavy stuff. I had to get a job to support us. It was a bar pretty much like this, only in those days it was full of smoke."

"We still smoke in here."

"How does the Florida health department feel about that?"

"They don't have much pull at the Dog Trot."

"I'm thinking they've never even been through the door."

I tried Rena at the store twice on the way back to town. Still no answer. I tried her house. Nothing.

"Shit."

I didn't want to go back to Blossom Avenue, but lots of horrific scenarios were running through my mind and I knew no matter what went wrong, Rena didn't close the store. What had I started? And what was I going to find in that neat little white house?

CHAPTER 16

Outside the white bungalow everything looked quiet and normal, no police cars, ambulances or yellow crime-scene tape. Only one vehicle stood in the drive, Rena's sedan. I had a good look at the house — nothing that shouldn't be there, no broken windows, nothing out of place. No one was screaming for help.

Should I take my gun? I felt exposed and vulnerable without it but how likely was Ray John to be here if his SUV wasn't? And I had nothing to fear from Rena, right? I took a deep breath and let it out and then I left the safety of the pickup, the ping, ping, ping of the open door calling me back.

I pressed the bell and had another good look around. Down the street a guy was pushing a lawn mower around a square of already perfect grass. If I yelled for help, would he hear me? Not likely over the racket he was making. The grass smelled nice though, nice and normal. I was growing real fond of normal.

I waited for Rena to open the door, going from apprehensive to bored and then, when I'd pushed the doorbell three times, I went back to worried. Finally I decided she'd gone somewhere with Ray John. But why? And would she have left Lacey behind? Ray John sure as hell wouldn't. And Rena wouldn't close the store for anything. Like me she was swimming too close to the mouth of the shark not to pay attention. Something was wrong here.

A new possibility occurred to me. How did I know Lacey was still at school? I decided to go back to the truck and call Rena's cell one more time before I called the police. If Rena and Ray John had taken off with Lacey, I was sending the cops after them and let the shit fly where it may.

I turned for the truck just as the door cracked. No words were spoken and I couldn't see who was there in the dark. "Rena?" I asked. The door opened a little more.

I started to make a joke then I saw her face. "I was worried about you," I told Rena through the four-inch opening.

I took in her condition. She looked like she'd crawled out of a concrete mixer. Her whirlwind hair had been combed by a blender, matted in places and sticking out from her head in others. An angry bruise was forming on her left cheek; a trickle of blood crept from her cracked lip. One eye was already closed and blood stained her satin top.

Through stiff lips she lisped, "Don't worry about us, stop thinking about us, get out of our lives." She started to close the door but I stuck my foot in the wedge.

I put my face closer to the crack. "Why aren't you at the store? What happened?"

"None of your business."

"I want to help."

"Go away." She was pushing hard on the door now, squeezing my foot. "I don't need your help."

"All right, all right but open the door a little. I have to get my foot out."

As she opened the door a crack I pushed hard, sending her flying backwards into the hall. She recovered fast and flew at me, pushing and shoving me and slapping at me. "Get out, get out. I don't want you here."

My hands went up to fend off her blows while I was screaming back at her, "Ray John beat the crap out of you, I didn't. Why are you taking it out on me?"

Slowly her rage ran away and she went perfectly still. Tears ran down her face.

"Are you satisfied?" she sobbed. She put her fingers up to her face. "You did this."

"No I didn't. I didn't hit you. Ray John did and he's been doing a lot worse to Lacey."

She swung at me, first with her right and then with her left hand, more to shut me up, to stop me from blurting out the horrible truth she didn't want to know than to really injure me, but it hurt anyway, battered my arms I'd put up to protect my head.

"Get out," she screamed. "I don't want to hear any more of your filth." She was a whirlwind of blows and then she pushed me and I stumbled backwards out through the open door, slamming into the black wrought-iron railing. The door banged shut before I regained my balance.

I was left with a dilemma. Should I call the police and report Ray John for spousal abuse? Would that make the situation better or worse? And there was another question digging its way out of my brain. School would be out in twenty minutes — who, besides me, would be there waiting for Lacey when she came through the door?

I headed for the high school. I wasn't equipped for this shit and I didn't want to be responsible. But who else was there? Styles was the one who'd signed on for this when he'd picked up his badge. This was his problem, not mine. I dialed his number.

I cruised around the block checking out the cars waiting for kids while his phone rang. I left a message on the voice mail and tossed the mobile on the seat. I couldn't wait for Styles. I turned around and drifted back up the block past the school.

No sign of Ray John unless he'd changed vehicles. I double-parked in front of the door, waiting and watching. Kids spilled out the big double doors, laughing and yelling, some lighting cigarettes before they were off school property — but no Lacey. The owner of the car I was blocking came out. I backed up, barely taking my eyes off the door. The rush dribbled down to a trickle.

I had to move for another car to get out. Now I was starting to panic. No good to call Rena; she might know where Lacey was but she wasn't going to tell me.

My finger was punching Styles' number again when Lacey came out. But she didn't come far. She stopped on the stairs like a wary animal and looked around. Only when she saw the little red pickup did she come down the stairs, still cautious, still ready to turn and run back inside to safety. Twenty yards from the truck she bolted. I reached over and opened the door for her. Safely inside, she turned and hit the lock.

"Take it easy," I told her.

She was already looking out the rear window, searching for her tormentor.

"He isn't here. I checked while I was waiting for you."

No answer.

"Let's start over. Hi. How was your day?"

She looked at me but didn't answer.

"Hungry?"

She shook her head.

"Has your mom called?"

"No," cautious and wary, waiting for the other shoe.

"She wasn't feeling well, closed the store this afternoon. I was just wondering if she still wanted you to work."

"I have a key."

"Maybe we'll just leave it closed for today."

"No, no." She shook her head in denial. "We can't afford to have it closed."

She couldn't be talked out of it.

Rena wasn't at the store when we pulled in. I went in with Lacey and watched her open up. Efficient and reliable, she had it all under control. How can a kid be so together in one part of her life and have the rest so messed up?

Styles called back when I went up the stairs. Our conversation didn't make me feel any better. "I'm on my way to talk to Leenders."

This was only likely to make Ray John madder and more desperate, but there was no way Styles was going to back off. I didn't have a real good feeling about any of this.

I hung up and called Marley. "I've got a little problem."

"Gee, that must be a novel experience for you."

"Yeah, it is a pleasant change from my dull life."

"Well, if it's money you want, forget it. I'm only staying with you 'cause you've got food in the fridge. When it's gone, so am I."

"I can always use money, but at the moment it's Lacey I'm worried about. Ray John beat Rena up today."

"Shit," Marley said when I told her about my little chat with Rena. I was too worried to take any joy in her lapse from grace.

"Lacey is alone in the store. I'm right upstairs but it's kind of scary. What if Ray John comes for her?"

"He wouldn't dare kidnap her in plain view of all those people coming and going."

"I don't know what he'll do. I think he's over the edge. Will you pick her up at nine and take her home? I'm short-staffed and won't be able to get away until closing, and I don't want to just take her back there and dump her, leave her alone at the apartment."

"Sure, no problem. Better yet, give us each a free dinner and I'll go to the store as soon as I get off work and hang out with her."

"I don't know if I can afford your friendship. You're going to eat me into bankruptcy."

"Who knew? You and food is still a novel concept but I knew if I hung in there long enough, knowing you would pay off in something besides laughs. My magnanimous forgiving nature and the bounty of my friendship is finally being rewarded."

"You aren't doing drugs, are you?"

"That would be your other best friend."

"All right, dinner on me but you aren't eating the whole damn menu. Chicken off the kids' menu."

She made a gross sound.

"Okay, okay, I'll throw in a couple of salads."

"What are you going to do, Sher? This situation is out of control. You need help. Get that guy off the street."

"Styles tells me that won't happen. If Rena denies Ray John hit her, nothing happens. And even if they do arrest him I have to be prepared for him to be back out in twenty-four hours. Best we can hope for is they'll have a restraining order against him and he won't be allowed back into the house but how will he react to that? Maybe it will just make him crazier."

A new thought hit me. "For sure, Rena will take Lacey back now. I'm surprised she hasn't yet. I bet she doesn't want Lacey to see her face and know what happened. It might buy some time. I need to do something, but what? Where's Miss Emma when I need her?"

It would be good to have someone older and wiser to help with this problem. Older, but not necessarily wiser, made me think of Tully. "I told Tully about Ray John."

"Phew!" Marley spat out. "So sorry I missed that. How crazy did he get?"

"Took it fine. Didn't break anything, shoot anything or even threaten to kill anyone. He did offer to off Ray John though. Wasn't that sweet?"

"That would be mildly amusing if I didn't know it was true. For sure he'd do it. Remember setting up bottles for him and your Uncle Ziggy to shoot? They barely waited for us to get out of the way before they started blasting away. Those two set a whole new standard for bizarre."

"I learned to shoot out there. I'm quite a good shot."

"Great, I'll tell that to the reporter who interviews me after your arrest. You with a gun is just bad news." I'd heard this before, which was why I hadn't mentioned what was in the fanny pack.

I told Marley, "Things are bound to get nasty when this comes out. I'll sound like just the sort of trash Bernice always said I was."

"Hey, your mother-in-law is a whole lot trashier than you ever thought of being, just trash with money. Gotta go, my patient is here."

All night I kept calling down to the Beach Bag to check on Lacey. Everything was fine. Nothing happened. Instead of reassuring me, it was freaking me out. When Skip dropped a tray of dirty glasses I jumped about two feet in the air.

The night slipped away with still no sign of Ray John, but he was out there waiting. Ray John wasn't going to give up his victims that easy; I just didn't know where or when he was going to come after them — or after me.

Marley called to say they'd closed the store. We stayed on the line until they were safely in Marley's car. At the Tradewinds she called again and said, "We're home but we were followed. He didn't do anything. Didn't even get out of the truck, but just his being there behind us freaked Lacey out."

After the Sunset closed I had Miguel walk me to the truck.

"You all right?" he asked.

"Sure, no problem." But I wasn't fooling him.

"Want me to follow you home?"

The answer was yes, but he'd already worked twelve hours and babysitting me wasn't part of his job description.

"I'm fine, Miguel, just tired."

I headed for downtown Jac to make a night deposit. Even at the best of times I hate going to the bank at night. I usually just lock the receipts in the bottom draw of my desk and don't worry about it, but I hadn't gone to the bank that afternoon and the insurance company has rules about how much cash I can have on the premises.

I looked over my shoulder as I went up Beach Road. I watched all the pull-offs and all the driveways, waiting for a dark monster to shoot out and trap me.

Not a sign of Ray John.

At the bank I sat in the truck, checking out the empty parking lot, sure he was there someplace just waiting to get at me.

CHAPTER 17

My plan always was if anyone came close to me when I was making a night deposit, well, I planned to throw the bank deposit bag as far away from me as possible and run like hell. But Ray John wasn't interested in money, so he wouldn't follow the cash and leave me alone. He'd come after me. I'd seen what he'd done to Ruth Ann and Rena, what would he do to me?

Even though there was no other vehicle in the lot, fear anchored me in the truck. In the end I squealed out of the parking lot, taking the money with me.

When I got home Marley was still up. I dropped my keys and the fanny pack holding the Beretta on the counter. "How's she doing?" I asked, nodding in the direction of the den.

"I think she's waiting for that bastard to come drag her back. Of course, my hanging around pretty much says she's right to worry."

I opened the bread drawer and stuck the night deposit bag inside. "I'm going to see Brian tomorrow and charge Ray John."

Brian Spears was my lawyer as well as my friend and although he was a real estate lawyer, he'd help me through this.

"And I'm going to have another go at Rena. She has to under-stand what Ray John has been doing to Lacey. Rena wouldn't listen today but I can't wait, can't keep Lacey's secret anymore. It just helps Ray John. Sooner or later Lacey has to go home; this is just a time out, and if he's still there the whole thing will start over. I can't let that happen. I can't wait any longer."

"It ain't going to be pretty," Marley said. "Are you ready for that?"

I opened a packet of hot chocolate and poured it into a cup. "Do you want some?"

"No." She shook her head. "Answer the question, are you ready for the bomb that's about to go off in your life?"

"If you want to reconsider your choice of bridesmaid, I'll understand," I told her.

"Like hell you would. You'd do something painful and nasty to me. So you're still in, even if you end up on Dr. Phil's show." Her face clouded over. "That's if it ever happens, the wedding I mean."

"Have you talked to David?"

"Nope."

"Hasn't he called?"

"Nope."

"What exactly did you do?" I took the steaming mug out of the microwave and sprayed canned whipped cream three inches thick on top of the hot chocolate, taking comfort in calories. I led the way out to the balcony.

"The church needs a new roof and donations aren't cutting it. I was just trying to get the bloody garage sale organized." Marley picked up a silk cushion off a rattan chair and plopped down cross-legged on the chair, hugging the cushion to her chest.

"Seeing how you're the greatest garage sale fanatic in the nation, they had the perfect person in charge."

"I know," she wailed and punched the cushion. "You should see the neat stuff I've got stacked in the Sunday School nursery room." Her emerald eyes gleamed at the thought of the loot. Every Saturday and Sunday she cruised up and down every back street on the island buying vintage stuff. She often talked about opening a small antique store on Hope Street, one street over from Banyan. Hope Street is full of antique stores and tea shops and packed with bargain hunters.

"They're just so sensitive. I was really into it, but those women just wouldn't get with the program. Everyone with their own ideas but no one was ready to do any work. I was trying to be efficient."

"I'm thinking you were a tad bossy."

"I'm not bossy; I just have the best ideas. Besides, what we needed was labor, not ideas. We had a great handmade quilt to raffle and some antique furniture for a silent auction. It was going to be terrific."

"Words were exchanged?"

"Some."

"I'm betting not ones that are normally heard in Sunday School."

"Not exactly." She reached a finger out and scooped up a dollop of whipped cream. I refrained from slapping her, knowing she was going through a bad time. "A delegation went to David. David asked me to step down as chairperson." The cushion came in for some more punishment. "He took their side over mine. Don't you think he should have told them to get stuffed?"

"I don't think ministers are allowed to use those words."

She frowned. "He should have been on my side."

Suddenly I was exhausted. That's what happens when you start the morning cleaning toilets — you just don't have enough juice to finish the chocolate.

Before sleep found me my cell rang. No caller ID. Ignore it or take a chance? It could be Clay or it could be a crude reminder that I was annoying a real bad guy. Curiosity is a terrible curse.

CHAPTER 18

"I give in," Clay said.

"To what?"

"Love, that's what it is, I know that now. I admit it, I can't live without you."

"What's happened since I talked to you two hours ago?"

"The sky, big and full of stars, do you realize how unimportant we are? The only thing we have is each other and love."

I smile into the dark, figuring a little booze was involved with the stars and the love, but even though I like to take advantage of other people's weak moments, it had been a long day. "Look, it's one-thirty in the morning and I'm beat, too tired for philosophy. Let's talk about the meaning of life tomorrow."

"It's love I want to talk about. Meet me in Miami."

For a nanosecond I thought about it, thought about leaving the mess for someone else to sort out. "Can't," I said. "Marley's here."

"Marley can look after herself. Let her stay there if she wants, although I can't quite get why she's there."

"Hiding out from the church ladies. They want to lynch her. Also she knows I've had trouble being alone."

"And how are you doing with that?"

I laughed. "I haven't really had a chance to find out. But I'm okay. No big panic attacks, no waking up screaming all in a sweat. Mostly now I just wake up horny."

"Come to Miami. I have the cure."

"There's something else, or rather someone else." The wrong time for this conversation but it couldn't wait. I told him about Lacey and to tell him about that, I had to tell him about Ray John.

The silence dragged out between as long as the miles. "Were you ever planning on telling me about this?"

"Not really."

"Why?"

"I just wanted to forget it."

"You don't trust me, do you?" Clay asked. His voice was heartbreakingly gentle.

"Why are you taking this so personally? It has nothing to do with us."

"Everything about you has to do with us. No secrets. Isn't that what we agreed?"

"There's a tall order."

"If we're in for the long haul, that's how it's got to be."

"We've never really talked about longer than next week. Can we talk about this when you come home? I need you closer for a serious conversation like this. Need to be able to see you."

"And yet it seems to me we always have our serious conversations long distance."

"That's because when we're together you can't keep your hands off me long enough to talk."

"I'm not the only one doing the grabbing."

"It's true. I never knew I was a nympho before I met you."

"You're trying to distract me. It's working, but there's one more thing I want to say before we go right off topic. Call Styles and charge that bastard. Do you want me to come home? Screw the race."

No excuses now.

"Don't come home. I'm calling Brian in the morning and bringing a civil suit against him. But thanks anyway. Got to go."

I dropped the phone and slipped into sleep. Hours later, pounding on the bedroom door woke me. Fuzzy-headed and annoyed I sat up in bed. The door slammed open and Marley shot in.

"He's dead," she said.

CHAPTER 19

I shot upright in bed. "No." One word was all I could manage. My lungs no longer worked. Clay dead? I couldn't conceive of it. I always felt I'd lose him but not this way. More likely one day he'd wake up and see what a fool he'd been wasting time with me, but to lose him in a stupid race? I couldn't lose him to water. "No, no," I was shaking my head in denial, wanting Marley to take back her words. "I told him not to go. Why did he go?"

For a minute Marley's face wrinkled in confusion. "Oh no, not Clay." She came farther into the room. "Sorry," she said coming to the bed and dropping down to its edge. She was wearing white cotton pjs with black sheep on them. How strange was that? Death and black sheep.

The world righted itself again. "Who?" I croaked. It didn't matter as long as it wasn't Clay. I'd give up anyone to keep Clay.

She wrapped her arms around my knees. "Ray John."

I could function again. "Good." I was relieved that it was no one I cared about. "I hope it was painful."

"You don't mean that," Marley said gently.

"Yes I do. You don't know how much I hated him." I took air deep into my belly and let it out slowly. Relief washed over me. "It's over now. Lacey is free."

"It's only just beginning." Marley's face held concern and

something else. "The radio said his body was found about three in the morning at the recreation hall of the Preserves."

"He was head of security there. Did they say anything else? What happened? How did he die?"

"He was shot."

And now I knew why she didn't share my relief upon hearing he was dead. "Funny but I would have thought he'd be the one doing the shooting. He was a violent, dangerous man, hard to think of someone killing him. Do you know what I mean?"

"You mean like violence came from him not to him?"

"That's it," I nodded. "I thought he might try to kill me or even Rena, never thought of anyone killing him."

"But surely," Marley said, "there must be more than enough people who wanted him dead. Isn't it a surprise it hasn't happened before?"

"Maybe. Who shot him?"

"Don't know."

She worried the inside of her cheek with her teeth. I knew something was coming I wouldn't like. My chest tightened.

"The police are looking for a pickup truck seen leaving the area shortly before he was found. That's all there was on the news."

"Tully." I buried my hands in my hair. "Oh my god, I told Tully about Ray John." All those years I kept my mouth shut, why did I have to blow it now? "He went after him. Oh god, why couldn't I keep my mouth shut just this once."

Marley lunged at me, wrapping her arms around me. We clung together, Marley saying, "You don't know that, don't know it was Tully. Don't jump to conclusions."

I pulled away from her and looked into her face. "But it's true, isn't it?" I said.

Her green eyes wavered and a tear slipped over the rim of her eye. Her freckles stood out like a rash on her ashen skin. She couldn't hide the truth we both knew.

I pushed down the covers and slid from the bed. "I have to find him."

"Whoa," Marley said, grabbing at my oversized sleeping shirt. "Think about it."

"You think." I pulled away and grabbed a pair of jeans from the closet. "Be sure and let me know what the results are. I have to find Tully." I tried to stuff a foot into the twisted pant leg of my jeans, hopping on one foot and kicking, fighting the fabric. "If I'd gone on keeping my mouth shut this wouldn't have happened."

"Okay," she said and picked up the bedside telephone and started punching in numbers.

I conquered the jeans. "What are you doing?" I asked sucking in my stomach to do up the zipper.

"You're not going alone."

"I need to see Tully before they arrest him." I took the phone away from her as the dental-office answering machine picked up. "Need to talk to him."

She looked doubtful.

"I have to do this alone."

She plopped back onto the bed. "Poor Tully. This just can't happen to him," she sputtered. Hugging my pillow to her chest she wailed, "I love him." She was crying for real now.

"Why?" I was really curious about this. Why would anyone love Tully? I'd spent most of my life hating him and wishing I had another father, a normal one, someone I could do normal things with, someone I could depend on, someone who showed up when he said he would, someone to be proud of.

Marley didn't have to think about her answer. "He was just so different from mine," she said. "Always a laugh and never giving advice." Marley's father was in insurance and had high standards, a hundred and eighty degrees from my old man. "Tully didn't expect anything."

"How could he? He's one of the world's great screw-ups. He's just proved that. How could he ever think this was making things better? It will hit the papers big-time now, murder and child abuse. The *Jacaranda Sun* is going to love it."

My pillow slammed into the wall. "When did you start caring so much about what people think?"

True, I did care. My don't-give-a-shit attitude had deserted me.

"You're getting to be just what you always hated," she said, her voice accusing.

"And what's that?" I dropped my nightshirt on the floor and pulled a tee off a hanger.

"You're turning into a social climbing…" I turned to look at her.

"You're turning into your mother-in-law, you're turning into Bernice," she yelled.

Her words rocked me before fury ripped through me. "Oh, thanks a whole hell of a lot. Don't you think I have enough to deal with without you taking a piece out of me?"

She bit the inside of her cheek. "Sorry." It was reluctant and insincere, dragged out of her because of sympathy and not because she believed it.

I turned away from her and pulled on the tee.

"I'm just scared for Tully," she wailed. "What if he does something stupid?"

"Oh, you think he can do something more asinine than killing Ray John?"

"What if he runs from the police?" She was crying again now. "What if he…" She couldn't finish the thought.

It took my breath away. What if? Here I was thinking about my problems when Tully was up to his ass in alligators. And Marley was right, somewhere along the way I'd started desperately seeking normal and belonging. Truth was, maybe I'd never been the rebel I thought I was.

"What's happening?" Lacey stood at the door. In her plaid pajama bottoms, white cropped top and bed head. She looked shockingly young.

"I have some bad news for you, Lace," I said. "Come and sit down."

"What?" she wailed, backing away. "Is it my mom?"

"God no." I took her arm. "It's Ray John." I told her what Marley had said.

She looked confused, shaking her head in denial. "But I didn't do it," she whispered, looking at me in confusion. "I didn't shoot him."

I led her to the bed and she flopped down. Marley wrapped her arms around Lacey and tried to pull her close.

But Lacey resisted the embrace and demanded, "How could he be dead? I didn't kill him."

"No one is saying that you killed him," Marley soothed.

"Don't think that," I said. "No one is accusing you."

"I wanted to," Lacey blurted out.

"We both did. Doesn't mean we're responsible. You can't kill someone by wishing." I knelt down in front of her. "If wishing could kill, he'd have been long dead before he ever got to you."

"My mom will be upset." She was trying not to cry, sucking on her lips and hunching her shoulders together, trying to hold it in. "She really loved him." Lacey wiped at her eyes. "When she called me last night she said she wanted me to come home. She said RJ just wanted us to be a family and if that wasn't going to happen he was going to leave so Mom and I could be together again. She was terrified of him leaving. I told her what he did to me but she didn't believe me. She said you'd put those ideas in my head." Now she folded her arms on her knees and buried her head in them. We could barely catch her next words, "She said I was lying."

I looked at Marley over Lacey's shuddering back. "Poor kid," she said.

"I'll take you home, Lace."

When I picked up my keys off the bar I didn't spare a thought for the fanny pack with the gun in it. I didn't need it anymore so I didn't notice it wasn't there.

Not noticing the Beretta was gone was only the first of the mistakes I made.

CHAPTER 20

Rena was a mess, barely coherent and unable to recognize us at first. The police had come and gone, leaving her alone after delivering their news and offering to call someone, but Rena had kept to herself as she always did. Lacey wrapped her arms around her mother and rocked her gently, saying there, there, the eternal murmurs for a bad situation. Rena let it happen, not reaching out for her daughter or pushing her away.

"Have you got a doctor?" I asked.

"Yes," Lacey answered and pointed to a drawer in the end table holding the phone.

I took out the list of numbers and called the medical clinic. The doctor on duty called me back within five minutes. Then I drove to the pharmacy to pick up the prescription he ordered when what I really wanted to do was to go find Tully. I wanted to talk to him before the police got to him. I tried calling his house while I waited at the drive-through window of the drugstore. Tully didn't have a cell and he wasn't at home; perhaps the police had already picked him up. There was no answering machine, too hi-tech for Tully.

On the way back to Blossom Avenue my mobile rang. Hoping it was Tully, I grabbed for it before the second ring. It was Styles.

"Where are you?"

"I took Lacey Cagel to her mother's, then I picked up a prescription for tranquilizers and I'm about to drop them off."

"I need to talk to you."

"Okay, when?"

"Now, my office."

"Can't right now. Meet me at the Sunset about three."

"Now," he bellowed.

"See, ya." I hit End. He could show up at three or not. It was all the same to me.

I left Rena and Lacey to sort things out between them. When I pulled out onto the divided highway a cruiser turned onto Blossom behind me. Perhaps Styles had really lost his cool and sent them to pick me up.

My purse rang and I fished out my mobile. "We need to talk," Tully said.

"Well, good morning to you too. Where are you? I've been phoning."

"I'm at Zig's. Come over."

"I'm ten minutes away."

He hung up without saying goodbye but then he never did.

I picked up donuts and coffee and headed for Uncle Ziggy's.

Ziggy Peek isn't a real uncle. He and my dad were in 'Nam together where they'd sworn some undying devotion to each other in combat and when they got home they bonded over shooting rats out at Uncle Zig's junkyard, a wasteland of wrecked cars and junked appliances surrounded by an eight-foot-high wood barricade.

As a kid, Uncle Zig's junkyard was my Wonderland and amusement park, home away from home. When other kids went to adventure parks, I built my own out of ruined vehicles, rusted appliances and broken furniture while Dad and Zig drank beer and told lies. I escaped out into the jungle of crap and into a world of my own creation. I built little rooms furnished with old car seats and crates for tables. With pocket books stolen from Uncle Zig's stash to transport me to exotic worlds, I dreamt long hot afternoons away. And though it wouldn't be anyone else's idea of heaven, some of my happiest hours were spent fantasizing in that junkyard.

Twenty years ago Uncle Zig's property sat all alone on an empty stretch of the Tamiami Trail. Now strip malls and car dealerships had moved in and housing developments blossomed behind him. In fact, a gated community with four-hundred-thousand-dollar homes sat smack up against his back fence. Irate homeowners, who'd known the junkyard was there but built their mansions anyway, complained about rodents and other things coming from Uncle Zig's scrap heap. They sent letters to the newspapers and lawyers to court to make his life hell.

Uncle Zig was now in the interesting position of being land-rich and money-poor. The citizens' group got a zoning change to prevent him from bringing in any more junk, so now he eked out a living selling used auto parts and running a small dirt-moving business. He could barely pay his taxes, never mind my friend Brian's legal fees to fight off city planners and local homeowners. He was poor as dirt while owning millions of dollars' worth of land.

The walls of the barrier around Uncle Zig's property were decorated with hubcaps of every conceivable model. I pulled into his turn-off and honked my horn while I searched for new models along the fence. The gates, rigged by Uncle Zig and Tully, opened magically before me.

Against a backdrop of rusted steel and green mold, a strutting peacock stepped delicately across the hard-packed shell yard in front of me. I stopped while it stood and displayed its jeweled feathers, shaking them and crying mournfully. I laid on the horn. It yelled indignantly but pranced out of the way.

I pulled in beside Tully's piece of crap which was parked before a dilapidated construction trailer where Uncle Zig lived and worked.

Tully and Uncle Zig sat on wooden captain's chairs in front of the trailer. An empty white plastic lawn chair sat between them waiting for me. I was about to get double-teamed.

Uncle Zig's fat face split with a smile that warmed my heart and made me grin in response. At six-four and over three hundred pounds, Uncle Ziggy always looked like he was made up of leftover parts from the construction of other people, pieces that didn't quite fit together on one person, especially one as big as he was. His long legs looked like they were better suited to a man at least a foot taller, but his arms were short and ended in slim delicate hands, hands surely meant for a surgeon or pianist. He always wore work gloves to protect those hands, whether out of vanity or caution I could never decide, and as a result his hands were always pale and soft, unlike his other weathered parts left bare to the sun. His face didn't add up either. His nose was large and bulbous while his sparkling blue eyes, dots sunk into folds of fat like raisins stuck in a bun, were graced by long curling lashes, startling and feminine.

He got up out of his chair and held out his arms to me. I set the coffee down on the empty lawn chair and walked into his embrace. He smelt of sweat, grease and something like sandalwood that I'd never been able to figure out but always identified with him. It was like Uncle Zig was wearing his own special scent.

I stepped away from him. "What are these?" I asked, snapping yellow suspenders with black markings, looking like giant yardsticks holding up his oversized greasy black jeans. Stiff with grime, the jeans could probably stand up alone.

"Your dad." He hooked his thumbs in the suspenders and pulled them away from his chest, tipping backwards on his heels. "I'm always losing my damn tape measure. Your dad thought these would be a two-for. 'Course if I use them, my pants will fall down." He threw back his head and laughed uproariously. "Bare-assed but accurate, that's what I'll be."

Tully didn't even break into a smile, just lounged in his chair, one long leg stretched out, chin resting in his hand, waiting and watching. He may look relaxed but I knew he was a coiled spring, holding it together while we did our small talk.

I kicked his foot. "So what did you get up to last night?"

"I've been wondering the same about you," he replied, lowering his hand and folding his hands across his waist. "Why don't you tell us about it?"

I handed Uncle Zig a coffee from the cardboard container

and then gave Tully one. He took it, watching me, never letting his eyes drift from mine.

Suddenly I got it.

CHAPTER 21

"Hey, wait a minute, are you crazy? You think I killed him?"

"Did you?" he asked.

Stunned into silence, not something that happens to me often, my brain was taking in the irony of it. Here I was sure Tully had done the deed and he was thinking it was me. So if neither of us did it, who did?

"Look, kid," Tully said, "I don't care if you blew the shit-head away. We just got to decide how we're going to handle it."

I picked up the cardboard tray with my coffee and the donuts and flopped down on the chair. Giddiness was bubbling in me.

"Should have come to me or your dad," Uncle Zig put in.

I handed Uncle Zig the bag of donuts and popped the top off my coffee. "Shouldn't have done it yourself," Uncle Zig added. "That was foolish."

I stared from one to the other trying to make sense of what I was hearing. "I should have come to you to kill someone?" I asked Uncle Zig.

"Damn right." He took a bite of donut, covering his lips in powdered sugar and asked around the donut, "What do you know about killing?"

"What do you?"

He hesitated, studying me, and then shoved the rest of his donut into his mouth. He looked at me while he chewed and then stretched his neck out and gave a huge swallow. "What do you thing I was doing in 'Nam?"

He had a point there. I hadn't thought of that. Vietnam was another life, hard to think of Uncle Zig running through a jungle or actually killing someone. At three hundred pounds he looked more cuddly than dangerous.

Tully sat up straight in his chair. "As I see it we have a couple of options. You could go up to your mother's but they'd have you in no time. No use hiding out in the States, so the first thing is we get you on a boat today and head south. I can take care of getting a boat, no problem. Don't want to use my own, too easy to trace. We need one that no one will connect with us." Totally intense, totally absorbed, thinking it through, he was planning our great escape.

"We stay well away from any marinas, except for gas. From the Keys we can head for the Bahamas and from there down to South America and just get lost." It was a route I'd planned on taking once before in my life. Maybe it was an example of genetic wiring. Maybe generations of Jenkins had run from every conceivable crime, a perfect example of survival of the fittest. Hysteria was bubbling up in me.

"But we need to leave today, now," Tully insisted.

"Don't even go back to your apartment to pack," Uncle Zig said.

"Right, stay here with Zig. They'll never look for you here. Zig will take us to the marina and we'll leave our trucks here behind the barricade where no one will ever find them."

"I'll strip them for parts. There'll be nothing left for the cops to find."

"But we need to make them think we've gone north," Tully added.

"When you're gone, I'll drive up to Georgia and use your credit cards," Uncle Zig put in. "That will make the police think you're heading north."

My head swiveled between them. "Have you two done this before?"

"Naw," said Tully. "Haven't been out of the country since 'Nam but I'm pretty sure we can get to Venezuela or someplace like that without ID — boats come and go without people paying much attention — but I'm taking Zig's and maybe we can get some for you. How about Marley's birth certificate? That would work."

"And don't worry about money," Uncle Zig said. He reached out and patted my knee. "We've got that figured too. I'll get some down to you wherever you end up."

"Well, I'm glad you've thought this all through," I told them.

"There's another choice," Tully said, hitching his chair around to face mine and leaning intently towards me. "The other thing I was thinking is that I go in there and confess to killing Ray John, god knows I wanted to, but you have to tell me everything and give me the gun." His forgotten cup of coffee, hanging from his hand between his knees, emptied into the earth at his feet. "It's up to you which way we do it."

"Gun?"

"Yeah, I need that. I'll shoot it, have my prints on it." He pointed a forefinger at me. "And I need to know about the time and everything, need every little detail you can think of. There can't be any holes or anything to trip me up."

"Let me see if I understand this. You're going to confess to killing Ray John even though you didn't do it?"

He just nodded his head, more intent on going over the details than bringing me up to date on reality. "I drove out to that place this morning but it's gated," he said. "How did you get in? Did anyone see you, 'cause if they did that's going to be a problem. If they have a witness we've got to get the hell out of here." He reached out for my arm and shook me. "Talk. This is no time for you to go white lily on us."

I started to laugh. These crazy old buggers just weren't to be believed. My dad's face turned to confused concern at my hysteria. He dropped the coffee cup in the dirt beside him and reached out to shake me. "C'mon, kid, get it together."

I wiped my eyes and raised a hand to him to stop him from slapping me out of hysterics. "Okay, okay." I turned to Uncle Zig. "What about you, aren't you going to confess too?"

"Your dad thought it should be him, but I will if you think it sounds better."

I laughed. "No," I choked out, shaking my head. "Not necessary."

They looked from one to the other and waited impatiently, watching me, until the madness passed. "Not me," I babbled, shaking my head.

I jabbed a finger at Tully. "I thought it was you. But I sure have to tell you I wasn't about to confess and go to jail on your behalf."

"What are you saying?" Tully asked, sitting up straight.

"Are you telling me you didn't shoot Ray John Leenders?"

"Yes." My head was bobbing up and down wildly. "That's exactly what I'm saying."

He looked confused or dubious, I'm not sure which, and told me, "But a pickup was seen leaving the scene. That wasn't you?"

"Nope." I had to ask again, "Was it you?"

I watched my dad. He pursed his lips and shook his head. "Damn, I wonder who did it for us."

"Wasn't me," said Zig. "Although I sure as hell would have given it some thought if I'd known about that bastard. Why didn't you tell us, kid?"

"Because of this. Do you think I wanted you to get fried? Florida has the death penalty, you know."

"Damn," said my father. "Damn."

"Indeed." I raised my cup to Tully and toasted him. "Here's to two innocent people." He picked his cup up out of the dirt and touched his cup to mine. We grinned at each other over the rims. My coffee was barely lukewarm but I didn't care. It tasted the best I'd ever had.

"I have to call Marley. She'll be waiting to hear what I found out. Man she won't believe this." I dug around for my cell phone. "She made me promise to call her as soon as I talked to you. For reasons that escape me she would hate to see you incarcerated."

Marley picked up on the first ring which made me think maybe she doesn't work as hard as she likes to tell me she does. I told her about Tully, trying to keep it light around the lump in my throat.

"Tell him I love him," Marley said.

"Wait." I lowered the phone. "Marley says she loves you," I informed my dad.

"Yeah, all the girls do," he replied.

"What about me?" Uncle Zig protested. "I wanted to confess too."

"Oh yeah, he was ready. He wanted to arm wrestle me for the honor," Tully said.

"A pair of old fools," I told Marley.

"Lucky you," Marley said and hung up.

And she was right. These two old men were no one's idea of happy nurturing family and the pet adoption people would never let them near a stray cat, but they were mine. The one true thing I had in the world, the one thing I knew for sure was mine without question, something I didn't need to deserve or earn and definitely something that wouldn't desert me in times of trouble.

CHAPTER 22

Kimmi Yost called in ill and I was filling in as hostess when Detective Styles showed up at one o'clock in the middle of the lunch rush. Joy of joy, nearly every table in the main dining room was in use.

I gave Styles my biggest smile and picked up a menu. "Table for one, sir?"

He didn't return my smile. "You were supposed to be at my office. I told you to come by at three."

The elevator opened and four people emerged. I ignored Styles and took them to a table. When I got back, Styles was really steaming.

"Do you want me to arrest you in front of a full restaurant?"

"I'll sue," I promised. "False arrest. You have no reason to arrest me."

"How about a red pickup seen leaving the scene of a murder, a red pickup with a Florida license plate that says RIF RAF? Is that good enough?"

I could see my life swirling around the bowl. I spun around on my heel and signaled for Gwen to take over before I headed for my office, just on the edge of running.

Styles sagged into the chair across from my desk. His eyes were etched with red; his hair was tousled; his tie was undone and a shadow of whiskers crept along his jaw. Normally he was an extremely fastidious man, impeccably dressed and turned out. Actually, the tired, world-weary and jaded look worked, gave him an edge that I much preferred to Mr. Clean.

"Have you been up all night?"

He drew in his chin and said, "Never mind about me. You're in real trouble."

"Since birth." I picked up the phone to call the kitchen. "You probably haven't eaten either." Styles grabbed the phone out of my hand and slammed it onto the desk.

"Never mind that shit. Just answer my questions." He was shouting. This man didn't swear, didn't go unshaven and he certainly didn't shout. I was in trouble.

"What questions?"

"Did you kill Ray John Leenders?"

"No."

"Are you sure?"

"What kind of a stupid question is that? Of course I'm sure. True, there are a few incidents in my past that I don't fully recall but murder? I'm sure I didn't murder anyone."

He ran a hand through his disheveled hair. "Then why was your truck at the murder scene?"

"It wasn't. I was home in bed and the truck was downstairs in its parking spot."

"Can anyone verify it?"

"Well, Clay is away but Lacey Cagel was there in the apartment all night and so was Marley. They weren't sleeping in the same room but they were in the apartment. And Clay called at one-thirty and woke me up. He can tell you I was there."

"Cell phone?" he asked.

"If you mean did I talk to Clay on my cell, yes I did."

"Then you could have been anywhere." His brow furrowed. "Then how did your truck get out to the Preserves if you were home in bed?"

"Someone made a mistake. Has to be."

He shook his head and got to his feet. "No." The word came out long and slow. He paced the floor, working through it. "No, it was one of the security guards. He was pretty sure about it. Besides, RIF RAF is a pretty distinctive license plate."

"It's Bernice's favorite name for me. My ex-mother-in-law has lots of names for me but that's the only one they'll let me put on a license plate."

Styles was caught up in his thoughts. "The security guard is sure. He's used to taking note of license numbers and at three in the morning they notice any vehicle. I checked his background myself. Mark Cummings was a military MP."

I picked up the phone and ordered two specials and coffee. Styles glared at me. "I'm not hungry," he told me. "You're not going to make this go away by feeding me."

"Look, you aren't going to do anyone any good if you kill yourself. Besides I'm hungry."

"You're always hungry." He gave me a small smile and sat down on the corner of the desk. "Let's start at the beginning."

"But first, do you believe I had nothing to do with it?"

He listed my sins on his left hand. "You threatened him. You didn't want to go the court route. You were worried about this Lacey Cagel. Your truck was seen. And yes I think you could kill someone."

"Thanks for the stirring endorsement."

"But you're more likely to do it in a moment of anger, not sneaky like this."

"Well, thanks a bunch."

"What was I supposed to think? Can anyone get your truck out of the parking lot?"

"Sure. We all have these electronic buzzers, kinda like garage-door openers, to get us into the parking garage. I keep mine on the visor. But they would have needed the keys to the truck."

"Do you keep one of those little magnetic boxes under the bumper with an extra key?"

My face answered his question. "Shit," he said. "So much for security."

"But how would anyone get into the garage?"

"Trust me; I could get into that garage. It's all for show. Or it could be someone in the building."

I shook my head. "Who else in the building not only knew Ray John but knew that I knew him. That's a lot of knowing if you know what I mean. Doesn't make sense. And why take my truck?"

"No idea."

"Tell me what you do know."

He took a deep breath and let it out in a long loud sigh. "Okay." It took him a moment to get started. "It happened about three. Mark Cummings, a security guard at the Preserves, made his hourly rounds and came back to the recreation hall where the security guys have a little office. He was about to turn into the parking lot when a red pickup shot out. He took down the number as a matter of routine but he didn't drive in. Seems he knew about Ray John's bad habits and he wanted to give him time to collect himself. Ray John was given to accusing people of trying to sneak up on him."

"Which way did the truck go?"

"It was heading towards the entrance to the Preserves."

"What are they trying to preserve there besides their money?"

"Can't say but they definitely are willing to pay for it. They have eight guards on staff, security twenty-four hours a day. They have it covered." He scratched the side of his nose. "There's one on the gate from seven in the morning until eleven at night and after that you need a transponder to get in. A guard patrols the community all night."

"Tell me again, how does someone get in after eleven?"

"Like your building they have transponders or if you have a guest you give them a code to punch in on a number pad. It's always the same, the date. Or you can go down and let them out."

"Can someone walk in at night? Slip under the gate?"

"Yeah, but you couldn't get a car in without the number."

"Well, there you go. How would I get in? I didn't know the code, never even been out there."

"But it's pretty easy. I bet half the walled communities around use the date as the security number."

"One night, just for fun, I'll go out and try a whole bunch of gates but until you told me what it was I'd never have thought of the code."

"Rena could have told you."

Before I could call him something colorful there was a knock at the door and Gwen Morrison entered with a huge tray covered in white linen. She had a good look at Styles and then set the tray on the desk and pulled off the cloth. Styles' eyes were riveted on the food, while Gwen, grinning like she'd found out something delightfully naughty, raised her eyebrows and pointed at Styles, asking a silent question.

"Police," I told her. "Official business. They're looking for a terrorist and I'm turning you in."

"Nice," she said. "Being arrested could be fun. Especially if there's handcuffs involved."

"Don't wait for a tip."

"Well, you two have fun," she said and left.

"That's it," I told Styles. "My reputation is ruined. You'll have to marry me now."

"Wouldn't be so bad," he said, picking up his silverware and going back to his chair. "At least it would never get boring."

I remembered he'd just separated, started to say something smart but for once in my life managed not to put my foot past my tonsils. "Go back and tell me what happened when this guard found Ray John."

Styles pointed his knife at me. "This isn't for public consumption by the way."

"Yeah, yeah, yeah." I poured coffee from a flask. "Talk."

"Cummings decided to drive around for a little bit before he went in. Seems Leenders often had late-night visitors, entertained some ladies there and the guards knew enough to stay away when he was doing the nasty. Leenders was real sensitive about people knowing too much. Cummings waited for about twenty minutes so Leenders wouldn't know he'd seen his lady friend leave."

I stopped him there, "Did he know it was a woman in the car? Did he see a woman?"

"I asked that. He just assumed it was a woman."

"Okay," I said, pouring coffee into my cup. "Go on."

"Not much else. He went in and found Leenders dead, shot with a small-caliber weapon. Forensics isn't back yet, that will take a while."

"In the office? I mean was the body in the office?"

"No. The recreation hall has meeting rooms and a kitchen. There's also a small room, like a sitting room, with couches and chairs. That's where he was. The door to that room is normally locked but he had keys to the whole building, all the rooms. All the guards do."

"Do all the members have a key to the building?"

"No."

"So Ray John had to let his killer into the building."

"That's the assumption we're going on. Ray John knew his killer and let him in or he had a key, which would make it one of the guards or four people on the board."

"Maybe the killer just found an unlocked door."

He had his fork halfway to his mouth. He froze, looked up at me and said, "Damn. I hate it when you do that. You're not supposed to see things I don't."

"I haven't been up all night. Besides, it's unlikely they'd take a chance of finding an unlocked door if they were going out to murder him."

"Well, so far we've been assuming Leenders let his killer in and knew him or her." He was going through it, thinking out loud. "Probably her, and looking to get it on. That's why the room with the couch. If it had been a man, he would have taken him into the office."

"Your bias is showing. Maybe he was a double hitter."

"Did you ever see any evidence of that?"

"No." I thought about it a bit more. "But I wouldn't have thought of it back then. I was only eleven when he moved in and not even I grew up that fast."

"How long was he with your mom before he started hitting on you?"

"Right away, overly friendly, wanting us to be chums and all. I wasn't comfortable with him from the get-go, but Mom was madly in love. Well, not that that was anything new. They moved in together within weeks of the first date."

"Does your father know about this?"

Alarm bells went off in my head. "I told you, if I'd called my daddy up and told him that Ray John tried to rape me, he would have killed him. Daddy and I weren't real close but still I didn't want to see him in jail. He did show up occasionally and take me for burgers, or out on his boat." I grinned at the memory. "Now I think about it we had some real good times. He just wasn't good at everyday things, birthdays or keeping promises like picking me up after school. If I had to wait for Daddy it always ended in tears."

Styles went right by the filler and grabbed hold of the meat. "I mean does your father know now? Have you told him now that Ray John resurfaced?"

"No," I said. "There's cheesecake for dessert." Always hide the truth behind the cheesecake. "Running a restaurant can be dangerous for your waistline."

"You look okay to me."

CHAPTER 23

Did Styles know something about Tully he wasn't telling me? Tully had been out to the Preserves that morning. Maybe the police took license plate numbers. Not a good thing. Maybe Tully even called up Ray John and left a threatening message on his answering service. That was more likely. Or maybe Tully, after a few drinks, had got big-mouthed and told someone he was going to kill Ray John Leenders. Even more likely. Tully did some mighty stupid things when he was drinking. Like the time he rode a horse into the Presbyterian Church on a Sunday morning. I don't know why, maybe he was still drunk from Saturday night and it seemed like a good idea.

When I was a kid and people heard my last name they'd say, "Was your daddy the guy who rode a horse into Jacaranda Presbyterian?" Tully stories abounded. Unexpected and strange things were done by my father and people were going to be bringing up adventures of my daddy long after Tully was gone.

The cops would have lots of notes on Tully, starting with stealing a car when he was fourteen, so I didn't like any policeman asking about Tully even if I didn't think he was involved in Ray John's death. They just might uncover some other little escapade better kept hidden. Oh no, he wasn't out of the woods yet. There were still lots of things out there to rise up out of the mud and bite us on the ass.

But not for a minute did I think Tully was lying to me. He just wouldn't. Well, not about this anyway. Then what about Uncle Zig? Did he go out to the Preserves and shoot Ray John? Loved him madly but the man was no genius. Sneaking into a gated community and shooting someone wasn't his style. He was more likely to go to Ray John's home with a bulldozer and run over him. Flatten his house first and then run over him. But he'd never lie about it or try to hide it. Nope, if Uncle Zig murdered Ray John it would be perfectly obvious. Besides, he would have told us.

What about Rena? You mess with my kid, I'm going to have your balls for breakfast, but Rena hadn't believed Lacey or hadn't wanted to. She wanted Lacey to go back home as if nothing had happened. But what if Ray John had said he was leaving? She was madly, passionately in love with him. Would she rather see him dead than lose him?

Lacey could have done it, but like me she'd been tucked up in my apartment sound asleep.

I didn't like any of the candidates. There had to be someone else, someone from Ray John's past, someone with a long memory and a reason to get even.

I knew a woman who lived in the Preserves. Sheila Dressal and I played against each other in amateur golf tournaments all over the state of Florida, not close friends, nevertheless we'd connected and shared some laughs. She often came into the Sunset for dinner. I called her and was told to come right over. I was guessing the unnatural enthusiasm at hearing from me was induced by a liquid substance.

The Preserves, a gated community on the mainland about three miles east of the intra-coastal waterway, had seven-foot-high white plaster walls covered in scarlet bougainvillea full of thorns to keep out the riff-raff. At the entrance, tall ornate black wrought-iron gates, with an eagle in the center, stood open. It was impossible to tell if the gates were just for show or if they closed at night. Being locked in behind gates would be like living in a prison, more claustrophobic than safe. I'll take my chances with the folks on the outside.

Beyond the gates a small white kiosk with hanging baskets of red geraniums sat in the middle of the divided road. A guard came out with a clipboard in his hand. I checked out his name tag. The guard was R. Brandt, not Mark Cummings. He checked off my name on his list, gave me directions and went back to his hut to put up the zebra arm that barred my way.

The community center was just to my right on the edge of the compound, its parking lot up against the high wall facing the street. Yellow police tape blocked off the drive to the parking at the back of the building.

No way was anyone going to be allowed in the building, so I pulled up out front. The largest jacaranda tree I'd ever seen grew in front of the building. The base was encased by a low stone wall, lifting it about three feet from the ground. Come April the tree would be covered with pale blue flowers and alive with the hum of bees. Sheltering beneath the tree on the stone patio were a dozen round glass tables with black wrought-iron chairs tilted up against them to keep falling leaves off the seats.

I got out of the truck. A mockingbird sang and somewhere in the distance a dog barked and a child laughed, while off to the right of the recreation hall came the thunk of balls from the tennis courts. Life was going on as normal even though there was trouble in paradise.

In front of the community center was a small lake with a fountain of water arching into the air. On the left, the road curved along the edge of a walking path bordering the lake. To the right of the lake were houses, with caged pools and lanais, facing the water but with another walking path between the houses and the lake. Pedestrians had access to the whole lake as well as to the recreation hall. At night it would be easy enough to go down that tree-lined path to the hall without being seen.

I walked along the left side of the water towards the excited squeals coming from a children's playground. A little boy, shrieking in delight and looking back over his shoulder at a young black woman, crashed into me. I reached down to steady him and he wrapped his arms around my leg and raised big blue eyes to me, not at all alarmed. "Sorry," the young woman said, taking the boy by the shoulders and turning him back to the play area. He immediately ran away from her again.

A white swan on the lake flapped its wings and raised itself up off the water before settling down and sailing gracefully on to join its mate that was dipping down beneath the surface for food.

I walked on towards a small gingerbread gazebo connected to a dock. Four hanging baskets, overflowing with scarlet begonias, hung around the outside of the gazebo. The inside was lined with seats. A white sign at the entrance identified this as Swan Lake dock. A half-dozen white pedal boats were tied to a rustic wooden dock. As I stepped onto the planking a duck squawked and flopped into the water ahead of me.

This was heaven. Never mind penis envy, I had property envy big-time. What had I done so wrong in life not to get a piece of this? I gave up on the greed and headed back. A jogger, a man wearing a tee-shirt and very short shorts, ran by me and that wasn't bad either. Clay better get home soon or I was going to get arrested for something besides murder.

The sound of voices made me turn back from admiring the retreating jogger to the clubhouse where a line of men were pulling on wetsuits. I watched them enter the water and then I watched the two men in business suits waiting for the divers to do their thing. The police were searching the lake, but for what? The answer came close on the heels of the question; they were searching for the gun.

Sheila lived at the back of the development, down twisting and turning roads with small cul-de-sacs running off them. The guard had explained to me that Signet Creek emptied into Swan Lake and divided the community. He'd given me exact directions on how to find the only bridge over the creek to Egret Way, but in the spaghetti-looping roads it was easy to get disoriented. If Sheila asked why it took so long to get to her house from the gate, I could honestly tell her I'd gotten lost.

But the question of when I'd entered the Preserves never came up. Perhaps the security guard didn't call to tell her I'd entered the Preserves — a small chink in the security web I'd file for future use.

Brick is a rare building material here in Florida. Mostly it is stucco over concrete block, so I figured the brick made Sheila's house even more valuable. Set on about half an acre, everything about it said money, but the two sandhill cranes walking delicately across the lawn and pecking at insects were unimpressed with the price of real estate. They raised their red-capped heads as I pulled in the drive but had little concern beyond that and by the time I walked up the flagstone path they had gone back to pecking at the manicured lawn.

Sheila, tall and thin and in her early forties, about ten years older than me, opened the door squealing in delight at seeing me there. She held an oversized goblet of wine in her left hand, explaining the warm welcome. She leaned forward to air-kiss me. When she pulled away she overbalanced and nearly went on her can. I caught her and helped her right herself.

"Oops," she giggled and gave me a silly little smile as she sagged back against the door.

"How's life?" I asked.

"It got a whole lot better today. And you?"

"Drugs, sex and rock and roll, baby."

"Really?"

"Yeah, *Prilosec*, *Desperate Housewives* and the radio."

She took me through to the back of the house past a dark gothic dining room; then we entered a great room, coldly modern and full of bright-colored glass objects. This house had more than just brick; it had everything, well everything except taste. There was just too much happening, too many styles and way too much stuff. She must have bought it by the truckload and hired a psychotic decorator.

But the best part was the family room. Decorated in French Country with pale furniture and blue toile, it overlooked a wild area. Truly stunning, the view was of tall pines surround-ing a marshy area of wild grasses.

Sheila followed me to the windows. "The Preserves is

named for this spot." She pointed towards a tall slash pine. "See that tree? That's where the eagles' nest is. There used to be another on the far side but the hurricane blew it away. Don't know where the eagles went."

"Probably blew them all the way to Georgia."

As we watched, a large eagle flew in and settled itself down into its broad nest of twigs. "Wow," I said, "that's awesome."

She smiled at me, delighted at both my response and the eagle. "I'll get us some wine."

I was about to turn her offer down but Miss Emma was whispering in my ear. "Secrets and confession go better with booze, girl. Remember that." I smiled. "Fine," I told her. "That would be nice."

CHAPTER 24

She seemed to have forgotten the glass she'd left on the coffee table and came back with a bottle of white wine and two enormous etched wineglasses. She filled the glasses to the top.

We talked. Excited and happy, she giggled outrageously at my jokes. Finally, she confided, "I've met the most wonderful man, a heart specialist. He just moved down here from Boston. I think this is the one."

"Congratulations! You've been on your own for a long time, haven't you?"

"Four years." She waggled her hand back and forth. "A few mistakes in there." She giggled some more. "A few mistakes and a couple of big disasters."

"We've all had those," I assured her. "I hope this guy is everything you deserve."

"God no, don't wish that on me." She doubled up with laughter. "I so don't deserve this guy, but if you don't tell, I won't." An echo sounded through the room. Hadn't both Marley and I said this about David and Clay? Rena even said the same thing about RJ. Did every woman feel this way?

She leaned forward to replenish her wine, looked at my glass and frowned before flopping back against the cushions.

"Did you know the security guard who was killed last night?" I asked.

The laughter left Sheila's face. "Ray John?" Cautious, and suddenly more sober. "What about him?"

"You knew him?"

"Everyone knew him." Her nose curled up in distaste. "This was his little fiefdom. At least he thought it was. He hassled the teenagers, flirted with the old women and agreed with the old men that the country was going to hell in a handcar. Snuck around and spied on us, knew every dirty little secret. Good riddance, I say."

"You didn't like him?"

She snorted. "How can you tell?"

"Why not? Why didn't you like him?"

"He was a pain in the butt. Thought he owned the place and we were just here to do his bidding."

"Like what?"

She shrugged. "Graffiti freaked him out. He caught a kid writing naughty words on the security wall last year and really worked him over. The board nearly fired Ray John's ass for that. They would have too except for Quinton Beckley."

"Who's he?"

"Chairman of the board of directors."

"Were they buddies?"

"God no. It was just sex."

"You mean they were…" I tilted a hand back and forth.

She curled her feet up under her on the sofa, settling down with relish to the topic of other people's sins. "Naw. It's just that Quint is always on the make." She started to tell me something else but stopped herself. "I've heard rumors about some of the parties at his place. Ray John probably was creeping around and saw more than Quint would have liked."

I was pretty sure this was a sanitized copy of what she'd been going to say.

"And one night I saw RJ bringing him home. The next morning I was out jogging and Ray John was delivering Quint's car from the rec hall. RJ had a security guard in his SUV behind him. Ray John didn't walk anywhere."

"Control, Ray John had control over Quinton."

"Yup, I bet old Quinton paid big-time for that, bet he voted just the way RJ wanted him too."

Ray John had always been about control, telling my mother who she could see, what she could wear and even telling her where she could work. He didn't want his girlfriend working in a bar, so Ruth Ann gave up her job. She had to take two cleaning jobs to replace it and make up for the lost tips. "Any idea how we could find out what he used to manage Quinton?"

Her face went white with shock. But then a smile returned and she giggled, "Well, I don't think Quinton is going to tell and sure as hell old RJ can't." A hoot of laughter exploded out of her and she pounded her feet on the floor in delight.

"What kinds of things would Ray John hold over people?"

Suddenly she went from amused to angry. "Why you want to talk about that? It's none of your business."

"Curiosity. I've never lived in a gated community."

"Lucky you."

"How did he hassle people?"

She gave an exaggerated shrug. "I don't know." But in a second she added, "If someone was driving drunk he'd follow them home and talk to them." She screwed up her nose and made a moue of disgust. "More than that, he even thought he had the right to pull you over, cut you right off with that SUV the board bought him. He never let anyone forget he'd been with the sheriff's office. He still acted like he was the police."

"That would be a good thing, wouldn't it?" I prodded.

She looked confused. "What?"

"Stopping people from driving under the influence."

"You'd think so but not with RJ. Big on not driving after one little drink." She leaned forward and set her glass down, hard. "There was always a veiled threat in his warnings. If he pulled you over he threatened to call the cops. You don't know what it took to stop him."

"Money?"

"He really wasn't into money."

"Yeah, power was his thing, wasn't it?"

She pulled out a pillow from behind her. "That and sex." She pounded the pillow and tucked it in behind her lower back. "Well, he isn't going to bother us anymore."

"Did Ray John have favorites in the community?

"He did favors for people."

"Like?"

"Like driving them home after a party." She picked up the bottle and poured herself another drink. The wine that slopped over onto the wood table didn't seem to worry her. "You're right about the power trip. He liked having power over people." She turned her head to look out the window. "He was always showing up at weird times of the day and night. He always seemed to be drifting around, watching." She gave a shudder and turned to me. "Like, if you were saying goodnight to people on the doorstep he'd be drifting by, watching. Then he'd pull over to the curb and stop until they pulled out and then he'd follow them to the gate."

"I thought you had to take them to the gate and let them out."

"Naw, you just give them the code."

So, pretty much anyone that had ever visited the Preserves would know the code was the date and be able to get in and out.

Sheila's mind was on something besides security. "People would call the next morning to thank me and tell me he really creeped them out."

"So, there's a price to be paid for feeling safe?"

"Yeah, about twenty-five hundred bucks a year per household."

"More than money, playing it safe can be dangerous if you let a man like Ray John into your life."

"Yeah. Imagine paying to have that Nazi around."

"And was there lots of stuff for him to find out?"

"Sure. He knew about every affair and every bad habit. Lots of secrets, but did you ever live in a neighborhood that was any different?"

I laughed. "They were mostly worse. I guess you can't hide from evil although we sure like to try. Evil is always there, it just hides and adapts to suit the environment."

Sheila looked away from me, out to the small piece of wilderness. "And he was evil. I couldn't hide from him."

"Did you kill him?"

My question surprised us both. She swung round, her jaw

clamped tight and with a small muscle twitching in her cheek. Finally she said, "What kind of a question is that?"

"One that the police are going to ask everyone, so the sooner they find the person who killed him, the safer all our secrets will be."

"They have no reason to question me. If they do I'll know who set them on me." The steely tone contained a threat.

"If Ray John knew your secrets, others might. Maybe he told someone or wrote it down. I'm guessing he had something you wouldn't want made public."

"Oh god." Her hands went to her mouth, her eyes closed and her face froze with pain and fear as she thought it through. Slowly her body melted. Her shoulders rounded and her back bent as she slumped over into an attitude of defeat, her head in her hands.

"How bad is it?" I asked.

She didn't answer.

"Talk to me, maybe I can help."

Sheila gave a harsh bark of disgust. "Sure, I tell you my secrets so you can take over where RJ left off."

"No, so we can find a way of making things better. You're a smart girl and I've seen you under stress, you're not easily rattled. I know because I've tried. Out there on the course, you never give it away, you have to be beaten. You're a survivor, Sheila, start thinking like one."

She raised her head. "In a place like this your survival instincts get blunted. On the surface everything seems so easy and charmed. You forget to pay attention. And by the time you get here you have more to lose. One little slip and you can lose everything." Her blue eyes held mine. "How did you know him?"

"Ray John lived with my mother. He was a bully and liked power. And he sexually molested me. One day he tried to rape me. He was gone the next day."

"Shit. I guess you're as glad as I am he's dead."

"I'm not shedding any tears but I'm concerned who's going to get hurt in the fallout."

She jabbed a finger at me. "We all have to stick together and keep our mouths shut. The cops will just put it down as a burglary or something. Someone from outside did it." Her hands gripped her knees and she nodded firmly.

"I'm from outside and the thing is, well, this is a pretty secure area. How could an outsider get in?"

She thought for a moment. "The north gate. It isn't manned. There's just a big iron gate that slides back with our remotes. Maybe someone came in that way."

"He'd still need a remote."

"Naw, just walk in and then walk out. No one would ever know he was here."

"It would have to be someone who knew the Preserves."

She didn't like that idea. "Why? And why does anyone care? There are lots of crimes that are never solved."

"The police aren't going to walk away from this. No way. They're going to find out who did it. Turn over every rock and ask a whole lot of questions."

"But they can't know anything."

"If Ray John knew stuff, the cops can find it out." I felt like a rat, feeding on the insecurities of a drunken woman, but once she sobered up, she'd shut up.

Her face collapsed into despair and her wine happiness spiraled down into depression. "I thought it was over," she whispered. She straightened. "But I'm still glad he's dead. He was a monster."

"The quicker the cops catch his murderer, the better. The less they'll be poking into other people's lives."

She tilted her head. "Yes," she said with a nod of agreement. "Yes. I just want it to end."

"Ray John liked young girls. Have you heard any rumors, know anyone he might have been messing with?"

Her eyes did a funny thing, like they weren't seeing me or anything around her but looking at a list deep inside her head. Then she gave a little nod and said a name. "Charters, Thia Charters. I was playing bridge at the clubhouse, when I went to the john and I saw them together. He was leaning in really close, holding onto her arm and whispering down into her face. Something was going on. I started to make a joke but he shot me a look that made me want to pee even more. Thia looked upset but I wasn't getting involved."

"I'd like to meet Thia."

"What's with you?" she protested. Even drunk, her brain worked. Up until now she'd just been celebrating Ray John's death and then she'd been shocked into fear, but now she was asking the right questions.

"Detective Styles, the guy in charge of the investigation, came to see me," I explained. "I'm right up there on the hit list of suspects."

"And did you do it?"

"No."

"Well, if you did they should give you a medal."

"No medal for me. I'd like to meet Thia Charters."

"And her mother." She wagged her finger at me. "You have to meet Anita too."

"Would Anita kill Ray John if she knew he was fooling around with Thia?"

She squinted her eyes at me, probably trying to focus but looking like she was concentrating real hard and expecting me to know the answer. "Don't know," she finally said. "But I'll tell you one thing — RJ only had to crook his little finger and Mommy would have been jumping into bed with him. She had the hots for him. Well, to be honest she goes for anything in pants, gay divorcee." She giggled. "Don't mean that, can't use gay like that anymore." She gave a big yawn. "Shit, I'm bagged." She yawned again. "Got to go out tonight."

"Have a nap. I'll call you in the morning. I'd really like to meet Thia. See if you can arrange it, will you? If you do I might even let you win a golf game."

"What?" She jumped to her feet to protest, misjudged and sat back down hard.

I held out a hand to her and pulled her off the couch.

"You can't beat me," she said when she was on her feet. Her right hand was making wide vague circles like a hawk looking for a place to land. "Even if I gave you strokes you couldn't win."

"Let's find out." I started walking to the front door.

"Wait."

I looked back at her. She had this enormous smile on her face. "I know how you can meet them. I'll check and call you tomorrow."

CHAPTER 25

Marley was waiting up for me when I got home from the Sunset about midnight. Normally an early-to-bed girl, she was curled up on the leather couch. As soon as I came into the room she sat up and said, "I can't keep up this pace." Yawning and stretching, she tossed back the mohair throw and planted her feet firmly on the hardwood.

"Go to bed," I told her. "You look like you're done."

"We need to talk first. There's something I didn't tell you." She sat very still with her hands folded in her lap.

This wasn't good. I felt the great big axe hanging over my head drop closer. I was too tired for whatever grief was coming but I sank down in a chair across from her and waited for it.

Marley's eyes locked on mine. "Lacey went out last night."

"Sweet Jesus, is this nightmare never going to end?"

"I came out of the bedroom about two-thirty — the door to the den was open. I peeked in. She wasn't there. I thought she might be having a bad time, you know, with everything going on, so I went to look for her on the lanai. She wasn't there. She wasn't anywhere. I thought she was either in with you or had gone home to her mother. Either way, I let it lie and went back to bed. Then there she was in the morning. It didn't really sink in until this afternoon that she was out of the apartment."

I blew out the breath I'd been holding. "She took my keys off the bar and drove the truck out to the Preserves." What she'd done next was beyond my ability to say.

"But she doesn't have a license," Marley protested.

"I knew those Baptists were going to be a bad influence on you. You're talking like a tight-ass Sunday School teacher. Driving without a license is still a lesser sin than murder."

"But can she drive?"

"Seems she knew enough to get out to the Preserves. Ray John was paying for lessons. Ironic, isn't it?"

Marley's brain made the next connection. "Now we know what your truck was doing out there."

I pushed out of the chair and headed for the kitchen to look under the bar where I'd left my pouch with the Beretta in it. It wasn't there. I'd picked up my keys to take Lacey home and never noticed it was missing. With Ray John dead I didn't need it anymore.

Marley had followed me into the kitchen. "What is it?" Marley asked.

"My gun is gone. I left it under the bar but it's not there anymore. Lacey must have taken it."

"Gun. You have another gun?"

"Yup, well at least I did. It was in the fanny pack. It's gone now."

"You have to tell Styles."

"I have to think about that."

"Sherri, you can't protect her. If you try, you're only going to land in it yourself."

"I'm already in it."

"It's going to come out that it was your gun."

"Only if Lacey tells them."

"She will once we explain to Styles that she was out of the apartment. Besides, can't they check and see who owns a gun? They'll know from the registration, won't they?"

"I'm not sure about that. The gun came from Tully. What are the chances of it being registered?"

"Zip," Marley said. "Call Styles first thing in the morning."

"I'll probably be charged with some gun offense. All the gossip and stories will start up again. This is going to be nasty."

"You're thinking about Clay, aren't you? He loves you."

I laughed. "Miss Emma used to say that when trouble came in the door, love went out the window."

"That old lady just had far too much to say." Marley turned away and started for her bedroom.

"Oh my god," I said.

"What?"

"Miss Emma also used to say, 'Don't rake the coals if you don't want to start a fire.' I sure as hell raked the coals, didn't I — getting involved in other people's lives? Do you think I'm responsible for Ray John's death?"

"Yes, and you're probably responsible for the sun coming up tomorrow. Go to bed." She started for her room and stopped again. "My first two patients cancelled and I didn't rebook. I'm all yours. Quality time, babe — a morning walk on the beach and breakfast. I want to hear all about Tully, the white knight."

Marley dragged me out of bed obscenely early. Out on the beach not another soul disturbed our view of the crashing waves and diving pelicans. Marley had the shells she could never resist all to herself. Walking a beach with Marley is a waste of time; she never gets farther than a few yards before she's bent over and moving like a snail. But that was okay with me. I used the time to think things through.

We were back at the apartment and Marley was frying bacon while I was mixing pancakes when the phone rang.

"Hi, it's Sheila."

"How are you?" I asked.

"Better than I deserve. My head is about the size of Mt. Rushmore and my stomach is a Maytag, but I'm functioning. That's the trouble with that kind of partying. It's no fun the next day."

"God got you for celebrating someone's death."

"You mean you weren't too?"

"Oh yeah, but I was a little bit more distracted by the details."

"Anyway, I've solved your problem of meeting Thia and Mommy. You and I are lunching with them today at the Royal Palms."

"How did you manage that?"

"I'm the chair of this charity luncheon and fashion show. Mommy's on my committee and Thia is in the fashion show. I found an extra ticket."

"Now that's a good thing."

Ever notice how one good thing is always followed by numerous bad things? I didn't even have time to drop a pancake on the griddle before my mobile rang.

CHAPTER 26

"Ziggy had a fire out at his yard last night," Tully told me. "He's in the hospital."

My heart rate shot up. "Uncle Zig? How bad is it?"

"He suffered some burns but it isn't life-threatening. His trailer is gone though."

"Son of a bitch! This was no ordinary fire, was it?"

"Fire marshal is still investigating but one of the firemen told me it started in more than one place."

"Why, why would anyone do this?"

"Those folks have been trying to drive Zig out for a long time. Things started to get real nasty about five months back. It's in the courts but it looks like they didn't want to wait any longer."

"I'm on my way to the hospital," I told him and hung up without a goodbye.

I was stopped at the nursing desk and told only immediate family could see Ziggy. I was still begging to be allowed to see my father, Ziggy Peek, when someone touched my arm. I swung to face Tully who just walked away without speaking, heading for a door down the hall. I followed.

Nothing creates panic like the foreign and inhuman environment of an ICU room. Stark cold surfaces, mixed with strange sounds and smells, ensure thoughts of the worst out-come. Nothing like the clang of metal, the silent drip of liquid into a vein, measuring out life drop by drop, to say, "This is serious shit," and grab your attention.

Uncle Ziggy's big belly, covered by a blinding white sheet, was the only part of him visible from the door. It didn't seem to be moving. Tully gave me a nudge forward and I slid cautiously into the room. It was strange to see Uncle Ziggy in all this whiteness and neatness; I was accustomed to seeing him against a background of decay and destruction.

Closer now, I could see the devastation. His shaggy grey hair was gone. What was left was blackened and singed, the skin blistered below. His eyebrows were gone, his fine lashes burnt away. He'd never been an attractive man but now he looked grotesque with his greased red face, the features obliterated by swelling. On the flame-colored cheek closest to me were stitches. His graceful hands, with their long slim fingers, were encased in what looked to be plastic bags. Everything that was beautiful about Uncle Ziggy had been destroyed by the fire.

"Oh, Uncle Zig." My low wail of pity brought his pale blue eyes around to find me. Now I could see the man I knew and loved. I moved closer, wanting to touch him, to comfort him but afraid of causing him more pain. "What have they done to you?"

"Hi, pumpkin." Even the voice sounded charred and raw, the melodic bass turned into a harsh rasp.

"Don't talk." I reached out a hand for him and then drew it back. "There isn't even any place left for me to kiss you."

He gave a harsh huff of laughter. "Ain't no big thing, girl."

The oxygen tubes in his nose, the IV bag stuck to his arm, told the lie. Uncle Zig was in real big trouble here.

Uncle Ziggy's eyes shifted to my father.

"Is the old buzzard still alive?" Tully asked, moving up beside me. "When I was in before you didn't open your eyes. Thought you might be planning on checking out."

"Too mean to die," Uncle Zig wheezed.

"And too ugly." Dad reached past me and laid a hand on Uncle Zig's chest. "You hang on, you hear?"

Uncle Zig lifted his chin, as much of a nod as he could manage. "Want to tell you," he wheezed out, "before the nurses come and chase you off."

"It can wait," I said, but he ignored me and concentrated on Tully.

"No accident."

"I know," Tully told him. "I talked to the firemen."

"Tried to burn me out. Ohio, two of them." He stopped and concentrated on his breathing. "Something else, pickup with a cap on it and a trailer hitch." Some more time out as he let the prongs blow more oxygen down to his lungs. "Bet they're camping somewhere."

"Tell the police," I urged him.

His eyes stayed fixed on Tully.

I turned to see my dad give Uncle Zig a little nod.

"Now listen you two, none of that." My voice rose an octave. "Leave it to the police."

"Sure," said my father. His tone wasn't convincing and I wasn't believing him.

"Look after Ralph," Uncle Zig said. His eyes fluttered closed, tiredness or drugs overtaking him.

I turned to my dad. "Ralph?"

"The peacock."

"Damn, you mean that peacock has a name?"

"Didn't I just tell you?" He turned away, now everything had been said, he was gone. We stopped for a nurse pushing a cart of equipment out of the next room.

"Ralph?" I asked. "Who would name a peacock Ralph?"

"Apparently Zig would."

"Thank god he never had children."

"Well, a man named Zigfried is bound to be partial to the unusual," Tully said and pushed the elevator button.

"So, what are you planning?" I asked as I watched the numbers.

"You've always had a vivid imagination, haven't you?"

"Along with a crazy old man — two things that can deliver interesting possibilities."

We left the hospital together. Another fine clear day, the kind you see on brochures, palm trees waving and birds singing, it was about seventy-five degrees at eleven in the morning but Tully didn't notice. He was in a world all his own, plotting and making plans — revenge was his new mistress.

"I'm asking again." I tugged on his shirt. "What are you planning?"

He let his breath out slowly and snarled, "The sons of bitches, they were going to drive him out, going to win in the end, but they just couldn't wait. The city already passed a law that he couldn't live there anymore, said it was for commercial purposes only, not residential. He was coming out to live with me. Every month they're finding more and more ways of making it difficult for him to hold onto his property. Zig was coming around to the idea of leaving, had even made plans to sell out, but they just couldn't wait." Tully kicked a pebble off the sidewalk.

"I understand how he feels," I said, "losing his home and the business he built, but won't he get filthy rich off the sale of his property?"

Tully glared at me. "What good is money going to do Zig?"

"Oh, I can think of a few things."

"Yeah, well it isn't right. Is that what we gave up three years of our lives for, so some dickhead with a lawyer can push him off his own land? A man can't live his life the way he wants anymore."

"That could almost pass as a political opinion. You're really upset about this, aren't you?"

"Aren't you? You think this is right?" he roared.

"Nope, but I'm not planning on doing anything dumb."

"And you think I am?"

"Absolutely. The question is just how dumb?'

His shoulders relaxed and he grinned at me. And then he did an extraordinary thing. He leaned forward and kissed the end of my nose. "See you later."

I watched him walk to his truck in his loose-jointed amble. No use telling him to be careful or think twice before doing whatever stupid thing he was about to do. Dumb and getting dumber, that was my daddy.

I gave in to my fears as he squawked open his truck door and yelled, "Be careful." He didn't respond, just peeled out of there like some brainless teenager.

At the restaurant no yellow police tape cordoned off the elevator or the stairs, so Miguel and Isaak hadn't swung for each other with cleavers. No one had been killed in the kitchen yet. The two of them were getting closer and closer to open warfare every day, something I was putting off dealing with as long as I could. I liked them both, needed them both, but honest to god the drama of them each trying to be top dog was giving me an ulcer.

I ignored the pokey little elevator and took the stairs two at a time, racing to my office to check my messages. All the disasters were manageable. No supplier had closed me down and only one waitress had to be replaced for dinner.

I headed to the kitchen to see that all the food supplies had arrived. I stepped through the door and was overwhelmed with delicious odors, spices mixed with the smell of roasting meat, reminding me that I hadn't had any breakfast.

It was strangely quiet in the kitchen, everyone had their head down, working like crazy, beating and chopping and flipping. Watching a good kitchen work is like watching a dance routine — it's organized and smooth and flowing. I checked with Isaak. He said, "Yes, yes, everything is fine, now go away."

I went to check that the beer order was in.

By the time I'd returned my calls, yelled at a few suppliers and sweet-talked a few more it was too late to go home and change for Sheila's luncheon. My black staff skirt and the white blouse that I wore when I filled in for missing staff would have to do. There was a spot on the blouse, which I removed in the ladies room, leaving a large wet blob, and of course I had to be wearing a lacey black bra which showed through the white blouse. I undid the top button to show more of my black bra. Perhaps it would look like a fashion statement, trashy but hip.

Or perhaps they'd throw me out of the Royal Palms where the dress code was probably tougher than at Buck House. I put on extra makeup and found a pair of Fuck-Me black-patent stilettos under my desk.

It would have to do.

Downstairs, I went around to peek in Rena's store. There were no lights on and the door had a sign saying, "Closed due to a death in the family." I recognized Peter Rowell's handwriting. The fact that Rena hadn't asked me to put up the sign told a story in itself.

CHAPTER 27

The Royal Palms is gated to keep the riff-raff out. I guess the guard missed my license plate. I got that particular plate because I don't like there to be any misunderstanding. But of course the way I dressed and what generally comes out of my mouth, a minute after meeting me you'd figure it out.

The drive curving up to the clubhouse was outlined with a hedge of red hibiscus. Past the hibiscus I could see the manicured course. White sand traps were draped along the far edge of the fairway like a string of broken pearls on a carpet of grass in a color green that only occurs when nature is given lots of help. Royal palms towered above it all.

The drive swung up in front of a two-storey clubhouse with a row of tall white pillars holding up a broad balcony on the second floor. I pulled up under the portico and a valet attendant ran out to get my keys. I handed them over and minced to the double front doors. A woman in a black skirt, just like me, and a white blouse, just like me, opened the front door. I was pleased to see she had on a silly white apron and I hoped all the wait staff wore them so none of the ladies would ask me to bring them a drink. I undid another button. More trash, less chance of being taken for staff.

I walked around the mahogany table in the middle of the

foyer. It held a fresh floral arrangement, massive and meant to impress, featuring mutant reeds and bird of paradise that climbed at least three feet above the stone urn. The urn itself was three feet tall. That sucker ever fell on you, you'd be dead. I pressed the elevator button and looked around the elegant vestibule while I waited.

It had been a long time since I'd been here. Jimmy's parents were members and had brought us to the Royal Palms for every major holiday or family event. The elevator doors sighed open and I turned to them. Behind me I heard the maid say, "Hello, Mrs. Travis." Too late to run and nowhere to hide, I put out my hand to block the doors from closing and turned to face the enemy, prepared to get down and dirty. There was a muttered response and then Bernice Travis, my darling mother-in-law, walked around the table to join me at the elevator.

She was dressed in an elegant Chanel-style black suit with white trim. Her impeccable coiffed blonde hair gracefully cupped her masklike face, tight and pinched, and surgically wiped clean of expression. With a husband who is a plastic surgeon it must be tempting to try all the latest techniques, as she had done. Her eyes tried to look startled when they saw me. Then Bernice's mouth opened and closed. And then it did it again.

I smiled.

She stepped back from me and clutched at her chest, giving me hope all was not lost. Maybe the bitch would die right at my feet. Her eyes tried in vain to widen against their surgical tautness. "What are you doing here?" she whispered.

"Oh, lunch and a fashion show. And you?"

Her eyes dropped to my cleavage.

"I was going to wear my spandex with this glittery tube top but my mom is wearing it."

She closed her eyes. For a moment I actually thought she was going to faint. But she was no quitter. Instead, she whispered, "You can't come here."

"Excuse me? Has someone passed a new law?"

"You don't belong here."

Well, that was the understatement of the day. If there'd been a railroad near the trailer park where I grew up I'd definitely have lived on the wrong side. I grinned at her. Up to that very second I'd been feeling twitchy and uncomfortable, like someone was going to come along and say, "Staff must use the kitchen entrance." But if Bernice Travis was unhappy, I was having a ball.

"Will you have time after lunch for a drink and a chat?" I asked, sweet and nasty, like arsenic in melted chocolate.

"No." She didn't add "not 'til hell freezes over," but it was there anyway. "No," she repeated. Her voice rose to a shout in case I'd gone deaf. "No."

"Oh, that's a shame. I've been meaning to call and have you over."

She sputtered and started to turn away. She didn't get far. She couldn't leave. Some strange fascination, like a train wreck, awful but strangely fascinating, held her there. She just had to know how bad it was going to be. Slowly she walked forward on stiff legs, never taking her eyes off me, and staying as far away from me as the space in the elevator would permit. The elevator rose silently with her staring at me the whole time, both hands clutching her handbag in front of her as if to shield her from contamination. When the door opened she jolted forward but not fast enough.

What thing in the world would make Bernice Travis the most miserable? Why, being seen with Sherri Travis! I stepped up beside her and linked my arm through hers. The Travis women had arrived. My face must have looked like I'd just won the lottery 'cause that's how I was feeling. Hee haw, revenge was definitely sweet and why hadn't I thought of amusing myself in this way before?

The room had an eighteen-foot-high ceiling and the far wall was glass from floor to rafters. Packed with elegant, sophisticated women in the latest fashions, all with drinks in their hands, it was as if the pages of *Vogue* had come alive. I was wildly underdressed but I didn't think undoing any more buttons to show a naughty lace bra would help. Beside me, Bernice had gone into some kind of shock. She wasn't moving, wasn't trying to get away, just standing there waiting for the social axe to fall, like some dumb beast at the abattoir.

"Smile," I whispered. "I certainly am."

Heads turned to look at us, eyebrows raised, before they went back to their drinks.

The scent of mingled perfumes, expensive and exotic, teased my nose. The perfume was overlaid by the smell from towering vases of lilies and small rosebowls filled with gardenias. I wanted to scream for someone to open a window. I wanted to sneeze. I did.

I don't sneeze quietly. Don't know how to. For me it's Whiplash City and dramatic. Heads turned. Bernice sagged against me, close to fainting.

Damn, this was fun, made me want to yodel. I propped her up and whispered, "Sorry about that but all the best people are doing it." Pressing a knuckle to my nose and breathing through my mouth, I fought for supremacy over my sinus.

Fortunately for Bernice, the ladies were more interested in whether their panty girdles were taking off the promised five pounds, or maybe they were concerned with how much of their martinis remained and how soon they could order a refill without garnering attention. Whatever it was, we had fallen off their radar.

I pushed Bernice forward to meet Sheila, who was coming to greet us.

"Hello, Bernice. Hi, Sherri."

"You know her?" asked Bernice, aghast.

"Why yes, of course." Either Sheila didn't know the history or she had as warped a sense of humor as I did; she made my being there seem perfectly normal. Sheila wore a linen dress in an aqua green color, with a matching jacket, and looked model perfect. "Come get a drink," Sheila said, drawing me away.

"You do know that was my ex-mother-in-law?" I said to Sheila.

"Yup."

"Okay, so you pulled me away so she wouldn't have the big one and ruin your party. Understandable, but I really would have liked a few more minutes to torture her."

Sheila laughed. "I thought you wanted to meet Thia."

"Oh yeah, that too. Lead me to them. No wait! I definitely need a drink first." I gave a dramatic shiver. "Alcohol will kill the Bernice germs."

Anita Charters came up to us while we gave our drink

orders to a waitress in a silly white apron. Seemed I could have undone another button; for sure Mrs. Charters was displaying more cleavage than I was. Tully would say she'd caught ten pounds of fish in a five-pound net. The fish were definitely wiggling and jiggling and trying to get back to the ocean and you couldn't help but watch the roiling to see how they made out.

And her skirt was too tight and too short. Standing about five-foot-three in three-inch heels, she was decidedly plump, with a round face perfectly made up like a Kewpie doll. In a little girl's voice she gushed and made happy over meeting me, and I was thrilled that someone finally thought my presence was an asset. I was sure this nice lady wouldn't lie. I chatted to her, maneuvering her out of the crowd, saying all the nice things I had heard about Thia, great big liar that I am and then got to her with, "Wasn't it awful what happened at the rec hall?"

Bingo. Her face clouded up and then moisture filled her eyes.

CHAPTER 28

"It's so awful! How could this happen to us? This isn't supposed to happen in the Preserves. We pay a lot of money to be safe."

"You knew Mr. Leenders well?"

"He was an employee." Her lips hardened into a firm straight line before the delicate flower returned. "He was such a wonderful man." Anita Charters sniffed delicately.

"I understand Thia and Mr. Leenders were close," I said.

"He helped me out a lot. He was good to Thia. He talked to her as a father would. Her own father isn't involved in her life. She really needed a male influence. RJ gave it to her." The babbling stopped with that suggestive statement.

"He spent time with her?"

Her eyes hardened momentarily and then she said, "He was a father figure to all the teenagers here."

"Did he spend time alone with her?"

She stopped dabbing at her nose and lowered the tissue. The Kewpie doll's eyes narrowed. "That's a strange question."

"I just wondered how well Thia got to know him. He has a stepdaughter about her age. I wondered if Thia knew her."

"No, I don't think so." Wary and watchful, she wasn't going to commit until she knew where this was going.

"His death must be painful for her if she got to know him well."

"She knew him as an employee. Thia is a kind girl, so of course this news is bound to distress her." She smiled sweetly. "He was a good man."

"And yet someone killed him."

She was back to dabbing at her nose with a tissue. "I just can't understand. It must have been something from his private life, something he brought in with him." It was as if she were talking about dog crap he'd stepped in and dragged with him to the Preserves. Maybe that's how she thought of everyone outside their enclave.

A shockingly beautiful young woman floated towards us. Her skin, clear and pale, her nearly black hair and her disturbing violet eyes would make her stand out anywhere, but in this crowd of aged matrons with their national debt's worth of procedures and products, this child/woman, the goddess whose image we were all trying to attain — in this room she was a shooting star. I felt a sharp bite of bitter envy. Had I ever been this young and beautiful?

She drifted to a stop beside Anita.

"This is my daughter, Thia," Anita Charters said. She beamed at her daughter with delight.

Neither the introduction nor the murmurs of admiration registered with Thia. Her face remained totally blank. She neither smiled nor frowned. Around us people moved in to be near Thia, drawn to her. They spoke animatedly and warmly to her but nothing seemed to penetrate her wall of indifference, and she remained unresponsive through the further succession of flattery and laughter that grew with her at the center.

Was she on drugs? There were none of the obvious signs that I could see and, believe me, I have a doctorate in identifying a buzz. The girl just seemed immune to everything, frozen inside her own little bubble that no one could pierce. Definitely not normal.

Thia and Anita were seated at the same table as me, thank you Sheila, and all through lunch I tried to get a reaction out of Thia, talked about music and movies and names in the tabloids. If she answered at all it was in monosyllables. I tried future plans, vacations, books, favorite beaches and surfing. Nada! She wasn't rude, just indifferent. When dessert came, a wonderful raspberry sorbet with fresh raspberries and a sprig of mint, she excused herself, rose gracefully from the table and left for her modeling chores. I ate her dessert.

Sheila left to be master of ceremonies, or is it mistress — whatever it was, she was terrific at the job, poised and witty.

Thia came first in the parade of fashion, floating elegantly into the room, a born model. Sighs of regret rose behind her as the ladies watched an unattainable perfection. She strolled from table to table, turning this way and that so everyone could see how beautiful the clothes were, but it was Thia everyone was looking at and a hum of adjectives went up after she passed by. She paused at each table, posed and turned, responded to remarks but never reacted to the compliments that followed her.

Anita watched joyfully, her hands joined in front of her mouth as if in prayer, worshipping at the shrine of Thia's beauty, as enraptured as the rest of the guests.

Thia had been given the lion's share of the clothes. The other people modeling were just there to fill in until she could change and return to the room. No doubt about it, whatever "it" was, the girl was loaded.

As the fashion show ended and the room started to empty, Thia slipped back into her chair beside me and picked up her lukewarm water.

"That wasn't so bad, was it," Anita asked.

"It was okay," was Thia's bland reply.

"You didn't want to model?" I asked.

"My mom volunteered me." Her tone was edged with anger, the first emotion I'd seen in her.

Anita's hand trembled as she picked up her wineglass. "I should have asked first." She gave a little laugh. "I promise I won't do it again. Okay?"

There was no response from Thia.

A large woman came to the table to talk to Anita and she turned away from us.

"Do you know Lacey Cagel?" I asked Thia.

Thia turned her blank violet eyes to me.

"Did you know that Ray John Leenders lived with her and her mother?"

She gave a small shrug. "So?"

"Ray John had a thing for young women. He had a thing with you." The face was no longer blank.

I leaned towards her. "Come to the washroom with me," I whispered. "I need to talk to you."

She hesitated, on the verge of telling me to get stuffed, and then rose without speaking and led the way from the room. People stopped her, congratulating her and complimenting her, but she sailed through the storm of admiration, barely hesitating. She walked past the entrance to the washroom and down the hall to an exit that brought us out on a long balcony overlooking the first tee. We were alone.

She stood with her back to the view, leaned against the railing and stared at me, challenging me to I didn't know what.

"You were…" I started to say "molested" but it didn't fit her attitude, "involved with him."

Thia neither denied nor confirmed it, just waited. I could've used some of her poise. She made me feel like an awkward fool, like I was the kid and she was the adult.

"Does your mother know?"

"What business is that of yours?"

"Absolutely none. Do the police know?"

The magnificent violet eyes narrowed. "Is that a threat?"

It certainly sounded like it. "I just need to know about Ray John. I'm not trying to cause you a problem."

She looked away, down the first fairway where two carts worked their way along the emerald carpet to the small flag in the distance. In profile she was even more stunning, with high chiseled cheekbones and a long patrician nose. She swung back to face me. "You got it all wrong. RJ didn't force himself on me. I was willing. I loved him."

Well, shut my mouth. Just in case I still had it all wrong, I tend to get things all wrong, I asked, "You were willing?"

"Oh yes," she said lightly. "I was willing. More than willing, I was eager for it."

"He was a lot older than you, old enough to be your father. What he did was illegal."

She laughed out loud, enjoying either my naivety and stupidity or my shock.

"Didn't that worry you?"

"No."

"I don't get it. What did you see in him?"

She laughed. "He loved sex and so do I. That's all that mattered."

"You had sex with him at the rec hall?"

"The rec hall, my house, his truck, wherever."

"Did he meet the other girls there too?"

Her jaw hardened as she came off the railing. "If there were others, they were nothing to him. Just shit. I was the one he was really into."

An unfortunate choice of words in my opinion. "So, it wasn't just sex?"

She shrugged and looked away. "We were good together. I suppose I'll have to go back to those stupid boys now." She sighed.

"Tell me about the other girls. Who were they?"

"I don't know that there were others, but if there were, they didn't mean anything." She dismissed the thought with a flick of her hand.

"Did you meet Ray John the night he died?"

My luck ran out. "It's none of your business and if you go telling anyone this, I'll make you sorry." She drifted away, back inside to her fans, completely composed. A hell of a lot more composed than I was.

Her attitude shocked me as much as Ray John's rutting ability. He definitely had to be on drugs of some kind to keep up his schedule. What was the number now — Thia, Lacey and Rena, at least three. That would take lots and lots of drugs.

CHAPTER 29

I begged off the golf game Sheila offered. The Royal Palms was freaking me out. I could take the zombie girl shagging an older man, but I knew my mother-in-law was lurking somewhere about. Normally, I don't even like to be in the same county as her if I can help it, and by now the shock had warn off. Bernice would be out for blood and there were sharp instruments, knives and forks, on the tables. Run-away, Run-away!

I went to see Uncle Ziggy. In the hospital parking lot I took a minute to call Styles.

"What?" he answered.

I hate call display. No more civility from your nearest and dearest or even the cops. "Will the autopsy report on Ray John show steroid use or drugs to push up his sex drive? Do they check for things like that or do you have to ask?"

I could tell by the quality of the silence I had his attention.

"Perhaps you'd better explain that," he suggested mildly, but I wasn't fooled, I knew it was really an order.

The pickup was turning into an oven with the air conditioning off so I stepped out of the cab, dragging my bag behind me and slamming the door closed with my foot.

"I saw him. That kind of definition doesn't come from just

working out. Also I heard a rumor that he was sexually…well, pretty active. There was more than just Lacey's and Rena's name on his dance card. Man his age, he's going to need a little help to keep that up, if you know what I mean."

"Men our age may not have lost as much energy as you might think, if you know what I mean."

"I choose to ignore that remark. Did they find any drugs in him?"

"Goodbye, Ms. Travis."

"Wait. Have you found other women that he was involved with?"

"Goodbye," he answered and hung up.

"Shit." I slammed the cell phone closed and tossed it in my bag. What would it hurt the man to share a little — wasn't I always telling him things, keeping in touch? I'd forgotten to ask him about Uncle Zig. I stopped at the door to the hospital and dug out the phone to call Styles back.

"What?"

"Have you forgotten how to say hello? I pay your taxes, remember? You have to be nice to me."

"I repeat, what do you want, Ms. Travis?"

"My Uncle Zig." I told him what had happened.

"Sorry," he said. "I'll check for you, although it may take me a bit to get to it, too many curious people calling me and asking questions that are none of their business. I'll call you later and let you know what I find out. Or I could drop by the Sunset and have dinner with you. That's a good idea. I'll tell you about the fire over dinner."

"For which I'll pay?"

"Hey, you own the joint, right?"

"It ain't no joint and I won't own it if every freeloader in town expects free meals."

"You want to know or not?"

"That's blackmail and yes I want to know. I'll call you back and let you know if it's going to work. Oh, and did they find the gun that killed Ray John?"

He mulled it over before he finally said, "No, goodbye," and hung up.

So, if my missing gun killed Ray John, where the hell was it? And could I find it before anyone else? Not likely, since I didn't know where to begin looking. A gun was a thing that wouldn't go unnoticed and if it was anywhere easy they'd already have found it.

"How are you, Uncle Ziggy?"

He tried a smile. Only one corner of his mouth stretched up. "Had better days."

His eyes were glazed, his lips swollen and chapped. He was worse than he'd been in the morning.

Anger blazed in me, as hot as the one fueled by the gas out in Uncle Ziggy's junkyard. People who likely thought of themselves as fine upstanding members of society had done this to him or paid someone else to do it. Like Tully said, sooner or later his neighbors would have shoved him out by legal means but they couldn't wait. The neighbors who wanted him gone or a developer who coveted his land, someone had been willing to cause pain like this to hurry up a process that was inevitable.

Uncle Ziggy's attempt at another smile wasn't pretty. "Your dad is coming to spring me."

"What?"

"Want to go home."

"It's too soon."

He gave a harsh dry laugh, painful for us both. "Never could be too early to get out of here. 'Sides, no insurance."

"Where are you going?"

"Out to your dad's"

"Bad idea. He'd make a horrible nurse and think of the germs."

He blew air out through his lips. "I'm immune."

Probably true; after all, he lived on a trash heap. "When you're ready to go, you're coming home with me." I held up a finger to stop the excitement lighting his face. "But not until all chance of infection is over and the doctors say you can go. This is a stupid time to try saving money." Besides, it would give me a little time to let me figure out how to tell Clay I'd turned his luxury penthouse into a flophouse. At least Lacey's leaving had freed up a room.

This good idea came with another complication. I'd always kept my life with Clay separate from my life before Clay, kept my various strange relatives well hidden. Neither Zig nor my dad had ever been in the penthouse; they hadn't even met Clay. I didn't try to fool myself. Bringing in Zig would mean that Tully came too. The sealed compartments of my life were starting to leak secrets — one more thing to worry about.

Uncle Ziggy gave me another weird little smile. "Thanks, honey."

Piss on it! Clay could to take all of us or none of us.

When I left the hospital, rain was pouring down. I was soaked by the time I reached the truck and at the exit to the parking lot the catch basin had filled up with debris, creating a small pond. I went through it carefully to avoid flooding the engine and headed for Blossom Avenue.

By the time I got to Rena's the sun was shining again. Love this place…it never gets boring.

When Rena opened the door I could see there was no sense asking how she was. Her misery was only too clear and there was a shocking anger on her face as if she might reach out and strike me. She pulled the pink bathrobe tighter across her chest and held it there with her arms. "I was hoping it was the police," she said. "I haven't heard a thing." She stepped aside for me to come in and slammed the door shut behind me.

"It hasn't been all that long. Besides, maybe they won't tell you anything until they arrest someone. "

She spun away from me, her bare feet making slapping noises on the faux wood floor, and marched into the long narrow living area along the front of the house. I followed her cautiously. The furniture was sparse and lined up against the wall like a waiting room in a clinic rather than a home.

"Is there anything I can do?" I asked.

She whirled around. "You really don't get it, do you?"

"Get what?"

"We were fine until you got involved. Now RJ is dead and our lives are destroyed, all because you stuck your nose into something that was none of your business. You're responsible."

"Now wait a minute…"

"No, you listen to me. I've heard the stories about you.

Why they let you walk around I'll never know. You're like some Typhoid Mary. Death just follows you."

I said, "You know that isn't true." I so wasn't to blame for any of this, except I provided the gun and transportation to the murder scene — best not to share that with Rena.

She wasn't giving up. "Somehow you caused it." Rena headed for a corduroy recliner, the only piece of furniture in the room that wasn't new and pristine. She flopped backwards into it, pushing out the foot rest and crossing her ankles and arms. Glaring at me, she muttered, "I wish I'd never met you."

"Hi."

I jumped.

"Sorry," Lacey said, putting her hand on my arm and patting it.

"I don't want you talking to her," Rena shouted, pushing the lever forward and vaulting out of the chair. "Stay away from her, Lacey, or you could be the next person to die."

"Mom, you're just being ridiculous." Lacey took me by the sleeve and dragged me down the hall to the first door on the left, pulled me inside and shut the door, pushing a chair under the knob behind her. The room was all bubble-gum pink and frothy and meant for a pre-teen. Nothing in the room spoke of Lacey, no teen posters, no overloaded bulletin board, and no pictures of friends or family.

"She's flipped," Lacey said. "If I have to listen to any more of this wonderful RJ shit I'm going to hurl. She just goes on and on."

"Have you told her what Ray John did to you?"

"I told her the last night I spent at your apartment, the

night RJ died. I told her on the phone. She didn't believe me. I can't bring it up again; she's suffered enough. I just want to forget it."

"That won't do you any good."

"I'm fine."

I shook my head. "It's going to come out. Styles knows what Ray John did to you, he's going to get into it."

She bit down on her lip.

"Hasn't Styles asked you about it?"

She nodded.

"What did you tell him?"

"I told him what happened to me had nothing to do with RJ's death." She ducked her head. "I was at your apartment all night."

"He knows one of us went out to the Preserves and it sure as hell wasn't Marley or me."

Her head shot up, panic on her face. Her tongue flicked across her bottom lip. She started to say something but went silent and looked away.

"Where's my gun, Lacey?"

"What gun?"

"The gun that was on the counter with my keys."

"How should I know?"

"Because you took it with you when you stole my pickup. If you took the keys, you took the Beretta. The question is, where is it now?"

I raised my hand to stop her denial. "Marley knows you left the apartment and the pickup was seen out at the Preserves. A guard saw the truck leave the rec hall just before he found Ray John's body."

"Get out of my house," Rena yelled, banging on the door. "I've called the police. They're on their way."

"Where's the gun, Lacey?"

"I don't remember."

Rena was kicking and banging at the door, yelling at me so I could hardly think, but I needed to know one more thing. "Did you use my gun to kill Ray John, Lacey?"

"No."

Her hesitation was gone now and I almost believed her. The pounding at the door went to a new level. Rena was using something heavy, trying to break through the door.

Lacey reached out and took my arms, hissing, "I didn't kill him."

I shook her arms off me and Lacey sank back onto the bed. "Please believe me."

"When you went out to the Preserves, you went inside with the gun, right?"

She worried her lip and then she nodded.

"Did you use it?"

"No." She shook her head wildly in denial. "No."

"The police are coming," Rena yelled through the door.

"What happened to the gun?"

"I don't know."

"Did you have the gun when you left the building?"

"No. Right, yes. I don't know. I…"

"Get away from my daughter," Rena screamed. "I don't want you talking to her." She punctuated her words with another blow to door. There was a loud cracking noise.

"I'm going," I yelled to the madwoman. I pointed a finger down at Lacey. "But you better call me with details."

Hunched over in misery and hugging herself, Lacey nodded her head in agreement.

I opened the door and Rena fell into the room, her momentum taking her over to the bed where Lacey sat.

"Great. This is a good time for a mother and daughter chat," I said. "Tell your mother all about it or I will, Lacey." I headed for the front door, righteous indignation propelling me along at a trot. Then again I wanted to be gone before any police cars showed up. I didn't go far, just around the block before I pulled over to the curb and started searching the truck. If I found the gun and turned it in I was sure it would go a whole lot better for me. I searched everywhere — under the seats, behind the seats, glove compartment and every possible combination; it wasn't there. No gun. I called Lacey.

"It isn't in the truck," I told her. "I want to know everything that happened and I want to know it now. You took the gun into the building, right?"

She hesitated, trying to find a way out, but finally she whispered, "Yes. The gun was under the bar. I took it with me in case...I took it with me."

"Did you take it out of the truck?"

"Yes," barely audible but an affirmation.

"Did you take it into the building?"

"Yes."

"Did you bring it out of the building?"

I could hear her tattered sobs but my sympathy was all used up. It was my own ass I was worried about now. "What did you do with it?"

"I just don't remember what I did," she choked out.

She was lying. I knew that. But what was she lying about. "Did you shoot Ray John? Surely, you remember that?"

"No, you have to believe me. I didn't kill him."

Before my mouth opened to tell her it was a jury she had to worry about, my brain flashed on a picture of her bandaged arm. I didn't want to push her over an edge she was already teetering on. "Have you talked to your mother?"

"She won't listen. I tried again but she got up and left the room. She went into her bedroom and closed the door." More sobbing before she choked out, "I think she hates me."

I took a deep breath and said, "That isn't true. Your mom is upset and not thinking straight. She has to deal with Ray John's death and also with what he did to you. Sooner or later she's going to have to deal with that; at the moment she's in shock and denying the whole thing. But it's you I'm worried about. Lacey, you have to promise me you won't do anything foolish, promise?"

I waited. "Lacey?"

At last it came. "Okay." The words were faint and the commitment was weak.

"No cutting. Promise?"

"Yes."

But could I believe her? In the distance came to the sound of a siren. I shivered in the hot sun.

Back at the Sunset things didn't get better. I parked in the alley and was coming out into the sun as Skip was lifting his trunk lid. Something in his body language told me to pay attention, told me he was up to something he didn't want seen. I stayed in the shadows and then quietly walked forward as he bent and took two bottles out of his rolled-up jacket and tucked them away in the trunk, shoving them deep in the corner under some beach towels.

"What's this?" I asked, but I knew exactly what it was. It was the same old, same old.

He started at my voice and swung to face me with the look of a husband caught with a pack of Trojans by a wife who'd had a hysterectomy. "Nothing, nothing," he said.

I lifted the towels off a bottle of Canadian Club and a bottle of Glenlivet. "We don't give out samples, Skip."

"I...I...just...I was borrowing a couple of bottles. I'll pay you back."

"Too right, you will," I told him. I pointed at the bottles. "Bring them." I headed for the door. He'd picked a really bad day for this.

CHAPTER 30

Thirteen minutes later, Skip left without his back pay. I figured he'd probably stolen more than that from me already. He was just lucky I hadn't turned him over to Miguel. Miguel would have diced him and sliced him and deep-fried him for lunch. Nobody messed with me with Miguel around.

So there I was, working the bar until I could replace Skip. I needed to do that fast, but I'd already spent an hour calling people without any luck. Something told me I wasn't going to have a whole lot of time to spend at the Sunset over the next few weeks. Until someone new came along, I was it. But being behind the bar wasn't really a hardship for me. I love bars, the easy companionship and the quick exchanges. Nobody comes into a bar who doesn't want to be there.

Styles came in about eight. After I told Styles about Skip, I filled him in on Rena and her belief that I was responsible for Ray John's death, "She's crazy with grief." What I didn't tell him was Lacey had driven out to the Preserves in my truck, taking along my gun. I intended to tell him everything but somehow I just couldn't get it out. Blame it on pulling pints and mixing margaritas. It's hard to start a serious conversation over a blender.

"I have to interview mother and daughter again tomorrow,"

Styles said, watching the beer he was sloshing around in his glass. This wasn't the Styles I knew, capable and in charge. This guy was going through the motions and just putting one foot in front of the other. A wrecked love life can do that to you.

"Are you going to tell Rena about the abuse?"

"Yup."

"Maybe you can make her believe it. She won't listen to anything I have to say and doesn't believe Lacey."

"We've found two other mothers with daughters. You aren't the only one she has to believe."

"And no one did anything?"

He gave me a look that made me sorry I'd asked. A guy down the bar was waving his glass at me. I set a menu down in front of Styles and went to fill some orders.

When I came back he told me about Uncle Ziggy. "That fire was set all right. He tried to stop them and got hit. My bet is our arsonists are already over the border into Georgia and headed north."

"So you don't think they're going to be caught?"

"Nope. They likely came down here to do the job, collected their money and left within the hour."

"Uncle Ziggy told you they had Ohio plates?"

"Yeah, that's why I figure they've left Florida." He pushed his half-finished glass away. "Bad guys who've moved on."

"So no way of knowing who paid them?"

He lifted his shoulders. "We'll keep looking but there's not much to go on."

A red flash went off in my head. I threw down the bar cloth I was holding and signaled Maxine that I was taking a time-out. I was so mad that I'd probably kill someone if I stayed.

Tears running down my cheeks, I went past the restrooms and out the exit door at the end of the hall. I looped the chain that hangs from the door handle over the railing so the door wouldn't automatically close and lock me out on the steel grating over the alley. I stood there and swore into the night.

If I'd known where to find those guys, even if it was a thousand miles away, I'd have taken a gun, got in my truck and gone to find them. The injustice of this happening to Uncle Zig and no one ever paying was making me crazy. I don't know, but it seemed that people like us just never win, never catch a break. Man, but I wanted to kill someone. Marley was right, I shouldn't have a weapon. My self-control was almost non-existent. And then there was Rena. Being blamed for something I didn't do already had me burning without this.

"You all right?" Styles moved through the light spilling out from hall to the shadows beyond.

"Crazy, that's how I am. This just isn't right."

He reached out to touch me, hesitated, and lowered his hand. "Let it go."

I gave a harsh huff of laughter, wanting to kick him off the grating. "Go away."

He braced his elbows on the top rail and leaned out over the alley below. "Sometimes things just aren't fair. Don't let it eat you up."

"Jesus." I shot away from the railing, jerking the chain loose from the rail as I went. I pulled the door closed behind me, locking him out on the exit. For one second I felt better, but it wasn't good enough. I went to my office and called Tully. Something told me that my old man hadn't given up yet.

CHAPTER 31

At ten o'clock the next morning I slid into the cab of my dad's truck. The air conditioning had given up long ago so the windows were cranked down and debris was blowing around the cab as we headed out of Jacaranda. It was the perfect day for a road trip, high seventies, sun shining and a breeze blowing.

At I-95 we headed north towards Sarasota, but I wasn't at all sure we'd get where we were heading. At seventy miles an hour the pickup shook and bucked and rattled; hard to believe that every bolt and every connection didn't spring loose in the washing-machine motion of the engine. Tully was unconcerned. Slumped against the door, his arm out the window and his hand resting on the mirror, he steered with two fingers. Not a worry in the world.

When we turned off the freeway onto a county road, the truck hit a pothole and the glove compartment flopped open. Stuff began to migrate out. I shoved it back in and slammed the little door shut. Another pothole brought more of the same.

"What makes you so sure they'll be there?" I asked, slamming the glove compartment shut for the third time.

"Checked everywhere else. If they're still around they won't waste money on a motel when they've got a camper; 'sides, these aren't the kind of guys who are going to be real social."

I planted my feet on the glove compartment and looked out the window as the world changed from walled and gated communities, with cute names like Quail Run, to open fields with long-horned cattle. White cattle egrets rode the backs of the beef, picking off vermin.

The Osacola State Park is about thirty-five miles inland from the gulf. When it was set up back in the twenties it must have seemed that development would never reach this sixty-three square miles of primitive nature, but every year expansion crept closer and closer. "I remember when we used to fish out here," I said.

"Yeah, 'til you hit that girly stage and didn't want to do any of the good stuff."

It was true. At about eleven or twelve I decided that I wasn't doing any of the things Tully wanted to do anymore. They always involved yucky dead things, hours without seeing a proper bathroom and lots of beer. Well, beer for him. He never would let me try it no matter how hard I whined.

I gave up baseball caps for boys and we hadn't seen much of each other after that. In my twenties I'd sometimes drift by his pork roast for an hour but that was pretty much the extent of our togetherness.

"I used to hunt with my daddy out here," Tully said. "Back in the old days when we could still hunt."

I half-expected him to go off on a rant about the government ruining his world. Instead he said, "We used to hunt with hounds." He looked over at me to see if I was even mildly interested before he went on.

"Daddy would build a fire and pretty soon four or five

other guys would arrive with their dogs, all whining and keening. What a racket. They'd all be in cages on the backs of the
pickups, anxious for the hunt. Had to keep them caged or
they'd be over the tailgate and gone 'fore you was ready. Every
man had an old dog, a dog that knew what's what, and a young
dog, eager and strong, willing to learn. And lots had a dog in-
between. There'd be a dozen dogs or more, yapping and calling
to each other." He turned to me and smiled. "The old stir-
rings, primitive and alive in man and beast, screaming in the
blood. We set them loose and they'd spread out, noses to the
ground casting back and forth for a scent. Then they'd find one
and be gone. But we could still hear them. Knew exactly where
they were and what was happening.

"Man and boy, we all took a seat around the fire, waiting
and listening. There'd be iced tea and homemade hooch and
sandwiches Grandma packed. We'd talk, lazy and rambling,
not important, but mostly we just listened to the calling of the
dogs, back and forth, telling each other what they'd found.
Each man knew his dog, knew if he was in the lead, knew if
his dog had caught a good strong scent. It was a good thing to
have the lead dog, the dog baying the loudest and holding the
scent of game in his nose. We'd sit there with the smell of the
fire and the earth and hear the sound change, know they'd
treed something. Or we'd hear something die. Can't mistake
the scream of death."

He fell silent while I held my breath, afraid of breaking the
thread of his memory.

"Sometimes all the game went to ground. After 'bout an
hour the men would walk to their pickups and lean on their

horns, calling the dogs in. Then they'd load them up and we'd go home."

He drove in silence.

"Nobody has hounds anymore." His voice was sad for something lost.

"Probably 'cause you can't keep them home."

"That's true; you can't change a hound's nature. It needs to hunt. If you want a lap dog don't get a hound. He ain't good but for one thing…hunting. He wants to be out and gone, just put his nose down and follow where it leads, no lying at his master's feet for him. Civilization will always fight nature, man or dog. Some just don't have it in them to settle. And when you teach a dog to hunt, to kill, you can't take him home and say forget all that, Dog, just sit out in the backyard and be quiet…damn, that's just so crazy. All anyone wants from a dog anymore is that he's quiet and housebroke. Piss on that!"

I laughed. "You never settled, did you?"

"Gotta be some excitement in life."

"Well, you always seemed to find it."

"The only way to live is like a dog." He took his hand off the wheel, stretching it out to the windshield. "Body stretched out, searching, straining to win the prize." His old truck wandered onto the shoulder and he grabbed the wheel and fought it back from the edge of the tar.

"You're crazy," I told him. "You do know that, don't you?"

He grinned at me. "Yup. But that doesn't mean what I say ain't true."

I looked away from him. The ditches were filled with arrowroot and pickleweed and six inches of water left over from the rains in the first two weeks of September. We'd have about another few weeks of rain and then we'd start into the dry season, months without a drop of moisture and the green of the swamps would turn into dusty brown prairie grass.

Tully slowed. Slash pines grew up to the edges of the ditches. We pulled into the park entrance and stopped before the barrier. Heat quickly filled the cab. A lady in a brown uniform came out to the pickup with a handful of papers. Tully handed over five dollars for the entrance fee and said, "Say, we got some friends from Ohio that might be staying here. They got a pickup with a cap on the back and Ohio plates. Have you seen them?"

"I don't remember seeing them but you won't have any trouble finding them if they're here. There's only one campsite open and not many visitors. This is the quiet time of the year."

"Thanks," Tully said, handing me the brochures. I dropped them on the floor with the rest of the garbage. The first pothole we hit, the glove compartment popped open and a manual slid out to join the brochures. I left it there.

A hundred yards past the entrance we came upon the first creek. Halfway across the wooden trestle bridge, Tully stopped so we could look down the broad lazy waterway with its flat mudbanks dotted with gators snoozing in the sun. Egrets and shorebirds, ignoring the giant reptiles, fed at the edge of the water. A log half-sunk in the mud was covered with turtles. Must have been over twenty of them all jumbled together.

I took a deep breath, sucking in the crystal air. It was a good day to be alive and a good place to be living. The truck jiggled across the bridge and down along a narrow road through miles of grass as high as my shoulders before entering a green tunnel through deep woods.

The park is a patchwork of grass prairies, hammocks and swamp. The whole thing, hundreds of thousands of acres, is cut with endless twisting waterways that disappear in grass beds. The creek or river, or whatever waterway you're following, just stops. It just doesn't exist anymore and now there's only grass in front of your canoe. You have to search through the grasses growing in shallow water for the channel, finding it and losing it and turning back on yourself. Even when you follow the stream through the palmetto and trees, matted with climbing vines, making your way under low hanging trees, you can get lost. The edges of the bank, covered with clinging plants, creep out into the water, hindering your passing. Criss-crossing and twisting, the streams lead to places only a few people can make their way through, my daddy being one of them.

Most people never venture off the five miles of road going to Osacola Lake, but there are also two smaller lakes in the park that can only be accessed by water — a long torturous paddle that Tully and I had made twenty years before.

Running off the main roads are dozens of forestry tracks, firebreaks and dead ends. These roads aren't maintained and are only there for emergencies. Poor maintenance is probably a way to keep people out of the real wilderness. As Tully drove I studied the map on the back of one of the brochures, trying to orient myself again, but I had no clear memory of how we'd canoed from one part of the park to another.

"It says here that there are five camp areas. Did the warden say only one was open?"

"Yup. But we ain't going to find them in the one that's open." He pulled over and took the map from my hand.

"Let's check out the main campground just to be sure," I told him. "It's on the way to the lake."

"If you like," mild and easy, not at all like my old man. Who the hell was this guy and what had he done with the real Tully Jenkins?

The main campground, with large log washhouses and electricity to every site, was nearly to Lake Osacola. We pulled in and drove through the winding roads. Fewer than a dozen sites — of the fifty or sixty spread out along the two- or three-mile trek — were taken. None of the rigs were from Ohio. Tully drove slowly, leaning out the opened window and resting his right wrist on top of the wheel to steer the truck. He studied each rig real carefully and didn't say, "Told you so," when there were no Ohio plates.

We went up to the lake where there's a large lodge that houses conference rooms, a snack bar, restaurant and gift shop. You can also buy tickets for airboat rides and rent canoes or launch your boat, as long as it has an electric motor — no motor boats allowed. There were only three cars in the parking lot and they probably belonged to the employees or the volunteers who kept the park running. September in Florida is quiet.

We cruised through the parking lot that circled the building. No Ohio plates.

"Let's check out those other campgrounds," Tully said.

"I remember those other campgrounds," I told Tully. "Pretty primitive, no electric or flush toilets."

"Some people can get along without those things."

"Not me."

"Good thing you've got such a fancy man then."

He reached out and turned on the radio. His acknowledgment of my living arrangement seemed to be as far as this conversation was going. That was fine with me. I'd rather listen to Gretchen Wilson singing about where she bought her underwear.

Three miles north of the lake we pulled off the road at the first campground. A chain strung across in front of us barred the way. We got out of the truck. Tully went left and I went right, walking around the posts holding up the chain. We walked down the grass-covered road about twenty yards until we came to a low place in the road covered with water.

"No one has come here in a while," he said. "The whole site is probably still under water. It'll be another month before it dries out enough to use." We started back to the truck.

The next two campgrounds weren't chained off, but they were empty and overgrown when we drove in and looked around. One was set deep in the woods, the other was on a hammock surrounded by prairie grasses. I started to relax, sure that Tully had guessed wrong and we weren't going to find the Ohio plates. Tully grew quieter.

The last campground, down a gravel-covered track, was also barricaded at the road by a chain. Tully didn't stop. He drove about a hundred yards past before he pulled over. "Two ways of doing it. Woods aren't too thick. We can make our way through there and try and stay out of sight. The other way is we just walk in there like we belong. Just like anyone would."

"Probably best just to walk straight in," I offered. "If we walk through the swamp and we get lost in there we'll never find our way out."

"Speak for yourself," Tully said, squawking open the door and heading back for the campground.

Within fifty yards of the road the gravel ran out and the track turned into grass and weeds. Flat and unditched, it wasn't meant to be used at this time of the year, but right away I could see this was different from the deserted spots we'd already checked out. The grass was freshly rutted and beaten down by tires. Tire marks skirted large puddles and dug deep wells into the sides of the track. Twice there was evidence that someone got stuck. There was definitely someone in here where no one was supposed to be. I wasn't liking this at all. My survival instinct was telling me to get the hell out of there. I glanced over at Tully. He could've been walking down any country lane on a Sunday afternoon.

"Let's go back," I said.

"Why? We paid our money and it's a nice day for a stroll."

A mile in we heard the scrape of metal against metal. I stopped and looked at Tully. "They're here," I whispered.

He moved forward, not trying to be quiet or to surprise anyone.

Ahead of us, someone laughed.

CHAPTER 32

We smelt them before we saw them.

"What the hell is that smell?" I whispered.

The air was rank with the odor of rotting meat. Think of throwing a Styrofoam tray that held raw chicken into the trash and then raising the lid an hour later. Now multiply that a hundred times.

Tully had his nose in the air like an old hound dog. "Blood," he said. "Innards and bad meat. Someone has been doing some butchering."

The rutted track swung right under a live oak, dripping with Spanish moss, and opened up onto the small campground. It was empty.

"Down there," Tully said and pointed.

Even knowing they were there you could miss them. They were at the very end of the campsite, tucked back in a little clearing along the river, the campers pulled up close under the trees, their noses deep in the undergrowth. There were two pickups, one with a fifth wheel on behind.

"Let's get the hell out of here." I was backing up even as I spoke. But it was too late.

A man stepped out of the woods behind us, blocking our way. "You lost?"

"Nope," Tully replied. "We're right where we intended to be."

"This campground is closed." The man was at least six foot and two hundred and ninety pounds and completely without hair on his head or his bare chest, which was covered in tattoos. Tattoos ran up both arms. His body was the canvas for a lot of art and a lot of pain. The little heart on my behind that said "Jimmy's" told me just how much he had been prepared to suffer for the animals that crawled over his body, a panther on his right bicep and some kind of lizard on his left arm. A snake circled his neck, the red tongue flicking onto his left cheek. Had he shaved the hair off his body to show off his tattoos? He pointed in the direction we'd come. "You'll find an open campground back towards the lake." His words were mild but he scared the shit out of me. Maybe it was his eyes, almost gold and shining.

I slid past him, breaking into a trot before checking to see if Tully was following me. He wasn't.

Tully said, "We'll have a look around first. Goin' to have a family reunion this Thanksgiving, thought we'd pick a campsite away from others so we won't disturb folks, if you know what I mean."

Tattoo Man stepped out in front of Tully and crossed his arms. They were about the same height but he had over a hundred pounds on Tully.

Moonwalking away, I called, "Let's go, Dad."

Tully didn't move.

"I'm going to be late," I called.

Tully's eyes flicked to me and then back. "Sure," Tully answered, but he wasn't moving. The two of them stood toe to toe locked in a staring match.

"Dad." I wasn't sure if Tully saw the two guys coming out from behind the camper, two man-mountains lumbering towards us.

"Come on now." Nothing. "Please, Dad," I begged. It was the please that did it, the surprise of it. Tully looked at me and then started towards me.

I didn't wait for him to reach me. I was gone.

Out at the road I waited for Tully to catch up, leaning over with my hands on my knees, trying to catch my breath.

He was grinning at me as he strolled towards me. "You almost broke a land-speed record getting out of there, little girl."

"Contrary to what public opinion might say, I'm no fool."

"You are a fast woman though."

"Is that what public opinion says?"

"Not around me."

"That guy was scary."

"Well, I'm guessing that's what he intended."

"He totally convinced me, and the two others on their way to do you an injury were pretty convincing too."

Tully laughed. "Told you it would take three good men to lick me."

"Oh, they weren't good men. Do you think those are the guys?"

"Maybe. What color are Ohio plates?"

"I don't know. But that guy talked funny, northern. Call the cops and have them check them out."

He didn't say anything which was the same as saying no. Tully's first thought would never be to call the cops.

"Uncle Ziggy never said anything about the tattooed man. It's probably not them."

"Zig never got a real good look at the guy that hit him."

"What are you going to do?"

He didn't say anything, just slouched along in that way of his.

Irritated and wanting to dig at him, I said, "You should wear runners out here instead of cowboy boots. Cowboy boots are stupid for anything but riding."

"I'll remember that when I come back."

I sprinted forward, grabbing his arm and jerking him around to face me. "Back?"

"I'd like to get a closer look. My nose tells me those fellas are doing some poaching. Gators likely, good market for them right now." That statement begged another question I didn't want answered. Lots of things about my father I just didn't want to know. I followed him back to the truck in silence.

The sun was streaming down on my door handle so that when I reached out to open the door it burnt my hand. I jerked my hand away. "Shit."

Tully climbed in and pushed open my door from the inside. The cab was a furnace — the seats burnt through my shorts.

"Let the cops handle it or the wardens. If they don't get caught for what they did to Uncle Ziggy, they can get done for poaching."

"A fine, nothing more."

"At least something." I could see by the hardness of his profile it wasn't going to happen. Something in him demanded justice, wanted pain, the old eye-for-an-eye thing that went back to Adam and Eve. But there was nothing to keep me from calling the cops, was there?

He started the truck and pulled away. "How do you know that some of the wardens aren't in on it?" Tully asked. "A few of them might turn a blind eye for a cut of the proceeds."

"You really think so?"

"I know so." He grinned at me.

"Man, you're destroying my last belief in saints. I so don't want to hear anything bad about them. If park wardens can be corrupted there's no hope for the rest of us."

"Some wardens feel there's too many gators since they stopped hunting back in the sixties. For the last two years this park has let out licenses to hunt gators. Two thousand dollars per license and a hundred licenses each year, plus you have to pay for the people you bring with you. A quarter of a million dollars a year, that's how much this park makes off gators. The park also gets money from the meat and the hides. You get about eight bucks a pound for the meat and a mature gator can dress out at about seventy-five to a hundred pounds. Then there are the hides. The belly is the most expensive bit, twenty-five to thirty dollars a foot. All and all you can make about a thousand bucks a gator. That gives the park another thousand dollars a license, over three hundred thousand each season. It's a rich man's sport. Rich guys are willing to pay big bucks for the fun of killing a gator."

"It's a crazy world," I said and watched the wilderness slide by, deep green and tangled and jumbled together, a whole world outside the hard surfaces, lights and steel of my world. "Did you and Jimmy hunt gators?"

"No, we never got the chance." His voice was full of regret. Jimmy had been like a son to Tully, a kindred spirit, and they'd fished and hunted together all over the state.

The truck rocked back and forth through potholes and rattled over a trestle bridge while I kept watch in the side mirror to make sure we weren't being followed by the gator hunters.

As we approached the little kiosk, I asked, "Are you going to report them for parking in a closed campsite?"

Tully snorted with laughter.

"Well, report them for poaching."

He shot me a look I remembered from childhood.

"Are you going to call the cops and tell them where to find Ziggy's guys?"

"How do we know they're the crew from Ohio?"

"Let the cops go out there and check. If they aren't the ones we say, 'Oh, sorry.'"

It so wasn't going to happen. Well, not if Tully was going to do it but I could call Styles. How would Tully take to me going behind his back? And did I care?

We drove back to Cypress Island mostly in silence, deep in our own thoughts. Tully was planning something that didn't involve calling any authorities. Did I want to be involved? Not really. A good rule of thumb is, if Tully Jenkins is involved it's bound to end badly. The man is just a natural born screw-up.

The closer we got to town, the more I worried. As we rattled over the humpbacked bridge spanning the intra-coastal I asked the question I'd promised myself not to ask. "Are you going back there?"

"Yup."

"Why?"

He laid on the horn as a tourist in an Avis rental pulled out in front of him barely missing the front bumper of the truck, which was fine; but then the tourist slammed on his brakes. I braced myself against the dash.

I asked again, "Why?"

"Want to see if they're from Ohio." The tourist decided he was going the wrong way and made a U-turn, cutting off traffic coming towards us. More horns.

"Going out there is a bad idea."

"Well, it won't be my first." He grinned like a kid planning a raid on the cookie jar. The man just had no good sense.

"How? I mean are you just going to drive in there again? They won't let you near their rigs. Maybe they've even packed up and moved by now."

"Been thinking about that and you're right. Those boys aren't going to hang around. They'll be gone by tomorrow. Maybe gone already. But my bet is they'll wait 'til tomorrow. They'll want to pull their hooks and they'll know how slow anything involving authorities is, even if we reported them today, ain't likely to be anyone out there to talk to them until tomorrow. They'll be gone by then so I'm goin' back today."

"How?"

"They're camped on the river mouth emptying into the north lake — Soldaat Lake it's called. That river, well little more than a stream really, broadens into swamp with no way to really get a boat through to the lake. But there's another stream that you can get a canoe down to Soldaat Lake. My guess is those fellas are taking gators out on the lake. That's where I'd take them." He grinned at me. "You can pull an electric boat up into the mouth of the river and not be seen, but no one can paddle up the other way and surprise you. Don't want company if you're doing a little poaching."

I didn't ask how he knew so much about poaching gators. Like in the army, my way of dealing with Tully's alternative lifestyle was don't ask, don't tell. "So how are you going to get to the lake?"

"From the north, off Jefferson Road, a little creek feeds into Soldaat Lake. Just a nice easy paddle away from where I park the truck. Take about an hour and twenty minutes down the lake to the outlet of the river those boys are camped on. No sweat, little girl, I'll get into their neighborhood real easy, see if they're from Ohio and see if they've set any gator hooks on the lake."

I took a deep breath and let it out slowly. "Okay," I said, nodding my head. "I'm coming with you."

"What? No way! You almost wet yourself back there."

"You aren't planning on confronting them, are you?"

"No. Not planning that." Somehow he didn't sound all that convincing. I didn't want to think about it, didn't want to look too closely at all the ways this could go wrong. Like I said, Tully Jenkins had a history of disasters. "I'm coming with you," I told him.

"Why do you wanna come?"

It was a sensible question and one I hadn't worked out an answer to. But primarily I was hoping I could save him from himself, dampen down the violence and stupidity. With me along he'd be more cautious; at least I hoped he would. I kept those thoughts to myself and said, "Why should you have all the fun?"

He thought for a minute and nodded. In his crazy world it likely made sense.

Paddling miles down a creek and sneaking up on some real bad guys just sounded like a barrelful. Hee haw! Bring it on.

Tully dropped me off at the restaurant and I spent time on the phone replacing myself. If I didn't get my ass back in there real soon I'd drive myself into bankruptcy or my employees would steal me into it, but that was tomorrow's worry. My worry bag for today was already full. I quickly called Clay, whose phone was off, thank god — no way I wanted to explain how I was spending my evening, so I left a message saying everything was fine. Another message for Marley and I shot off to the apartment to get into my sneaking-up-on-people kit.

CHAPTER 33

We turned onto Jefferson Road at the edge of the park, where civilization meets wilderness. Houses, weathered, unadorned and falling down, said life was hard. Strung out in a thin ragged line along the dirt road, the houses perched on concrete blocks in yards full of rusting cars and cast-off machinery. Squatting in a circle of bare dirt or struggling out of tall grasses, thick vines strangled both man-made and natural forms alike. Every yard seemed to have a lean, half-crazed brown dog that came out to yap at us through bared fangs as we rattled by.

The land here was neither one thing nor another. Swamp turned into fields of tall grasses dotted with hammocks. Close to the back of the houses crouched dense woods of pine and oak, waiting for a single season of neglect to claim back the occupied land.

When we got to the pull-off at the bridge, Tully cranked the old truck over to the very edge of the grass ditch. The engine coughed and died. "It's late," I said. "Not much light left."

Tully's door squeaked open. "We got two hours of full light to get to the lake, and then we got nearly another hour 'til deep black. More than enough. Don't worry, little girl." Right then and there warning sirens started going crazy. When this man said, don't worry, you sure as hell should.

I wrapped the bottom of my jeans tight around my legs and

pulled Clay's dark socks up over them. No nasty little critters were going to get at my bare skin — no white flag of sock was going to betray my presence. I was way into this survival stuff.

I pushed open my door. The truck was tilted towards the ditch and gravity pulled the door down the incline. Some of Tully's paperwork slid off the floor into the grass. As I stepped down out of the truck my foot hit the manual, shooting it out from under me. I slid down into the ditch, landing on my ass in the muddy water at the bottom. I quickly jumped to my feet, dripping but upright in ankle-deep muck. Water oozed between my toes. The water stank and now so did I. On the road above me, high and dry, Tully laughed. I considered killing him — would have if I'd realized what was coming.

I sunk my fingers into the tall grass and scrambled back up to the truck. My whole right side was wet, including the cell phone in the buttoned-down pocket of my black cargo pants. I took it out and pressed On. Nothing. "Shit." Already this adventure was living up to my expectations. On a branch in the underbrush a dove cooed softly in sympathy.

I wanted to tell Tully I'd changed my mind, tell him I was having second thoughts. Well, maybe even third and forth thoughts, but whatever the count I wasn't real eager to get started on this misadventure.

I wanted to tell him to call the cops and forget about it, but pride, that same old demon that would always make me cut off my nose to spite my face, kept me silent. I only hoped that Tully was wrong and they'd already gone. That was the only thing keeping me in this game. I was betting they weren't as cool as Tully Jenkins, weren't always ready to push things to the limit.

Tully muscled the brown-and-green camouflage-painted canoe out of the bed of the pickup, so I held onto the truck bed to keep from sliding down the bank again and picked up my end of the canoe. Together we slid it down the embankment and into the narrow stream under the bridge. The water was pretty clear here, not the dark tannin brown water of the woods. Perhaps here the grasses filtered the water. Tully scrambled up the bank and handed me down a duffel bag, full and heavy. I didn't ask what was in it, just stowed it in the canoe and waited for him. He went back to the cab of the truck and came back with the long sleeve of a rifle cover. Was this good news or something more to worry about?

Tully pushed the canoe away from the grass bank and anchored it with his paddle.

Keeping my weight low and holding the gunnels, I stepped into the canoe and settled in the bow. I took up the paddle. Ahead of us, a blue-grey heron lifted elegantly off the shore with slow even beats of its wings. Legs trailing behind, it flew ahead of us down the waterway, guiding the way to the entrance in the solid wall of deep jungle. I settled my hips and dampened down my misgivings. A nice little paddle with the old man, what could possibly go wrong? Yeah, right.

We paddled towards the wilderness crouching in front of us, waiting and licking its chops in anticipation of devouring us. The land between the road and deep forest had once been worked but now it had been left to go back to nature. Cabbage palms, our state tree, grew in abundance along the edge of the stream, their trunks cross-hatched with dead branches offering fiber for nests, their fruit feeding the birds and hiding the rats and the snakes that fed on the birds.

Somewhere farther down the road and beyond the palms on my left a dog barked, not loud or adamant but just to say it was there. A man's voice told it to shut up while another voice, a woman's voice, called for the man to come inside. Strange to hear people but not to see them through the dense foliage. I felt a little safer just knowing other people were close, wanted to call out to them and tell them I was among them and not to let me disappear into nothing. A door slammed somewhere in the distance along the thin line of dusty road.

Within minutes of leaving the bridge we reached the narrow arch into the wild. The man-built world slid away with the water under our craft as we glided back in time into a primordial world, base and immediate. Only the water mattered, sleek and shining and spreading out in front of us, leading us on. The stream was broad here and shallow, the water now like a dark brown sauce, colored with the tannin of dead leaves. The air was strangely quiet, as if nature were holding her breath and waiting to see what these new invaders brought with them.

The dip and stroke of the paddles eased my anxious heart, the rhythm relaxing and soothing. I said, "Tell me about the snakes," hoping he'd lie.

Dip and pull. "Which ones?"

"Start with the ones likely to kill me."

More strokes as he counted the reptiles to himself. "Really, only six likely to do that." He named them, "First the c-snakes:

coral, copperhead, cottonmouth. Then there are the rattlers: pigmy and diamondback and the canebrake. Other than that, no worries."

My paddle stopped in midstroke. I plunked it across the gunnels, the crack sounding loud in the stillness. I leaned on my paddle and looked back at him. He was grinning at me and paddling on. Not a care in the world.

"I hate snakes."

"Then you're in the right place. The theory is, the fellow upfront stirs them up and the guy in back gets hit. 'Course, theory is well and good as long as someone tells the snake."

I glared at him. "Sometimes I don't like you much."

He laughed softly as we ducked down under the overhanging branches of an oak leaning over the water and maneuvered around a fallen tree. We cut so close to the bank that the grasses combed the water from our paddles as we passed. Ahead of us an otter raised his head to look at us and then scurried, sliding and slipping, into the water and was gone.

We settled into a silent rhythm until the water grew too shallow to pass through. Tully said, "Get out" in a quiet voice, barely above a whisper. Did he feel it too, the strange waiting, the feeling of expectancy, of being in another world? Or maybe he'd just slipped into his 'Nam jungle mode.

I got out of the canoe, reaching down to grab the prow and drag it through the shallows, thinking of leeches and Humphrey Bogart in *The African Queen*. The mulch on the bottom sucked on my canvas sneakers, trying to vacuum them from my feet. In front of me a fish darted away, the fin on its back breaking the surface of the shallow water. Above us the canopy thinned as we skirted the edge of a marshy area. Dragging the canoe through tall grass, the late-day sun warming our skin, we found the stream again on the other side and re-entered the forest, startling a white egret that cried and flew up from a branch.

The waterway narrowed; the banks grew steeper. I sank into water up to my knees. "Okay," Tully said and braced the canoe while I entered. As I did, I waggled each foot in the water, shaking off the muck and searching for hitchhikers. Leaning on the paddle across in front of me, eyes probing the underbrush along the banks for danger, I settled again.

The canoe barely wobbled as Tully entered and we slid forward. Branches reached across the stream to each other, sheltering us from the last of the sun. It was cooler here. And darker. My senses came alive and I breathed deeply. The sweet smell of decay, rotting wood and leaves, mixed with the smell of the water. The stagnant, unmoving water of the swamp, the smell of death in our nostrils, the roots of a cypress tree jutting out like the arthritic knuckles of an old man's hand, these were the things I fixed on. My eyes searched the trees, noting air plants and mosses and moving on, searching for danger or information I might need. I didn't know what form danger might take; I only knew it was out there, waiting.

Behind me Tully began to sing softly, "Oh mama, I can't dance, the boys all got sticks in their pants. Oh mama, I can't…" The canoe rocked gently as Tully moved forward and swatted at something on the back of my collar.

"What?" I asked."

"Nothing, don't worry."

Hell girl, nothing to worry about out here, just bad men,

snakes and spiders and god knew what else. "I'm used to bars and things," I explained and laid the paddle across my knees. I watched the water run off the end. "I know what to worry about there, crazies and drunks and druggies but there's real scary stuff out here."

He laughed. "Don't worry, got you covered, little girl."

I wished I could believe it.

CHAPTER 34

"Look," he said. "Gator."

On the bank ahead of us was a ten-foot gator with his long, flattened snout pointing towards us. His armor-plated skin had spikes running along the edges from head to tail. "They feed at night...at dusk." Tully spoke quietly. "He's just about ready for dinner."

"Oh whoopee!"

"We'll stay well away. That thing's nothing but a seeing, smelling, eating machine." Tully angled his paddle, steering us to the far shore away from the gator, but in a thirteen-foot-wide stream it offered little comfort. The gator saw us and rose up on his legs as we passed. The horizontal line of his mouth opened in the massive elongated head. I couldn't take my eyes off him although my brain was saying paddle like hell.

"He looks like a huge set of pointed teeth with stubby legs."

"Never ignore that tail," Tully warned. "He can break your leg with one sweep."

The gator's jaw closed and he ambled awkwardly forward and then slipped silently into the water. Only the nostrils on the tip of its snout and the two hills of its eyes protruded from the water, watching us and coming silently towards us. Then it disappeared.

I paddled like some demented cartoon character on steroids.

"Easy, easy," Tully warned.

Panting with exertion, I asked, "Where is it? Why doesn't it come up?"

"It can stay under for hours."

"You're just full of good news...among other things."

A soft laugh. He wasn't perturbed by any gator.

I was still pulling hard but searching the water on the backstroke for any tell-tale signs of the monster. We were another hundred yards along before I started to feel safe. Then I saw two more gators, smaller ones this time, sleeping on the shore. They might be small but all the same we were within a dozen feet of them. "At this moment I don't feel poaching gators is a bad thing," I whispered to Tully as we drifted by. I took a deep breath and looked back over my shoulder at them. "Their backs look green. The ones I've seen have always been black."

"Duckweed," was his cryptic reply. Was Tully feeling it too, feeling this strangeness of the other world, the fear of the unknown and the alarm of a victim?

It wasn't just the dread of what was to come but the "what if" of imagination that was having a go at terrifying me. Nature was no longer benign and welcoming. Maybe it never had been and I'd just been too young and ignorant to know.

My heart rate settled but we weren't through with the gators. Now the water teemed with ones about four inches long, and as I watched a long-nosed fish broke for the surface, its mouth closing over a wiggling gator fingerling, and the hunter became the hunted.

The lake surprised me. One minute we were in a narrow, choked watercourse and the next, as we pulled free of the reed beds along the edge of the water, we broke out onto a broad flat lake with a cloud of white ibis rising up around us to signal our arrival. Tully steered the craft hard to the right. "Their camp is about five minutes down. No more talking."

A chill swept over me. I turned to look at him, wanting to ask to turn back. Out here only the men who beat Uncle Ziggy would be able to hear me scream.

A breeze came up on the lake, sending tiny waves dancing across the water in front of us and pushing against our hull, demanding more of us. I swiveled around to the bow and matched Tully's strokes.

We heard them before we saw them. They were coming from behind us, between us and the stream that led back to safety, to civilization where I wanted to be again. "Jesus Christ, hold it still you ass," one of them said.

I didn't need to be told to dig harder. We shot by the opening to the stream where their camp was, pulling hard to put distance between us and the men. There was no cover. The reed beds here were thick but only grew about a foot above the water.

Within seconds a curse went up.

A bass voice yelled from behind us, "Hey, you there."

"Pull," Tully said. I went hard. Another twenty feet and we cleared a small finger of ground snaking into the water. We passed it and veered right. "Out," Tully said. "Lie down in the water. I did as I was told, looking up at the sky, my paddle clutched to my chest and breathing hard. I didn't look to see what Tully was doing but I heard the sheath slide off his rifle.

"Where the hell did they go?" That was clear even with water covering my ears. There was a heavy clunk, a sound like a foot hitting against the side of an aluminum boat.

"Let's get rid of the gator and get out of here."

"No way. We'll drop you back at camp. You dress this out, Bob, and we'll keep looking."

"Why do I get all the dirty jobs?"

"Let's look on down farther," a new voice put in.

There was no sound of the electric motor or any more voices. I stayed where I was, flat in the water along the edge of the bank while overhead an osprey hovered and watched. Would it see my eyes and think they were food? Would it dive down to peck them out? I should close my eyes, but no way could I take my eyes off him. Then I saw it fold its wings and dive. A hand touched me. I jerked up.

Tully had his finger to his lips. I nodded. Waves echoed out from me and I froze.

He made a patting downward motion with his hand. I took it to mean he wanted me to stay down close to the water. Then he beckoned for me to come. I rolled on my belly and started to crawl through the reeds after him, no longer worried about leeches. Tully pushed the canoe ahead of him. I wanted to raise my head enough to search for the men but didn't. I was going strictly on instinct here, instinct and a thousand adventure movies. Mostly I was following my dad and trusting to his sixty years of survival.

We moved deeper into the reed bed in the shallow bay. Were we leaving behind a trail of broken reeds and stirred water to show our passage?

Here and there, where it was as much land as marsh, bushes were growing out of the reeds, offering us cover. We fled from one small refuge to the next, hovering behind them without moving, waiting until Tully decided it was time to move and then we went on to the next bit of protection, angling towards denser shelter, thicker than the last, but still I caught glimpses of the lake when I looked back. Tully leaned in close to me, his breath warm on my cheek. "They're waiting for us to break cover."

I stayed as still as I could, staring into the emerald green bush in front of me. Five minutes passed and then ten. A red-winged blackbird landed on the bush, startling me. Tully reached out a hand to my shoulder. More time passed before we heard them.

CHAPTER 35

"Have to be here. We lost them when they went around that point." The voice belonged to the tattooed man.

"What does it matter? Just tourists likely, if it was wardens they wouldn't have run away."

"Have to be somewhere hiding."

"Well, we can't get any closer, too shallow. Let's forget about it and go back to camp. It's time to get out of here."

"I want to know who's sneaking up on us. Bet it's that cocky bastard from this morning. I've got a bad feeling about him."

"We don't know that it's him and who's ever out here probably ain't got nothin' to do with us."

"How'd they get here and why? They didn't put their canoe in by our camp. Least not while we was there. You don't accidentally wind up here — you have to know what you're doing to find this lake if you aren't coming in from our camp. They came here on purpose. How many times we been around this lake? You ever see anyone out here in the last three years?"

Another voice joined in with, "He's got a point."

"You only stick up for him because he's your brother. I always get the dirty work and I'm always the odd man out."

"You're odd all right."

"Okay, I'm taking you back. I'll drop you two off and then I'll come back and look for them."

We waited some minutes more and then Tully motioned me into the canoe. I was trying to guess how long it would take for the men to make the trip to their camp and back. How long did we have to escape? Electric motors are quiet but slow. Maybe we could paddle as fast as they could go in a boat with an electric motor. But we couldn't paddle fast enough to cross the lake to the stream before they got back, couldn't paddle fast enough to go around the lake or any other improbable scenario I was coming up with to get us out of there without passing the men who stood between us and safety.

Tully motioned me to follow him as he pulled the canoe towards open water.

The jut of land protected us from them but I felt as if their eyes were boring into my back. Once at the water, we entered the canoe and paddled hard, focused on speed and distance.

We couldn't go back the way we came. Even I knew this. The men were between us and the stream leading us out of the swamp. And dusk was falling.

We couldn't sneak by them in the dark; we'd never find the mouth of the stream in the dark and no way would we want to show a light. If we were at the mouth of the stream at this moment, could we get out before blackness overtook us? And did I want to try slipping through those narrow banks with unseen danger waiting for us on either side in the night? Being the smartest of species wasn't a help in this situation. We had no advantages out here; this was where brute strength and the size of your teeth won.

My nervous heart trembled and I wanted to ask a hundred times, in a hundred different ways, what's going to happen to me? I wanted to ask where we were headed and what we were looking for, but our roles had changed. We weren't two equal adults. Not by a long shot. Out here I was following his lead, a neophyte at the feet of a master. He would tell me what I needed to know and I would listen. Until then I would keep my concerns to myself. I needed my strength for the paddle.

Tully steered us around the end of a cypress tree. There was a small narrow cut of water into the land. We nosed the canoe into the bank. I scrambled out without being told and reached down to pull the canoe up onto the bank.

Tully opened the duffel and handed me a thin blanket, a bottle of water and a power bar. The light of day disappeared.

Before long another light appeared and a bright shaft danced through the bushes and cypress at the edge of the lake. "Spotlight," Tully said. "They're looking for us. We can't show a light but we don't need to."

Night came swiftly. A full moon hovered over top of us, making me feel exposed. Although the humid air was still full of warmth, new sounds chilled me with their strangeness.

I drew my knees up to my chest and wrapped my arms around them. A chorus of peepers and frogs covered my hushed question. "Are there still panthers out here?"

"A few, I suppose."

"Did you ever shoot one?"

"Naw. Why'd I do that? Can't eat them."

"So, there's panthers. What else?" I meant, of course, what else is there to kill me besides men and panthers.

"Don't worry," he soothed, "you'll be fine."

A bull gator sounded. It had been a long time since I'd heard that sound but I recognized it; only now, instead of excitement, I felt fear and dread. "Yes," I replied, "we'll be fine." We fell quiet, with me thinking about what being fine meant. Heaven only knew what Tully was thinking about.

Somewhere up above us an owl called out, "Who, who." I wanted to answer him, "Me, me," wanted to say I was there, wasn't forever lost to the world.

And then in the dark some huge creature screamed in agonizing death.

Tully answered the question I hadn't asked. "Gator. They must have left a hook set. They won't take him 'til morning. Can't take a gator in the dark."

"Hook?"

"You take a steel hook, a great big whopping steel hook, and you spear some chicken on it. Gators only like dead things. They get you, they gonna pull you into the water and drown you before they eat you."

"A comforting thought and one I'll surely keep in mind."

A soft laugh. His strong arm snaked around my shoulders and pulled me to him. I let it stay. "Anyway, you take a rope and put it on a pole you've stuck in the water and then suspend this hook from it over the water. It has to be high enough off the water to make the gator jump for it, so's he sets the hook, you know?"

I nodded. I was so hoping I wasn't ever going to need this information.

"Anyways, then you tie the rope to a big old tree. The blood drips in the water, let's the gator know it's there, and that old gator snaps up that chicken, hook and all." His left hand flashed out in front of us and snapped shut in a fist. "Then the gator goes into this death roll. Gator will always do that. Roll over and over with prey in its mouth."

"Why?"

He shrugged. "Just does. Maybe it's to kill whatever it has hold of. Maybe it's to break off bits of whatever it's got in its mouth. Don't know. Anyway, that's how a gator does it. And as it rolls over and over the rope, see, the extra rope you've put over the pole, wraps around him. He trusses himself up like a Christmas turkey."

"And then it dies?"

"Nope. Then you have to kill it. That's the tricky part."

"I can see it might be."

We listened some to the night sounds, life and death in the dark, strange and foreign to me.

"How do you kill a gator?" I asked.

"You shoot it."

"What's tricky about that?"

"Well, there only one spot you can hit a gator that's going to kill it. Shoot it anywhere else and it'll ricochet off and kill you or one of your buddies. Or maybe you'll just make the gator madder."

"I wouldn't want that. That wouldn't be a good thing, would it?"

"Nope."

"Won't the gator just die?"

"It could live for days."

"Oh. So when I get this gator all roped up and ready for dinner, where do I shoot it?"

He let go of me and placed his right index finger low down on the back of my head and to the side. "Right here at the edge of that bony plate. Bullet will go right into its tiny little brain. Only thing that will kill it. Some fellas will tell you to shoot it in the eye. Doesn't work." He tapped his finger on the back of my head, "Shoot it right there."

"Good to know," I told him, nodding to let him know I'd taken it in.

"'Course there's one other tricky thing."

"Only one?"

"Only one important thing."

"What's that?"

"How to tell if it's dead."

I wasn't going to ask why that would be tricky. Dead is dead, isn't it?

"How do you think you can tell if it's dead?" he asked.

"If it passes on a beer?"

"No, that would be how you tell if your old man is dead. A gator's a little different." His arm went back around my shoulders and he hugged me to his side. I'd wait 'til tomorrow to correct this new and nasty habit.

"Hard to tell if a gator's dead. One time Zig and I took a gator, had it in this big old aluminum boat Zig used to have. Goin' along nice as you please, maybe an hour after we took it, when this damn beast rears up its big head, bucking and twisting on its back, its feet going like sixty, those big old claws scratching at the sides of the boat as it flipped itself over to its belly."

He was laughing softly to himself, remembering, until the laughter set him coughing, choking and gasping for breath. He hawked and spit into the darkness.

I asked, "What did Uncle Ziggy do?"

"Well, Zig and I kinda had this discussion when we took it. Zig always likes to take good strong tape and wrap it around the gator's mouth to prevent nasty surprises like the one we were having but I'd told him it was a waste of time and tape, so old Zig wasn't too happy 'bout now, what with the gator going crazy, tossing his head until the rope came free and there was nothing left to stop it doing pretty much anything it wanted. Don't know why Zig was worried, the business end of the thing was facing me and its smile didn't warm my heart. Now Zig, well he just got real excited like your Uncle Ziggy does, and he didn't think too clearly. He pulled out this big old hand gun and shot at the gator. Wasn't close enough to get under the armored plate so the bullet just bounced off and put a nice big hole in the boat — just 'bout the waterline."

"Oops."

"Big oops." He was laughing again and I was smiling a bit myself, two fuck-ups on their day off.

"Zig got him with the second shot. That one stayed in the gator but I tell you I was expecting the bullet to go right through and put a hole out the other side of the boat." Tully was collapsing with laughter. "Funniest damn thing you ever seen, that gator going crazy."

"So how do you tell if a gator's dead?" Why was I asking? Guess because we'd come this far, it was only natural to want to know the rest.

"Well," he said, "me, I always poke them in the eye."

"Does that work?"

"So far." He gave a hoarse chuckle and added, "'Course even dead they can still hurt you."

I didn't rise to the bait.

Layers and years of sophistication and independence were sanded away by fear in the night. I leaned into the shelter of my father's body, a solid barrier between me and the unknown. Tomorrow I could win back my cool indifference and urbane contempt but at the moment I was a child again in my father's arms and happy to be there. With his protection came a twinge of guilt at the selfish thought that whatever danger came for us it would have to get through Tully before it got to me.

CHAPTER 36

The world lightened around us, false dawn, not quite real. Hundreds and thousands of noisy raucous voices, more birds than I would have believed to exist, called and answered across the ragged bloody sky.

Somewhere in the night our bodies had curled together for warmth and safety. I stayed still, reluctant to wake him. Finally Tully awoke, turned away from me, stretched and yawned, sat up, hawked and spat into the bushes. He rose to his feet, shaking his legs and pulling the legs of his jeans down over his boots. He looked down at me and grinned. "Morning, little girl."

When had he taken to calling me that?

"Morning," I answered and tried to smile. My bones hurt. From the way Tully was limping as he walked back and forth along the edge of the hammock, searching every clump, every tree, I figured a night on the ground had been even harder on him. I pushed back the blanket and got to my feet. "See anything?"

"Nope. Let's get started."

I folded the blanket, stuffing it back in the duffel that had served as our pillow.

"We'll be across the lake and gone before they're up," he said as he righted the canoe.

I looked at my watch. We'd be back at the truck before seven. I slipped into the bushes for a pee, pushing the wet branches from in front of me cautiously, watching for snakes and bugs and trying my best to stay dry. Everything was sodden like we'd had a rain, the whole world dripping with dew.

When I came back, the canoe and Tully were gone. Panic, full out and complete, set me dancing with anxiety. "No, no," I moaned. A low keening wail escaped from my throat, fear no longer keeping me quiet but making me want to scream into the sky.

Tully burst from the trees, in a crouch with the rifle ready. "What?" he growled.

I swung to face him. "I couldn't see you. I thought you were gone."

He lowered the gun. "You thought I left without you? That's stupid. I went to have a look around."

"You did before," I accused. "You left me before."

"One time." He held his forefinger in the air. "Once."

"You left me behind at a bootlegger's."

"Keep your voice down. Sound carries on the water."

I was still upset, still angry and frightened after all those years, but I lowered my voice and I whispered, "I woke up and you were gone. There I was all alone with those strange old men playing cards. Who takes a kid to an illegal poker game? Who forgets they brought a kid with them?"

"I wasn't used to having a kid trailing along behind me. I came back for you as soon as I remembered."

I was five again and couldn't let it go. "It was a Sunday night. Ruth Ann was waiting tables at the Rookery and you were supposed to look after me. You took me with you to a floating card game at a bootlegger's. It was late, I fell asleep on the floor on someone's coat in that little room next door." My voice rose, but caution fought it back to a lip-curling snarl. "I woke up when the guy came for his coat. You were gone…I was five years old." I poked my chest with a forefinger to make sure he knew who I was talking about. "You left me."

"Yeah, well I'm sorry 'bout that. Like I said, I forgot. Anyway, your mother made me pay for it. I didn't get to see you for nearly a year and she wouldn't let me move back in." He frowned at me, head to one side, while he dug deep into the past. "I went to your school once, called to you when you came out of the school gate. You turned around and ran away like a rabid dog was chasing you." Hurt and indignation at being treated this way furrowed his forehead. Tully didn't get it.

"Is it any wonder? I wasn't going to give you another chance to leave me behind."

"You didn't tell your mother I was at the school though, did you?"

The "no" came out reluctant and slow.

He looked pleased. "I guessed you hadn't or she would have called and given me hell."

"Sorry I acted like a fool just now." I hate to apologize more than anything in the world. "Guess I'm a bit jumpy."

He just headed away with me on his heels. When we got to the canoe he said, "Stands to reason you'd be nervous." He put the rifle in the craft and tossed the duffel in after it. "You ain't used to sleeping rough."

He squatted down beside the canoe and stared across the

marsh before he said, "My life and my existence are like this." He reached down and wrote in the water with his finger. "Like writing my name on water — gone as it happens." He looked up at me. "Only thing I leave behind is you and the ones that come after you." He stood. "You're the only good thing 'bout me. I'll never let you go."

He motioned to the canoe and held it while I entered and then he pushed the canoe through the reeds and out into the water of the narrow channel.

We were nearly through the reed bed back on the lake. The stream split, going either side of a small treed hammock covered with dense plantings — a small rookery where birds roosted for the night. The trees hanging down to the water were dripping with white ibis and stilt-legged herons. As we broke cover and glided towards the rookery, a cloud of birds rose in the frail light, circled and swept over head. Hundreds of birds, calling harshly to others, lifted into the air while behind them, in ragged stick nests, their young screamed out to their parents.

"That's cut it," Tully said. "If they're watching and they're smart, they'll know we're here."

We swept around a bend while behind us the flock disappeared below the trees, settling back into their nests.

Tully steered us close to the bank, sheltering beneath low-hanging shrubbery, the only cover available at the edge of this marshy area.

I looked over my shoulder, questioning. He put a finger to his lips. He reached out and grabbed the branches and pulled the canoe deeper into the cover. I did likewise, hunkering down into the canoe, letting the grasses spread back along the edge of our craft.

I listened hard, harder than I ever had in my life but there were no voices, no soft sounds of an electric motor, no splashing against gunnels. It was as if even nature held her breath. We stayed like this for some time, waiting until Tully said, "Okay," and then we pushed away from the shore. "Maybe we got lucky."

Maybe. But then again, maybe not.

CHAPTER 37

Within seconds of breaking cover we were on them. Why hadn't we heard them? Guilt, always there and willing to jump up and tell me everything was my fault said it was probably because Tully and I were locked in the past and not paying attention to the present.

The three guys were drifting towards us, eyes glued on the bank, bodies leaning forward in search mode. And what they were hunting for was us.

Behind me Tully planted his paddle to stop our forward motion and to swing us around. I dug in, thinking, "It's going to work, it's going to work." There was only ten feet of open water to cross and then we'd be hidden from view behind a jut of land and able to take cover. And then from my pocket came a ringing noise. The wet cell phone, against all likelihood, was working again. And I hadn't shut it off.

I was wrong about two paddlers being able to outrun an electric motor.

To our left was the solid land of a hammock, to our right open water. Tully swung the canoe to face the shore as the sound of a gun echoed.

"Down," Tully screamed. I was down below the gunnels before his voice stopped reverberating across the water.

"Back off," he shouted. I peeked around to where Tully

knelt in the bottom of the canoe, the rifle raised to his shoulder. I lifted my head over the edge of the boat.

"We don't mean you no harm," Tattoo Man said, but the rifle in his hands put the lie to his words. "Just wanted to see who else was on the lake."

"If you don't mean no harm, just turn around and get going," Tully told him.

The men shifted uneasily, trying to catch each other's eye and see what the next move was, trying to guess how it was going to play out. "Sure," said Tattoo Man. "Sure, we're going, no reason to get upset." He held the rifle out high, away from his body.

Tully waited. I saw the large bearded man in the back of the craft shift, saw him reach into the bottom of the aluminum boat for something and saw him straighten. But then, so did Tully. "Leave it lay or he's a dead man," Tully yelled.

Hard to say what the bearded man planned, for at that instant out of the bottom of the boat something large reared up. The man screamed and stood up. In his hand was a rifle. He pointed down at the alligator and before the gun was to his shoulder he fired. And then the man in the front of the boat screamed and grabbed his leg. The alligator was on the bearded man before the boat tipped. The man screamed some more in a high falsetto, shrieking in pain and fear. He didn't stop screaming when he hit the water, didn't stop screaming until he was dragged under.

The tattooed man went after the gator and its victim, trying to run, pushing the boat away from him to get at the bearded man even as he fell.

We were moving as well, shooting forward without my

help, to get to the man in the jaws of the gator. But it was hard to see what was happening. The water was beaten into white froth as the alligator rolled over and over, showing first its dark back and then its pale belly. The heavy rope around his body was unraveling, snaking along in the water, jerking back and forth like it was a living thing.

Locked in the gator's jaws, the man beat his arms against the water, struggling to pull loose; but as the gator rolled, it took the man with it. The man's piercing screams sounded as he broke the surface and faded as he went under, twirled in the maws of death.

The tattooed man tackled the alligator, jumping on its back and trying to do…I know not what. The gator rolled, taking the second man with him.

Tully was shouting, "Back off, back off," at the second man. The guy wasn't listening.

"I can't get a shot," Tully said as we watched in horror as the water churned with man and beast.

The tattooed man let go of the gator, scrambling to his feet and gasping for breath just as the animal rolled again. The thrust of its spiked tail caught the nearly drowned man, knocking him backwards into the water.

Tully moved fast. As the gator finished his barrel roll, Tully was waiting. The barrel of the gun was up against the gator. The recoil shot us backwards, the sound exploding in our ears. And then nothing. We rocked gently away from the scene of carnage.

The tattooed man recovered first, trying to run in the knee-deep water and calling, "Tom, Tom."

Death relaxed the giant jaws. His victim floated free. The tattooed man took the man's body in his arms, brushing his long, straggly hair back from his face. "He's killed, he's dead," the man wailed to the sky.

I saw the third man on the bank where he'd pulled himself up. I could see the crimson patch seeping from beneath his fingers.

"Paddle," Tully ordered.

"Aren't we going to help?"

The look he threw me was the only reply I needed. I started to paddle. I wanted to protest but it would be a waste on Tully; even begging wouldn't help here. We paddled fast. I wasn't sure if we were still running away or it was from the adrenalin pumping through our veins.

Within five minutes we were on their camp at the mouth of the river. We could see very little of it from the water, just the remains of a fire with three aluminum lawn chairs before it. Anyone passing by farther out on the lake wouldn't even notice it was there, but for the putrid smell of rotting meat, foul and fetid. Two rigs were backed into the brush and from a tree hung the hide of a gator. Tully swung us in closer.

He handed me the gun. "Stay low and don't be afraid to use it."

I could barely hear his quiet words over the panting of my breath. He slid a sealed plastic pack of ammo along the bottom of the canoe; all the time he watched the camp. "Maybe there was just the three," he whispered. "But I hate surprises."

He used a paddle to work us a little way closer, cautiously watching.

Finally he called, "Hello the camp." No answer.

"Your men are in trouble out on the lake," he shouted. Still nothing.

"Two of them are injured." Only silence.

He got cautiously out of the canoe in water halfway up his calf and pushed the little vessel offshore. "Lay off a bit," he said. "'Til I see if anyone's home. If there's trouble, head upstream and don't stop."

I watched him wade into the bank, wanting to call him back. Tully climbed the bank, stood with hands on his hips and helloed once more. Then he started for the campsite.

CHAPTER 38

I unbuttoned my pocket and dug out the cell. The signal was loud and clear. I pushed in Styles' number but didn't hit Send. I waited, cell in my left hand, rifle in my right.

Tully reached the first rig and pounded on the door. No one answered. I watched him open the door and disappear inside, leaving the door agape.

He seemed to be gone for a long time. What should I do? The rifle or the cell? There wasn't anyone to shoot, so that left the cell.

Tully jumped from the rig as I was about to hit the Send button. He didn't seem in a hurry like he was being chased — he just hadn't bothered with the step. He ambled back towards me. I slipped the cell back into my pocket and put both hands on the rifle, watching the underbrush behind him.

Tully splashed through the water, grabbed onto the side of the canoe and pulled it to him while I watched the camp.

"Well?" I asked.

Tully said, "As my daddy used to say, 'Call in the dogs and piss on the fire, it's time to go home.'" The canoe rocked gently as he entered it.

"No bad news there?"

"Nope, you can put that gun away, sugar."

All the same I kept my eyes on the brush around the camp as he picked up his paddle and steered us out into deeper water.

I turned on the seat and watched behind us and asked again, "Well?"

"Guess you should put that thing down before you hurt yourself," he told me.

I put the rifle across my knees but I didn't pick up the paddle.

"They was from Ohio, all right." He pulled a piece of paper out of his shirt pocket and held it up. "Fools left this on their countertop with Ziggy's address on it. We found the right guys."

"Are we just going to leave them out there to die?"

"I don't care one way or t'other if they do but I can see it would bother you some. You always did have a tender heart." He looked saddened by this shortcoming in me. "Used their cell to call the Venice police. Let's go home, little girl."

I let out a huge sigh of relief. Later, I promised myself, I'd tell him a thirty-one-year-old-woman, standing five-foot-seven and weighing a hundred and forty pounds stark naked, wasn't a little girl. But not yet. The day was clear and bright and already warm. The sky, a perfect blue with cotton batting clouds, hung over the lake in a broad dome. Not yet. I was still too happy just to be alive to take offense. I'd be back in fighting form soon enough. But not yet.

I pointed the rifle at the sky and leaned back to hand it to Tully. He took it from me and emptied the chamber before slipping the rifle into its sleeve.

I laughed at nothing and said, "Call in the dogs and piss on the fire, it's time to go home."

Tully pulled his crapped-out pickup under the portico of the Tradewinds condos. I squawked my door open and propped a muddy shoe up on the hinge. It had been a quiet drive home. We'd mostly watched the scenery go by and it seemed we'd been gone for months or at least weeks, but it hadn't been much more than thirteen hours.

Tully said, "Well, that was fun, wasn't it?"

"Hell, yeah! No one can say Tully Jenkins isn't a fun date."

"So we'll do it again sometime?"

"Sure thing. About thirty more years ought to be about right."

Tully huffed with laughter. Then I started in laughing, not sure why, but I laughed until I couldn't breathe and couldn't talk, although I was still trying to do both. Tears ran down my face and both Tully and I were well into craziness when someone came up beside me and shouted.

"Where in hell have you been?"

Why do I have this effect on men? I seem able to turn the nicest, most sensible, reasonable man into a raving lunatic. Not quite the kind of passion a girl wants to generate.

Tully hugged the steering wheel and leaned forward so he could see past me to the guy doing the yelling.

"Why haven't you returned my calls?" Styles demanded before I'd even answered his first question.

Tully wiped tears from his face with the flat of his hand. "This guy going to be a problem, little girl?"

I looked back to Styles and said, "Not for me."

Styles jerked his head towards Tully and asked, "Who is he?"

"None of your business." Just like that my temper was off, heading for the fences. Sweetness and light never lasts long with me.

Now Styles noticed the state of my clothes and the crappy condition of pretty much my whole body. "Holy shit, what in hell happened to you?"

"Nothin' good," I said, but a cautious voice warned me to be real careful, no need to share all I knew. "Spent the evening with my daddy. We went fishing."

He looked around me at Tully, who waggled a couple of fingers at him.

Styles looked back at me. "Might want to try using a pole next time. No need to jump right in there."

"I slipped in a ditch."

"Yeah? Why'd you decide to stay there all night?"

"Bugger off." He stepped back as I hopped out of the truck.

"See ya, Tully," I said and slammed the door. Tully took off in a cloud of noxious fumes but when he hit the pavement he pulled into the curb and parked, not ready yet to believe Styles wasn't about to give me a real hard time. I gave him a big smile and an even bigger wave and started for the front door, Styles bird-dogging me. "Can't you take a hint?" I said over my shoulder.

"First you lock me out on the back step of the Sunset, then you don't return my calls and now you're downright rude." He grabbed me by the arm, bringing me to an abrupt halt. "What are you trying to keep from me?"

The answer was a whole boatload of crap, but I didn't think

I'd share any of that just yet. I shook off his hand. "Did you come to arrest me? If not, take off."

"You and I have to talk. We can talk here or we can go to the station."

"I have to take a shower."

"And not a moment too soon, if you don't mind me saying so."

Over his shoulder, I saw Tully opening the truck door. I waved at him and headed for the front door. Styles followed me into the building.

Inside the doors, I turned to him and said, "I'll come by later, promise."

"Nope."

"Are you crazy? I need a shower."

"I've noticed." He grinned.

"Look, what's the rush? We can talk for as long as you want later, only I have to tell you, I can't add a whole lot to the story." I was finding it hard to focus on what Styles was saying. My mind was still back on the lake, still seeing churning water and still hearing the screams of those men.

But Styles had his mind fixed firmly on the single problem of murder. "I want you downtown now. You have to come in and sign your statement."

I made a face. There were so many other things I needed to do first. I headed for the elevators. The only bright spot in the day was the shock of the immaculate woman at the desk when she saw me. Maybe it was the pants still tucked into the socks or what Styles had called the night-in-a-ditch look. Either way, I always like to give folks something to talk about.

At the apartment I asked Styles, "Can you cook?"

"More or less."

"Then make breakfast while I shower and make it more rather than less."

I stood under the shower forever, not even worrying about the water shortage that normally had me bathing like a bird in a saucer. I didn't feel like I'd ever be clean again. Can little microbes crawl up into your body out of the dirty water and give you parasites or something? And how come I'd never worried about that as kid? When did weird things like this begin to scare me? This was a nasty part of adulthood no one had warned me about and one more reason not to grow up as Marley was always advising me. Grown-ups just have too many awful things to worry about.

I got dressed but left my shoulder-length hair wrapped up in a towel. The smell of coffee and bacon had me salivating and I wasn't wasting any time on hair.

Out on the balcony, Styles had set the wicker table with placemats and everything. He pointed to a coffee carafe on the table beside a container of orange juice. "Pour the coffee," he ordered, "and I'll bring the food."

CHAPTER 39

When I'd eaten just about everything in sight, I asked, "So have you got Ray John's killer yet?"

Styles grimaced. "That's why I'm here."

"You think I've got him?"

"You have to come in, alibi or no. Your truck was there. Marley wasn't in the room with you so you're still the best bet for the killer."

"Do you really believe I killed Ray John?"

"No, but your truck was at the scene of the crime. You or Marley or Lacey Cagel drove it there, you being the most likely."

"Oh, come on. What happened to me was a long time ago and wasn't near as bad as what happened to Lacey."

He pointed his knife at me. Ruth Ann would have had a few words to say to him about that — it was a thing that was never done in her trailer. "You wanted to help Lacey Cagel. The question is, would you kill to protect her?"

"Of course not, she isn't my daughter."

He tilted his head to the side and considered it. "You still are capable of it if you thought it was the only way to stop him. And it was your truck. You are the most likely person to drive it out to the Preserves."

"Or someone who snuck into the parking garage and used

the key under the front bumper. What about the security cameras?"

"They show the truck going in and out but not who was driving it. The person who went into the garage was smart enough to avoid the cameras."

Which is what Lacey would do if she were stealing my truck. Ray John would have passed along everything there was to know about security cameras. He was the kind of guy who liked to show off his knowledge and he had nothing else to talk about.

"Both Marley and Lacey have made statements," Styles said, pouring me more coffee. "Now it's your turn."

"What did Lacey say about Ray John?"

"Everything was goodness and light — no problem, he never touched her, she never cut her wrists, and until we have some reason to, we can't push her any harder. Her mother backs up everything she says."

"So it's just me with a reason to kill Ray John."

"And the other women we tracked down whose kids he abused, but you're the favorite."

"Well, as I always say, it's nice to be popular but hell to be the rage. Accusing me of murder never gets old with you, does it?"

"I've been looking at other possibilities." He looked like he was in pain.

"And?"

His look of pain didn't go away.

"Are you having any luck with that?" I prodded again.

"Not so far. We've talked to dozens of people at the Preserves. It isn't what they've said but what they aren't saying. No one is sorry he's dead, that's crystal clear, but they all claim they know no reason for his murder. They all hated him but now he's dead they just want to forget about it. No one wants to stir up any mud and they're all insisting the reason for his death comes from outside the Preserves."

"How do they explain the killer getting in?"

"Various ways, it seems at sometime or other they've all snuck in or out without using the main gate. Maybe you can tell me how it could be done."

"How would I know?"

"You know who was there driving your pickup and you know how they got in and out."

"I've only been inside the place once, as someone's guest, so I'm not the best one to ask about the place."

"But you know who drove your truck out there."

"Says who? Did you find the gun that shot Ray John?"

"No."

"What kind of gun was it?" I tried to sound casual.

"Why?" Styles asked.

"I just wondered."

He was watching me closely as he replied, "It was a twenty-five caliber."

"And you didn't find it, so the murderer probably still has it."

"Or he threw it in the lake."

"But you dragged the lake."

"Now, how do you know that?"

"Someone told me the police were dragging the lake in the Preserves."

"We can't be sure it isn't still there."

"Or that the murderer won't use it again."

He sat up straighter. "Do you have reason to believe that will happen?"

"God no, absolutely not, but if you kill once, I'd think it would be easier to do it a second time."

"Rena Cagel thinks you killed R.J. Leenders. She's telling everyone who will listen that you did it. You need to come in and make a formal statement."

"Okay, but it has to be quick. I'll be bankrupt if I don't get my ass into the Sunset."

"Let's go now." He crumpled his paper napkin and tossed it on his plate. "I'm not on duty yet so I've got the time to take your statement."

I nodded, only half-thinking about making a statement, while the other half of my brain was working out possibilities. Somewhere there was something I'd forgotten. There was also something I wanted to ask Styles, but I couldn't remember what.

Styles started stacking up the dishes.

"Leave those," I told him. "Mrs. Whiting will be in. It'll give her something to do and something to tsk over, leaving dirty dishes, how disgusting." I got to my feet. "I have to do my hair and I need my own wheels. I'll follow."

He frowned. "You have a lousy record of doing what you promise."

"Scout's honor."

He still wasn't believing it and quite rightly too. "If you aren't there in an hour, I'm sending out a patrol car to bring you in."

He pointed a finger at me. "One way or another, you'll be there this morning."

"So get going already. The sooner you get out of here, the faster I can make myself beautiful."

"You're always beautiful," he said and then flushed. He turned quickly away from me and headed for the door.

"Of course I am," I said, picking up my keys off the bar and following him.

As we came out into the hall, the door to the penthouse next to Clay's opened and Mrs. Finestein came out, carrying her little Yorkshire terrier. Her eyes opened wide and she stopped. She was looking at the towel wrapped around my head and jumping to conclusions.

"Business," I said, pushing Styles in front of me. "Never enough time," I added, keying in the ground floor for him.

"Be there," he ordered as the doors closed.

I meant to follow him to the station, I truly did, but I still couldn't stop thinking about the goons from Ohio. On the way to the truck it hit me that Tully might not have told me the whole story. He said he found Ziggy's address in the camper, but had he also found the name or telephone number of the person who hired the muscle? What would he do if he knew the name of the guy who set the dogs on Uncle Ziggy? And an even bigger worry was where was Tully now and what was he doing?

It was the coffee that made me suspicious. On the way back to town, I suggested we go through a drive-through for coffee and Tully begged off, said he needed a shower. So did I, but not that bad. Coffee came before everything else for Tully and me, so what was the old bastard up to? Panic exploded in my chest and I started begging that deity that I disclaimed to keep Tully safe and for once, just this once, don't let him do anything stupid. I was promising all kinds of acts of contrition if Tully could only be somewhere safe.

I tried my cell but it didn't work in the parking garage. I pulled out and headed for the hospital. Maybe he went to tell Uncle Ziggy about events on Soldaat Lake. Tully's truck wasn't in the hospital parking lot and unless he snuck by the dragon on the desk he wasn't in the hospital. Visiting hours didn't start until ten and she wasn't likely to let anyone in.

Would I get lucky and find his beat-up truck if I drove through the neighborhood of new houses behind Uncle Ziggy's scrapyard? I headed for the over-priced suburb.

I drove slowly up and down the streets but there was no sign of Tully. What would he do if he found the person who hurt Ziggy? In Tully's old Baptist head it would be an eye for an eye or maybe fire for fire. Bad thought, bad thought — surely not even Tully would go that far, but I found myself listening for fire trucks and watching over the rooftops for black clouds rising into the crystal-blue sky.

None of those things happened. It was just a pristine suburban neighborhood, with people leaving the pale stucco houses for school and work. I gave up and headed for the police station.

Styles was livid. We sat in a tiny room across a small wooden table from each other on straight-backed wooden chairs. The walls were totally unadorned except for an apple-green paint, chipped and gouged where chairs had been pushed into it.

This small claustrophobic room brought back to me all the shock and horror, all the emotions and all the pain, of my husband's death. I tried to decide if it was the same room we'd been in when Styles showed me the plastic bag with Jimmy's wedding ring, taken off Jimmy's severed hand.

Styles turned on the tape recorder and started asking questions. One thing was certain, anyone listening to the tape wasn't going to think he was cutting me any slack. The man sure as hell sounded like he thought I shot Ray John Leenders.

But there was one question that really got to me.

"Did Marley Hemming kill Ray John Leenders?"

"What? Are you crazy? Why would Marley kill him?"

"Someone drove the pickup out there that night. If it wasn't you, then it had to be Marley Hemming."

"Why? Why would she kill him?"

"Perhaps you weren't the only one he abused fifteen years ago."

"Don't be stupid."

His face turned puce. "Sorry," I added quickly. "I just meant Marley had no reason to kill Ray John. She wouldn't kill anyone anyway. Oh, she might trample you if you got in front of her at a real good yard sale, but that would be an accident, wouldn't it?"

He didn't smile.

"So that leaves you," he said. "You drove out to the Preserves. You took a gun with you and you killed Ray John Leenders."

He held up his hand to stop my protest. "Your truck was there. You, Marley Hemming, or Lacy Cagel drove it there. You tell me which one it was."

"Or someone stole it."

"Let me see," he said, scratching his head, pretending to actually consider it. "Someone slipped into the parking lot of a high-security building, stole a red pickup with distinctive plates, drove out to the Preserves and shot someone and then took the truck back. How well do you think a jury will take to that story?"

Put like that, even I, loaded with optimism, didn't having a real good feeling about it but it was all I had to work with.

He started asking me about holding a shotgun on Ray John and threatening to kill him.

"Why is that still on my record? I was just a kid and no charges were filed."

"There isn't a record, just a cop with a long memory."

"Then I'm not talking about it."

"The fact remains, you had a gun and threatened to kill Ray John Leenders and now he's dead."

"But it wasn't loaded," I protested.

"Did you know the shotgun wasn't loaded when you picked it up, Ms. Travis?"

"Well, no, but I didn't shoot him, even though he was beating on Ruth Ann. Why would I shoot him now?" None of this seemed to be helping me. "I want a lawyer," I said. All those hours of watching *Law And Order* had taught me that much about the law, always ask for a lawyer.

"Why?" Styles said. "You aren't under arrest, at least not yet."

CHAPTER 40

I came out of the police station shaken but still claiming ignorance. Why hadn't I told him that Lacey had been at the Preserves with my gun? I guess because I was still hoping to wiggle out of it. When that little piece of news dropped on his desk, I was in shit up to my eyeballs. What would happen to me for letting a minor get her hands on an unregistered gun? I was sure that Florida had a new law — if your gun was used for a crime, you were equally as responsible for that crime as the person holding the gun. It would certainly have been madness to try and clarify this law with Styles. I didn't even want to ask a lawyer…best to worry in silence. I only remember this new law because of a horrific newspaper story about the first person tried under the new law, a grandfather whose small grandson had picked up his grandpa's gun and accidentally killed someone.

And then there was what would happen to Lacey if she were arrested for murder. Even if she could prove her innocence, and that didn't look likely, what would it do to her messed-up head? But then, perhaps it was one way she could get help for her problems and any jury would see it as self-defense — even if she had taken the gun and driven out there. Still, I was hoping there was another option. Maybe I could find someone else to blame, always my first choice.

The Sunset felt like the best place in the world to be that day. Miguel and Isaak seemed to have declared some kind of truce, no suppliers bugged me and the dining room was as full at lunch as the last Sunday before Christmas would be. Even the rain that started late in the morning didn't scare the diners away. Gwen Morrison told me that we were over half-booked for dinner which, with walk-ins, meant a full house. At least something was going right.

I settled down to work, trying to forget the hard decisions I knew were coming. But not yet, now I needed a little time-out for myself and for me that meant fitting into the ebb and flow of the Sunset. At four the rain was long gone and the sun had come out again. I went into the dining room to lower the mesh blinds against the setting sun. The dining room is two-tiered; the upper tier is part of the old hotel and the lower tier, two steps down, is the former balcony. Some might see it as a tribute to a lousy building job, but the two-level dining room gives the Sunset a wonderful theatrical feeling, with the sun sinking in the west being the nightly performance.

Standing there with the beach spreading out before me, I was struck once again at the beauty of this place I lived in. Between the Sunset and the Gulf of Mexico there is only a thin strip of road, some tall, elegant, black light standards in a whimsical Victorian style, and some beach grasses bordering seventy feet of sand before the breaking waves. Umbrellas in rainbow colors danced in the breeze out on the beach. People folded them up and took them away each night, but every morning they sprang up again like flowers opening in the sun. You can pretty much tell the temperature by counting the umbrellas on the sand.

On the beach a small pot-bellied boy of about three ran from his father, laughing back over his shoulder as the man flapped his arms, pretending to be some scary monster. I watched man and child race in front of the water that lapped at the sand. It was a dolphin day on the gulf. Flat and on the cusp of a changing tide, there were no waves. You can see dolphins better on such days, although I always prefer to think that the calm water brings them out to play. Right on cue, as this thought entered my head, a pair of dolphins breached the waves. With backs arched, they rose from the water, shining and graceful.

A woman, sitting on a red towel, called out to the man and the boy, pointing offshore to the dolphins. The man swept the child up in his arms and pointed to where the dolphins broke the water again. The boy stiffened in delight and threw himself forward as if he might join the watery creatures. But his father held him tight, twirling him around, making the child swoop and fly in arcs about him while in the distance the dolphins rose and fell, pure and innocent, sweet and joyful — laughter on a sunny beach. Hot tears bit my eyes and a longing tugged at my heart.

"Sherri," Gwen called behind me. I fingered away the tears and turned to her.

"Are you all right?" she asked.

"Sure, the sun got in my eyes," I told her.

"Yeah, that happens. A woman in the bar wants to speak to you. She says she's a friend." Something in her voice, an undertone of disbelief or wry amusement, warned me.

"I'll just close the shades and then I'll go find her."

"I'll do it," she said and moved beside me. "Go."

I took one last look at the child, now riding on his father's shoulders, and went to the etched-glass doors leading from the lobby into the bar. I stopped inside the door and drank in the smell of the room, smoky ten-year-old Scotch mingled with the musk of expensive perfume. Overhead the giant fans on pulleys creaked and groaned softly while Oscar Peterson played in the background.

I didn't see anyone who might be waiting for me. At the bar a string of middle-aged women, wearing bright capris with matching tops, perched on the wicker-backed stools, laughing one bit louder than was polite or necessary. Two businessmen I knew sat in the farthest corner deep in conversation, talking in hushed tones, probably about some future development that would change all our lives. Their body language said plans were being made and money was involved. I always figured if I were smart enough and eavesdropped on enough power conversations, I could figure out how to get rich. But instead of becoming disgustingly wealthy on real estate deals, I'd bought the Sunset and worked seventy hour weeks just to service my debt.

I stepped farther into the room and looked around the potted palms. Sheila sat at a small round table with two glasses of wine in front of her. She lifted her hand. I went to her table and sank into the leather club chair across from her.

CHAPTER 41

She looked like a runway model, exquisite in every way, with makeup that artfully highlighted her fine eyes and wide mouth. Her chartreuse silk pants and top and high-heeled backless sandals were the upscale version of what her plumper sisters at the bar were wearing.

With makeup this fresh and impeccable she hadn't come here from somewhere else, everything about her was too unwrinkled and just-applied-looking. So had she dressed like this to impress me? But why would she go to all this trouble for a drink with me? "Because she wants something or is hiding something," my brain replied. "She doesn't want to appear weak or needy in any way and being impeccably turned out says power." Interesting thought, but maybe she was on her way to somewhere else.

Her eyes were anxious and drawn and she wasn't her normal relaxed self. "I ordered for you," she said, following my glance.

"Thank you." No use telling her I never drank when I worked. That road led in a direction I knew well, straight to Disasterville. "Nice to see you," I told her and I meant it.

It took a while, several trips 'round the mulberry bush, before she said, "So, have you heard anything new about the murder?"

"Not a thing and I've been so busy I haven't even had time to read the paper. What's happening?"

She shrugged. "I don't know anything but rumors. The Preserves is full of them. Everyone is waiting for the next shoe to drop as they pass along the gossip, cruel tittle-tattle and idle speculation, while looking at their neighbor with suspicion and worrying about what the police know that they don't."

"Tell me about the rumors."

Her shrug was artful; her eyes were on her glass. "Stories of sex parties up at the clubhouse late at night involving RJ and one of the other guards."

"With residents or outsiders?"

"Residents."

"Do you know who was involved?"

She uncrossed her long slender legs. "What's the point of adding to the rumors, I don't know anything for sure." She leaned forward, knees together and elbows resting on her knees, and she looked down at her long slim fingers turning her engagement ring around and around. "I thought when he died it would be over, that I could forget about him." Around and around went the ring.

I waited.

"It hasn't gotten any better for anyone. Everyone in the Preserves seems to be on edge. Even golf games have been cancelled. It's like we've become afraid of each other and don't want to be standing too close in case we get splattered by mud thrown at someone else." She raised her eyes. "Will it ever end?"

"Sooner or later. The cops will discover who did it or something else will come along to take everyone's mind off Ray

John. People really have a short attention span for drama. They always want the new and fresh sensation."

"I just want it to be over. I thought it was when that bastard died."

"Have the police interviewed you?"

Panic, raw and naked, raked her face. "No." She straightened, rigid with fear. "Why would they?"

"No reason, I just figure they'll be talking to everyone sooner or later."

Her body relaxed slightly. She licked her lips. We were coming to the reason for her visit now. "Do you know…?" she hesitated, searching for a path through a minefield. "Did RJ's stepdaughter say if he left anything behind, records or journals, anything like that?"

This was a new and interesting idea. "Not that I know of."

"Do you think you could ask?"

"What exactly are you looking for?"

Her voice, normally rich and low, was tight with anxiety. "Maybe files on a computer. He didn't have a computer at the clubhouse. Do you think he'd keep files on people, you know the ones he talked to about graffiti and drinking? Wouldn't he keep a record of things like that on a computer at home?"

"Sounds like a possibility."

"That girl who is staying with you, can you ask her?"

"If something like that exists, don't you think the police already have it?"

"Oh shit," she said and closed her eyes.

"Try not to worry, Sheila. If the police had Ray John's records and you were in there, they would have been out to talk to you by now."

She opened her eyes, swimming in tears and said, "Do you really think so?"

"For sure."

She pursed her lips and nodded and then she set her jaw. The tough competitor wasn't about to give up the game.

"So where are you and the doctor guy going tonight?" I asked to change the subject.

"I'm not seeing him tonight. He's at a meeting."

"Well, you look great, too good to waste on a night of TV. Call someone and go out for dinner or a movie."

"How about you? Are you busy, Sherri?"

"Yes, unfortunately. I took last night off. Now I have to pay for it."

"Yes," she said, her eyes looking at something in the past only she could see. "Yes, paying for it — that's the hard part." Her smile was thin and sad, saying the bill would likely be more than she could bear.

Every table along the windows was full long before sunset and every seat in the bar was taken up by people waiting with their little square electronic pagers sitting in front of them. Isaak's fame was spreading. Every night he came up with a new culinary sensation and if I didn't go broke on his extreme use of exotic foodstuffs, he'd make me rich. He'd worked at the Bath and Tennis Club before coming to the Sunset and many of the diners from the B&T had followed him to the Sunset. Tonight he had a pot roast, mundane-sounding, but the meat had been marinating for three days in pickle juice and it had simmered in wine and bay leaf for hours. Heavenly nectar, like nothing

I'd ever tasted. With it he was serving a French-Canadian dish of root vegetables — rutabaga, parsnips, carrots and potatoes whipped with cream and butter. Even the golden color made the dish special, while the taste had me moaning like an orgasmic Meg Ryan.

Isaak had been going to throw out the mound of pickles left over from marinating the roasts when Miguel had stepped in and started putting the sweet pickles on the sandwich plates. Simple, simple but it had been a great hit on the luncheon menu. Now if I could just keep the crazy Israelite from killing the pugnacious Mayan or vice versa, I was golden. Isaak's talent and creativity were balanced by Miguel's practicality and understanding of the thin line between profit and loss in the kitchen, something I could never get through to Isaak. I needed them both and hoped I could hang onto them both. Yes, I was pretty happy until the first bad news of the night walked in.

CHAPTER 42

It was a sight I'd hoped never to see, the elevator opened and out stepped Dr. Travis and his wife, Bernice, my god-awful husband's god-awful parents. My shock and outrage must have showed on my face because Bernice actually smiled, a gloating winner's smile. I guess she thought if I could walk into the Royal Palms and turn her world upside-down she should return the favor.

Beside me, Gwen smiled and said, "Good evening."

They ignored her. "Dr. Travis, Mrs. Travis," I said, and I swear I even gave a little bow of my head. What in the freaking world would ever possess me to do that? "How nice to see you." This proved that all Clay's gentlemanly manners were finally rubbing off on me — but I didn't kid myself, I knew my festering emotions might turn septic, gangrenous and nasty, at any second.

"We thought we'd drop in for dinner," Dr. Travis said. In his late fifties, Dr. Travis was still handsome. There was only a wisp of grey at his temples and his fine square jaw was still firm. "We've missed your chef's wonderful cooking."

"I'll be sure to tell him that." Right after I told him to lace their dinners with arsenic. For the nine years I'd been married to Jimmy, these two people had gone out of their way to make my life miserable. "Give the Travises the next window table to come up, Gwen."

"But…" she started to say and quickly changed it to, "of course." She picked up a pager. I took it from her before she could hand it to them.

"Would you like to wait in the bar?" I asked and led the way.

Back at the hostess station Gwen asked, "Are we comping them?"

"Hell, no," I said. "In fact, charge them double so they don't make a habit of it."

Before I could even curse them out good and tell Gwen my tale of woe, the elevator opened and out stepped Tully Jenkins — just to keep life from getting boring.

"Is Uncle Ziggy okay?" I asked, sure his being there meant new and possibly fatal disaster had struck.

"Far as I know."

"You haven't killed anyone, have you?" I inquired, and held my breath while I waited for his answer.

He pushed the black straw cowboy hat off his forehead with his thumb, giving it some thought. "Don't think so."

"So, why are you here?"

Beside me, Gwen gasped, but then she's always been nicer than I am.

"Why, I just got to missing you, sugar."

"Bullshit."

He laughed. "Wasn't it you that left messages all over town telling me you needed to see me?"

"Oh right, I forgot." I'd called all his favorite bars and most of his friends, trying to find him before he did anything foolish, "Unless you have another daughter, that was definitely me."

"Nope, you're the only pretty thing I recollect that occasionally calls me Daddy."

A wonderful brilliant idea hit me. "Come with me," I said, heading for the bar. "I'll buy you a brewski." I took him to where the Travises were huddled together at a round table. Bernice looked up and saw Tully, denim from shoulders to ankles, with his straw cowboy hat pushed to the back of his head, and started gasping for air.

I turned to Tully. He was grinning, enjoying this way too much. "You sit," I ordered. "I'll grab you a beer."

"Anything you say, honeybunch."

The conversation was stilted when I got back with Tully's beer. I left them to it and went to tell Gwen I didn't think the Travis party would be waiting for their table. I was wrong. Forty minutes later when their electronic pager went off they came out of the bar together, Bernice hanging onto Tully's arm and talking earnestly to him. They didn't see me as Gwen led the three of them to the window where the sun was slowly setting over the gulf.

And then, while I was lending a hand behind the bar, the Charters family, Thia and Anita, came in. Thia was dressed in tight blue jeans and a startling white tee-shirt with a small Nautica label over the left breast. She was wearing red high-heeled sandals that matched a shiny red bag from Dooney & Bourke. Simple right? Nothing to get excited about, right? Except this was Thia. Conversation halted in the bar and everyone, man and woman alike, stared. Her lavender eyes coolly assessed the room.

Beside her, Anita looked like a sack of potatoes. How could a beer keg give birth to a six-foot glass of champagne? Anita teetered on stilettos with her feet puffing over the sides, painful to see, her black leather skirt, sitting below her hips, was too short and the leopard-print top was so tight her belly button showed. I felt embarrassed for her, wanted to run over and wrap a blanket around her. That woman just wasn't doing herself any favors, trying to compete with her daughter.

Thia saw me and headed for the bar, while her mother reached for her arm and pointed to an empty table. Thia jerked her arm away and then ignored her mother as she floated to the bar. You could hear men sighing all over the room. Behind Thia clomped Anita.

Thia pulled out a stool and said, "I'll have Scotch on the rocks."

"How 'bout a soda?" I replied.

She made a face but didn't argue. Anita struggled to climb onto the stool and said, "Why are barstools always so high?"

"Why are you so fat?" Thia shot back.

"My theory is, barstools are designed by men," I told Anita. "They like to see us struggle, makes them feel all macho. Or maybe they just like the view. What would you like to drink?" Anita's first vodka martini disappeared and the second one was mostly gone before Thia was halfway through her soda, and the kid's nasty streak got worse with each sip her mother took.

"Have you heard any news about the murder?" I asked as I came back to set a red wine on a coaster in front of Anita. I wasn't sure her plan of changing drinks was going to slow down her growing inebriation but hell, it was her choice, and her hangover, not mine.

"Has there been any more news about his shooting?"

Anita leaned across the bar. Her grin was lopsided. "Shot three times." She struggled to flip up three fingers to show the number just in case I couldn't count. "Must have been someone who knew him well." She giggled, amused by death.

"I heard that the police were talking to all sorts of people out at the Preserves. Have they interviewed you yet?" I was looking at Thia when I said it but Anita answered.

"Uh huh, told them I barely knew him, just the hired help." Anita smiled, pleased to be clever, then abruptly changed the subject. "Say, why we have to talk about him." She added an exaggerated wave, dismissing Ray John. "Thia's going to New York. She's got a contract to model for a big New York agency. She was supposed to go before but she wouldn't leave, wanted to finish high school. But she can do that in New York and still model. She's going to be famous, be on the cover of *Vogue* and *Elle*, television even. Goin' straight to the top." She set the empty wineglass down carefully on the bar. "I gotta go," she said and tried to slide off the stool, taking it with her. The guy standing next to her grabbed the stool and righted both it and Anita. "Thank you," she slurred, patting the man's chest. He moved quickly away and she tottered off to the ladies room.

"New York sounds pretty exciting," I said to Thia.

"Nothing to stay here for now, is there?" Thia said. Her beautiful features were blank. Hard to tell how much she was missing Ray John.

"Were you staying because of him?" I asked.

She raised an eyebrow, "I would have got bored eventually and moved on, but I was having a blast."

Were the fun and games restricted to Ray John or had other people been involved as Sheila had hinted. Prurient curiosity made me want to ask for details. "I hope you didn't start your modeling career out at the Preserves. Pictures have a way of coming back to haunt us."

"You sound like the voice of experience," she made a guess that hit too close to home.

"Where are the pictures?" I asked.

"I've got them."

"All of them?"

A small shrug said she really didn't care. "I think so."

"Didn't happen to retrieve them the night Ray John died, did you?"

"Are you accusing me of killing him?" Her lavender eyes had turned into ice but her voice didn't change.

Was I accusing her of killing Ray John? I was sure of one thing: this was a young woman who was capable of just about anything. "Can you use a gun?" I asked.

"Sure, but not as well as my mother. She's the family sharp-shooter. Grandpa was a diamond merchant and made all the family learn to shoot. They all carry."

I laughed. "That could make family get-togethers real interesting."

She smiled. "Mainly we just snipe at each other with words. We save the bullets for outsiders."

Ray John would have been the perfect outsider for target practice.

CHAPTER 43

Two hours later Gwen said, "I wish your family would quit with the yack yack and free up that table."

With all the fun I'd been having in the bar I hadn't realized that the Travis party was still going on in the dining room. They'd been there longer than they'd ever spent together through all the miserable years of my marriage, including the wedding. What on earth were they finding to talk about and why hadn't my red-necked old man given Bernice a cerebral hemorrhage like I'd hoped? I went in to have a look. They were laughing. Bernice was hugging herself and rocking back and forth with laughter. Had I ever seen her laugh before? Not that I could remember. Against my better judgment I sidled over within sniper range.

"We were just talking about a fishing trip Jimmy and I took," Tully said when he saw me. Of course they were talking about Jimmy, the one thing they all had in common. Jimmy had been everything Tully had ever wanted in a son and sometimes it seemed he loved Jimmy better than he loved me. Jimmy and Tully had fished and hunted and gone diving together, two sides of the same coin.

I smiled at the happiness on their faces and nodded in understanding.

Tully went right on with his Jimmy story. "We fished all day and didn't catch anything. Cold as a witch's tit out there and enough wind to give us a chop all day so you never really got comfortable, rocking back and forth for hours. After three hours of that misery Jimmy reeled in and declared the whole goddam Gulf of Mexico was fished out. Blamed it on the tourists, said there was nothing left and someone should do something about it, stop them from overfishing." Tully wheezed with laughter. "Just as he made this little speech a lady fish jumped right out of the water and landed in the middle of the boat."

The three of them went into gales of hilarity. Bernice's face was full of joy — for one fleeting second Jimmy had come back to her.

"Did you try the pot roast?" I asked Tully.

"Yup, best I ever had, better than Grandma Jenkins' and that's saying a lot."

I went to tell Gwen it would be a while yet before the table was free.

CHAPTER 44

Tully came into the bar and looked around.

"Jeff, I'm going out," I said.

"Okay," Jeff replied without looking up from the mixer. I went to join Tully.

"I just came in to say goodnight," Tully told me.

"I'll walk out with you."

We went outside to the railed landing with the broad steps down to the parking lot. I never take the elevator, that tiny little thing scares the life out of me, but when I led the way outside it occurred to me that maybe Tully shouldn't be using the stairs, even going down. I still hadn't read the pamphlet on angina I'd swiped from his truck. Damn, I didn't even know where I'd left it, bad daughter, horrible child that I am.

Out on Soldaat Lake I'd seen a side of Tully, a tender side, I'd never seen before, and decided he was sick, maybe even dying. Nothing else could explain it. "Do you want to take the elevator?" I asked.

"Why?"

"It's late, you've had a busy day, no matter that you've just survived Bernice."

"She's all right, you know, just wanted to talk about Jimmy, listen to stories. I guess that's all she has left. Horrible thing to lose a child. I don't think Jimmy was going around to see them much at the end. They bought dinner, they were just so grateful to talk about Jimmy and so was I." Tully laughed softly. "I loved that boy, more fun than a sack of monkeys."

"And more trouble."

"Ease up now, girl. He wasn't all bad."

"Just mostly."

"Well, time to forgive him and get on with your life."

I didn't even ask what that meant. I only said, "How's Uncle Ziggy making out? I didn't go see him today." More guilt to pile on guilt.

"Doing okay, stronger, but still the pain is bad."

"When can he come home?"

"Few days yet."

"The den will be ready. There's a TV and he can sit on the lanai and watch the beach. Someone will have to come in everyday to do the medical stuff. I'd be dead awful at that."

"Well," he said, "if you want to do it."

"I do. That's what families are for, isn't it, to help each other through stuff in the best of times and the worst of times?"

"It's hardly that," he said. "Hardly the worst of times."

"Bad enough, but we'll get through it, one way or another."

I didn't think either of us was talking about Uncle Ziggy.

He reached out and patted my shoulder and then ambled over towards the stairs.

"Are you sure you don't want the elevator?"

"Not dead yet, even if I'm not the man I once was."

"Daddy, I'm thinking you never were the man you once was."

"I love you too, baby."

I had to do something about this annoying habit of sweet names real soon — he was beginning to take them for granted.

He started down the stairs and I called out to him, "Did you find the guy who hired the Ohio goons?"

"Yup." He turned on the step and looked back up at me with a grin on his face.

"Anyone die, anything burn up?"

"Nope."

"So everything turned out fine?"

"Well, enough so's an anonymous donor paid Zig's hospital bill today."

"Good for you, Daddy."

"Told you I wasn't dead yet."

When I went back inside, Styles was waiting for me. Seems he wasn't afraid of confined spaces.

CHAPTER 45

"Let's go to my office," I said, not wanting to be seen with a cop any more than necessary. Everyone would be guessing what I'd done this time and if he'd come to arrest me. They'd be leaning in real close to get an earful, something juicy and colorful that they could distort, embellish and pass along. Having a colorful reputation was no longer one of my aspirations but something I was stuck with.

I led the way down the hall, asking over my shoulder, "Eaten yet?"

"Yeah, but I could use a coffee."

In the office I called the kitchen and then leaned on my desk and waited as he made himself comfortable. He hadn't stopped by for idle chit-chat, the meat of the matter came out immediately.

"Why didn't you tell me it was Lacey Cagel who drove the truck out to the Preserves?"

I sat down behind my desk and tried to think of a safe reply, but he didn't really expect an answer and this was only the start of his rant on all the mistakes I'd made in the past few days. I was waiting for him to tell me I was being arrested for unlawfully carrying a gun while my brain veered off topic and started figuring out who could replace me at the Sunset until Brian Spears bailed me out. How long would that take?

Styles got tired of listing my sins. "I brought Lacey Cagel in for questioning again today and she broke down and told me that she'd taken the truck out to the Preserves, said she told Leenders that if he didn't keep his hands off her she'd have him charged." He looked at me expectantly, as if he were waiting for me to fill in the blanks.

"And did her threat scare him off?"

"She seemed to think so."

"So she would have no reason to kill him if he wasn't going to bother her anymore." Could both Lacey and I wiggle out that easy?

"You and I both know that isn't how it works. Just because the abuse stops, it doesn't stop you from wanting to kill him. He stole her youth, her very life, and it wasn't coming back. She was still angry, and killing him was a real possibility. Even now, couldn't you kill him?"

I shook my head. "No." I hadn't realized it was true until the words popped out of my mouth. The hate that burned for so long had turned to ashes. "Ray John was in the past. There are more important things in my life now and I haven't the energy to be angry anymore." And how about Jimmy, was I still mad at my lying, cheating, scam artist husband or was I nearing that place where I could make peace with that part of the past as well — interesting question to be considered on those nights when sleep wouldn't come. "That doesn't mean when it came up again it didn't still hurt, but I was way past shooting Ray John."

"Why didn't you tell me Lacey took your truck?" Styles seemed very calm, not annoyed or even upset, just weary and a smidge frustrated, inviting me to share everything — all friends together.

Yeah right — even sleeping dogs can jump up and bite you.

"I left it up to Lacey. I knew she'd tell you sooner or later." It sounded very noble. I hoped he was impressed. I had no idea if Lacey would come clean. I'd have continued pleading ignorance until the judge delivered the sentence. I always go on the ignorance-is-bliss theory until proven very, very wrong and I can play shocked surprise as well as Meryl Streep can.

"You made me waste a lot of time. I could charge you with obstruction."

I pushed back my swivel chair. "You knew the truck was at the Preserves. You knew more about that than I did. I don't know who killed Ray John. Personally, I was hoping you'd arrest Marley. That would have been so much fun."

He rewarded me with a faint smile. "What else aren't you telling me?"

For once I honestly couldn't think of anything except the fact that my gun was missing. Lacey obviously hadn't told him about the gun or he would have jumped down my throat with both feet. And for sure I was keeping that bit of news to myself.

"Anita Charters has a gun. She came in tonight, got blasted and let her hair down. Great thing about a bar, sooner or later you get to hear all the secrets."

He thought about it and then gave a little determined nod.

"And another thing, ask her how…" There was one sharp rap on the door before it opened and Gwen Morrison sashayed in with a tray. It was a great production, tray held high, hips swaying, very femme fatale. Gwen and I shared a love of old movies, throwing out quotes and characters for the other to guess, so I knew she was riffing on the silver screen but had no idea who she was trying to be or maybe she'd just lost her hold on reality. In the Sunset it wouldn't be hard to do.

"You're working in the wrong place with that act," I told her. "You haven't any place for him to stuff a dollar."

"You'd know all about that, wouldn't you?" Gwen said and set the tray down. She smiled at Styles and slowly poured him a cup of coffee. "So nice to see you again, officer." She handed him his coffee and then swayed to the door. "If you want anything else just whistle. You do know how to whistle, don't you?" She gave him one last long lingering smile over her shoulder. "You just put your lips together and blow," she added before she closed the door.

I pointed a finger at the door and said, "Lauren Bacall, I'm sure she's doing Lauren Bacall. But what movie?"

"What are you talking about?"

"Gwen, that bit she just did at the door, she was doing Lauren Bacall but from what movie?" His gaseous look said he'd lost the thread of the conversation or I needed a new coffee bean supplier. I tried again. "It was from the movie with Bogie, South America and she had a hat." I deepened my voice and said, "If you want anything, just whistle. You do know how to whistle, don't you?"

His eyes grew rounder and I could see he was wondering how long I'd been off my medication.

"Oh never mind." I poured myself a cup of coffee. "Where were we?"

"You said there was something else I should ask Anita Charters about, what was it?"

I sat perfectly still and concentrated. Whatever I wanted to ask him was gone. "Her ability with a gun, maybe? You might even ask to see her handgun."

His pained look went away. Now it was all sweetness and light on his face. How wonderful it was for him to have a new suspect. Maybe I'd just dropped a notch on his list of who done it. If I could just give him enough names I might drop to say, number ten. Number ten would be safe, wouldn't it? I wanted to be safe. Who else could I throw at him? I'd give it some thought. Gwen was a possibility or maybe I could just pick some names out of the telephone book and keep him busy for a while.

"Is that all I should ask Mrs. Charters about?" Styles asked, "What else haven't you told me?"

I tried to remember. Somewhere, between Lauren Bacall and where I was on the murder list, it had slipped away. This had been happening a lot lately and I was getting really concerned about it, one more thing for my worry list. "It's gone. I'll call you when it comes back."

I offered the small plate of open-faced sandwiches Isaak had sent along. "Thia's supposed to be a rather good shot like her mother. Can you check out Anita's gun registration to see if her gun fits the caliber of the murder weapon?"

"I wish you'd mind your own business," Styles said.

"This is my business, remember? You'd never have known about Ray John's past without me and you've still got me down as a suspect. Don't deny it."

"I'm not denying it."

"Don't overdo making me feel better."

He grinned. "Okay, how about this. I'll take you off the top of the list."

"Gee, thanks, and while you're at it, when you go to see Anita, don't let on you heard it from me, about her gun. Could you pretend it was a man who told you? Make it a lawyer, yeah, that would work, he told you because he's an officer of the court. Tell her he was the guy who helped her off her barstool."

"Why do you care if she knows you were the one who told me about the gun?"

"Well, the number one reason — where I come from, you never, ever snitch, even if someone sets your pants on fire. And the second reason is I'm in the restaurant business. Like once, I saw this woman putting the salt and pepper shakers from the table into her purse. I started over to rip her head off and Miss Emma stopped me, said the woman and her friends could cost us a lot more money by bad-mouthing us than the cost of the salt and peppers. Miss Emma even said, 'Come again, ladies,' when they went out the door. Can you imagine that? She said if those old bats went out and said how awful the food was, or how terrible the service was and it cost us even one customer, one customer, we were out more than a salt and pepper shaker. When you live or die on the good opinion of others, you have to be real careful what you say and do." I gave him the evil eye, "Or who you're seen with."

"Is that why we're in your office?"

Damn, I always forget how smart he is. "Yup, don't be seen alone with a handsome man, rule number one for a virtuous reputation, although in my case it may be a little late for that. My unsullied name took the express out of town when I was about sixteen."

"So what does having a handsome man coming out of your office late at night do to your reputation?"

"Damn." I gave it a little thought. "I'll make sure no one's in the hall before you sneak out. But don't forget to spread the praises of the Sunset far and wide to make up for all the free stuff I've given you. Just get out there and tell everyone how great the food is here, like you just love eating here everyday and bankrupting me."

"These sandwiches are really delicious." He held up an open-faced smoked salmon with cream cheese on pumpernickel, topped with a sprig of dill.

"Yes, and they whipped them up so quick. Is everyone just sitting around in the kitchen waiting for an order, and if Isaak has time to do up sandwiches, how long before I go bust?" I tried worrying about two things at once. "And how long can I keep such a wonderful chef before someone else offers him more money and steals him away?"

"The chopped beef is great," Styles said.

"I thought you weren't hungry." I moved the plate away. "I was going to wrap them up and take them home for breakfast."

"So was I," he said.

"What about the guy who found Ray John, what was his name?"

"Mark Cummings, what about him?"

"He was the first person there. Maybe he went in and killed him after Lacey left."

"Maybe."

"What? You really think he did it?"

"There were issues."

"What issues."

"End of information."

Something else was worrying me. "Did you talk to your daughter about Lacey and me?"

He wiped his mouth with the linen napkin and sighed. "I tried. She didn't want to hear it."

"Still, I bet she listened. You just have to keep talking about the dangers out there without making her afraid of her own shadow, that's probably as bad as not saying anything."

"I try to talk to them every day even if I don't see them. My son is always eager to talk, but with my daughter it's always nothing, nothing and more nothing. Nothing is happening, she's doing nothing and the news is all nothing."

"But she doesn't actually hang up, does she?"

"Not so far.

"Good, keep calling and keep telling both of them about the dangers that are out there so they know what to look for. Some of it is bound to sink in." I don't know why I felt so strongly about this piece of wisdom. Never once has knowing the possible disaster that might occur from my actions…never once has that knowledge stopped me from doing whatever stupid thing I was about to do.

Best not to share this insight with Styles.

CHAPTER 46

Clay called. They were in Cuba and things were not going well.

"Something about a locker of booze. Seems the Cubans think we were smuggling it into the country although it's less than half of what we had when we started out. And if we were going to smuggle, sure as hell we could think of something better than booze."

"Is it going to be a problem?"

"Not sure yet, but there are worse places to be stranded."

"Don't start liking it too much, and in case it's already too late and you've decided to stay, let me tell you about a book I'm writing. It's called *A Hundred Things to Do in Bed on a Rainy Afternoon*."

"How Kama Sutra of you. But I don't understand, why does it have to be raining?"

"Don't distract me with minor points, let me just give you chapter headings so you can get…" I paused so he could picture it, "a feel for the material."

I was on the third chapter when he said, "There's a flight to Toronto leaving at ten o'clock tomorrow morning. From there I can catch a direct flight to Tampa and be home before you turn out your light tomorrow night."

"So you've already checked this out. Getting a little lonely, are you?"

"That's only one of the things I'm getting."

"But what about the race?"

"The rest of the boats will probably leave without us. The authorities aren't going to release the *Legal Dream* in time for us to sail with them."

"Can they sail *Legal Dream* home without you?"

"Sure, if they wait for the right weather, no problem. Two guys can handle her easy to Key West."

"Ooh, two guys can handle her easy. Are you talking dirty again?"

The conversation wallowed in the mud for a bit before I started my confession.

"Did I ever tell you about my Uncle Ziggy?" I knew full well I hadn't.

"What about him?" Clay's voice had turned suddenly wary and abrupt. The thought of my having family must have really been freaking him out and he hadn't even met them yet.

"His name is Ziggy Peek. Not really an uncle, no DNA involved, but he feels like family."

"Guess that makes him family then," Clay said.

"Yeah, that's what I think. Well, he owns this junkyard out on forty-one. You know, the one with the wooden barricade around it and all the hubcabs nailed up."

"Sure," he said. He sounded like he was waiting for real bad news, when I was the one who should be worried.

"Well, there was a fire out there and Uncle Ziggy was hurt. Someone set the fire; they've been trying to get rid of him for years, but I'll tell you about that when you get home. The thing I want to discuss with you now is…well, Uncle Zig doesn't have any family, no one to look after him when he comes home. I'd like to have him stay with us." Before he could get a word in, I hurried to add, "It won't be any trouble really. I'll get a nurse in and he's real easygoing."

"Sure," Clay said. "Zig's more than welcome."

"Zig? You know him?"

"Brian introduced us. Zig and I are partners."

"What?" I hope my screech fractured his eardrum. "What in hell are you talking about and why didn't you tell me?"

"Why didn't you tell me?"

"Well, this isn't going anywhere. How long have you known him and when did you become partners and partners in what?"

"The deal is, when Zig has had enough, we'll develop the land together. He'll put up the land and I'll develop it. We'll own the development together. In the meantime, I paid him a little bit to seal the deal and to keep him living there. The city consul has blocked him from doing any kind of business out there to drive him out, but with his lifestyle and what I paid him Zig can hold out for a long time."

"Why didn't you tell me?"

"Back at you."

"What else do you know about me you aren't telling?"

"What else is there?"

CHAPTER 47

The next morning, Saturday, I went to see Uncle Ziggy before I went to the Sunset. His color was better and his voice was stronger and not as raw.

"Your dad told me about your little adventure," Uncle Ziggy said.

"Little? It was the scariest night of my life — well, except for one night in a frat house, but you're too young to know about that."

His laugh no longer sounded like it hurt, less breathy and raspy.

"I'm so glad to see you getting stronger. You look loads better than the last time I was here. How long before you'll be able to come home with me?" I asked.

"They aren't saying for sure but I figure a couple of days. You sure about this, honey?"

"Oh yeah. I'm going to hire you the cutest little nurse you've ever seen. You aren't going to want to get better."

"Unlikely."

"You're right, when you balance my cooking against her cuteness, you'll be better in double time."

At the Sunset, I saw that Rena's store was open. I debated going in, but what was there left to say except maybe, "So, Rena, did you finally do the right thing and go out there and blow Ray John away?" Maybe not a good idea, so I kept going up to the restaurant and the load of paperwork waiting for me. I hate all that stuff, schedules, checking times and calling in orders, and some days I wasn't sure keeping the Sunset was worth the mind-numbing hassle.

Within minutes of entering my office there was a knock and Lacey peeked around the edge of the door.

"Hi," we both said. "Come in and sit," I added.

She was wearing shorts and flip-flops and her hair was pulled back off her face. Colorful plastic bangles jangled up and down her wrist, hiding the scars. For the first time since I met her she looked like what she was, a young beautiful teenaged girl with her whole life ahead of her. She gave me a tentative smile and perched on the edge of the chair facing me.

We were both uneasy, unsure of the new state of our relationship as we went through the "How have you been, how's it going?" stuff. Finally I said, "Styles was here last night and said you admitted that you took my truck out to the Preserves. But you didn't tell him that you also took my gun, did you?"

"No." She looked wary, waiting for me to jump on her for leaving this out of her statement.

"And are you still sure you didn't use it?"

"Yes. I wouldn't forget that, wouldn't forget if I shot someone."

"Shot? Was he only shot once?"

"Yes." She wrinkled her nose in the most appealing way.

"Wasn't he?" she asked. She leaned forward, and asked almost in a whisper, "You mean he was shot twice?"

If she was pretending not to know about the three bullets she was doing a real good job, but being a liar makes you suspicious of any display of innocence. Or maybe Anita was passing on bad info and he hadn't been shot more than once. "I'm not sure. I just thought you might know how many times he'd been shot."

"Well, I don't because I didn't shoot him." She was quite indignant.

"The police didn't tell you or Rena how many times he was shot?"

She shook her head. "Does it matter?"

"Not to Ray John. Have you remembered what you did with the gun?"

Again her nose wrinkled.

"Look, Lacey," I said, "I went out on a limb for you. That gun is going to come back to haunt us. Stop lying to me and tell me what happened." I was hoping she'd tell me she'd dropped it off a bridge or down a storm drain, anywhere that it would never be found.

"I was going to kill him." The words exploded out of her. "I pointed it at him, told him if he didn't leave me alone I'd shoot him."

My stomach rolled.

"I couldn't do it. RJ just laughed at me. Then he told me I'd been bad and he was going to punish me." Her voice went to a whisper. "Told me what I had to do to make up for threatening him with a gun. The whole thing was a joke to RJ, maybe even excited him a little. I wish I could have shot him but I couldn't."

"What happened then, what happened to my Beretta?"

"I don't know. He took it away from me. He wasn't afraid of me even when I had a gun. He was never going to let me go." And now we had come to what brought her up the stairs. "You aren't going to tell the police, are you? I don't want them to know I took a weapon out there. I just told them I went out to talk to him."

"I have to admit I don't want to tell them about it either; leaving a gun sitting around for you to pick up was pretty foolish on my part, but then I hadn't expected you to…" I reconsidered my words. "I didn't expect you to do any of the things you did."

"I'm sorry. I know I was stupid."

But hadn't she had a real good reason for everything she'd done? If I was on a jury and she was charged with Ray John's death, no way I'd find her guilty. It was self-defense as far as I was concerned, maybe even a public service. "Lacey, did Ray John say anything about the people who lived in the Preserves?"

She shrugged. "He hated them. He wasn't friends with them or anything; he just thought they were all stuck-up and stupid." She frowned and thought for a minute. "He never really liked anyone, either at the Preserves or in our neighborhood. He fought with the guy who lives behind us because he leaves his dog outside when he goes to work and it barks all day. It woke RJ up all the time."

Another guy to add to Styles' suspect list.

"RJ threatened to shoot the dog once. Things were better

for a while, but now RJ is gone, the guy is leaving the dog outside again and its barking is driving my mom crazy."

This guy was definitely someone to add to Styles' list. "Was there anyone special Ray John talked about at the Preserves?"

She gave it some thought. "This Quinton guy. RJ really thought he was a load of sh…" she stopped and looked at me, squirming a bit in her chair, "Well, RJ just had no respect for the man."

"Did Ray John spend much time on a computer?"

"Never," she said in a voice dripping disgust for dinosaurs that had been left behind by technology. "He hated the things, went on and on that they were destroying some great way of life. The way he talked, I bet he could barely use a computer. He never used the one at home."

"Did he keep a journal or anything?"

"Not that I know."

"Did the police look for one?"

Her teeth worried her lip for a moment. "I don't know what they were looking for or what they found. They searched through his desk and all his drawers. Mom nearly went spare but they said they had to find out everything they could about him."

"Did they take anything away?"

"A boxful of stuff. I don't know what was in it, except Mom was mad about missing bank statements from the store."

"How's Rena doing?"

"Not so good. I should get back." She stood to leave.

She was almost to the door when she asked, "Why are you asking all this stuff?"

"I'm asking because you and I are still under a shadow. The

quicker the police look somewhere else, the better I'll like it. Did Ray John talk about people breaking laws out there?"

"He hinted at all kinds of things but I don't know any names." She smiled. "There was one woman living out there who he arrested for prostitution back when he was in the sheriff's department. Can you imagine that, a prostitute living in a big house with rich people?"

Oh, yeah, I was imagining it all right. "Do you know her name?"

She shook her head. "He liked to put them down but he wasn't going to say anything that could get around. He was really careful that way. Didn't want to get sued or anything."

It didn't matter, I was pretty sure I could guess the name of the woman who had been turning tricks thirteen years ago, the same woman who'd been celebrating the day Ray John died.

CHAPTER 48

Lunch hour was crazy and it didn't back off until after two. By four the bar at the Sunset was already filling up again. By seven every seat at the bar was full and people were two deep in the vestibule.

I went to check with Gwen to see if we could get things moving. "There hasn't been any break since lunch," a harried Gwen said. "We were still serving lunches in the dining room right up until three and then the bar took over. We're fully booked tonight. I even had to turn down bookings. This is the best we can do."

"Hallelujah, I won't have to declare bankruptcy this week," I said and ran my finger down the list of reservations. Lots of new names, the word was getting around. In August no one needed to make reservations and no one had, but now in September the story had changed.

"And I actually heard Isaak and Miguel laughing," Gwen told me.

"Better and better."

"Maybe not." She turned away to say goodnight to a handsome couple just leaving. When they were gone she turned her attention to me and said, "I think you were the subject of the laughter. Can't be sure, mind you, but I did hear your name mentioned."

"Bitch, but not even you can destroy my gratitude for the lovely people dining here tonight."

"All and all, I think everything is under control."

A tray dropped and a glass shattered. The pen in my hand flew across the foyer and I ducked behind the stand-up desk.

"Geez, what's with you?" Gwen said.

My heart was beating too fast to speak. I forced myself to stand up straight again. I couldn't explain it, it was just this impending sense of doom that had settled over me, like something was waiting for me, a disaster ready to strike. It had been building all day and now it had me as nervous as a pig at a barbecue.

"Only a tray," Gwen said, patting my arm. "No need to jump out of your skin." She looked at me with concern. "Are the nightmares coming back?" Gwen knew all about my bad times.

I tried to laugh but my laughter parts weren't working. "Just a little jumpy." I took the pen, which a man waiting for a table held out. "Thank you," I said to him and then, when the man went back to hold up his share of the wall, I said to Gwen, "It's your fault." I told her, "You scare me when you make rash statements about everything being under control. Things are never under control." I didn't know how true those words were going to turn out to be.

We'd been short one busboy all night and there were cartons of empties I wanted moved from behind the bar. I went into the kitchen where everything was chaos and asked Miguel, "Where's Gomez?"

"In jail," Miguel said, not looking up from the blade flashing up and down, shaving parsley off the stock.

"What? What did he get arrested for?"

"Cock fighting." Miguel called to one of the assistants, "Leah, do the rest of these plates."

"Miguel, what do you mean he was arrested for cock fighting?"

He dried his hands on the towel hanging from the ties of his wraparound apron. "He has a trailer out on a sod farm three miles east of the interstate. He was raising roosters for fighting. Someone called the cops. He was arrested for cruelty to animals."

"You seem to know a lot about it."

Miguel shrugged and grabbed another stack of parsley draining in a rack. He shook it violently and slapped it on the wooden cutting board, frowning down at his young assistant who worked slowly and with extreme concentration to drizzle something red from a yellow squeeze bottle. I knew he longed to grab the bottle from her and take over, doing it in his mad frenzied style. "He talked about it. He made a lot more money off them roosters than what you pay him busing tables."

"Didn't you think you should tell me about the cock fighting and his arrest?"

"Why?" The knife stopped. "What would you do about it? It isn't your problem. Life would be easier for us all if you didn't try to solve every problem in the world." The blade started slicing through the parsley at speed.

"Well, first of all, it's left us one busboy short. And I'm in charge here, Miguel. What happens in this kitchen is my responsibility and in the future when you have information like this pass it on."

"Sure," Miguel said. "So now I'm telling you we need one more busboy."

The knife stopped and he raised his eyes. "Gomez was no good for here. I talked to Tommy Jackson, he can start tomorrow." He went back to the parsley.

I opened my mouth to blast him and then shut it again, waiting a beat before saying, "You take on too much. It's my job to do the hiring and firing."

"So you don't want Tommy?"

"Yes, I want Tommy." Tommy had worked for us full-time before Hurricane Myrna paid a little visit. He'd been working elsewhere when I started rehiring the following spring. Tommy fit in perfectly at the Sunset.

"Good," Miguel said and turned away with his silver bowl of parsley to oversee the plating of orders.

I really had to get my staff under control, but I didn't know how. The problem was they were friends before they were staff and I didn't know how to reconcile the two.

At the bar the bodies were two deep while they waited for something to open up in the dining room. I sent the barman out with the empties while I covered for him.

When he came back I called Sheila and then I went to find Gwen.

Before I opened my mouth she saw the purse over my shoulder. "Oh no," she said. "You can't run out on us again."

"I'll make it up to you," I promised, heading for the door.

"Don't tell me, tell the folks waiting for drinks," she called after me.

See what I mean, I just wasn't getting any respect.

CHAPTER 49

It was great to be outside. It still had to be in the mid-eighties, balmy and sweet, with a gentle breeze blowing in from the gulf and bringing the smell of saltwater.

In the parking lot, Rena was getting into her car. This was a new Rena, one I hadn't seen before. She wasn't wearing tight sexy clothes; now she was dressed in something that looked as if it belonged to an older, heavier person. The slacks were black and bagged at the knees and even though the day had been sweltering she wore a long-sleeved blouse in a striped grey material. Her hair had flattened and drooped and no longer shone, while her face had slipped into middle age.

Where Lacey had been made younger and lighter by Ray John's death, Rena had gone in the opposite direction, sunk under the weight of her loss.

She looked up and recognized me, hesitated, and then got into her car. She sat there for a moment while I watched and then she got out of her car and carefully closed the door behind her.

"Shit," I swore under my breath. I really didn't need any more confrontations, didn't need an angry woman dumping on me. Would I be wiser to go back into the restaurant, give her some time to cool off, a few days, say, or maybe a few years?

Truthfully, she didn't look like there was enough strength or life in her to raise a hand to a fly. I walked towards her.

Awkward and uneasy, I faltered within five feet of her.

"You were right," she said, a tired and defeated concession. "Lacey was cutting herself."

"Didn't you know?"

"No…maybe. I don't know." Her shoulders slumped further.

I searched for something to say and decided, with my track record, silence was best. I didn't want her to get back in her beat-up sedan and run me down.

She pushed a hank of hair back from her forehead. "I'm leaving as soon as I can find a buyer for the store."

"But you're doing so well. How will leaving help?"

"Do you think I want to live in that house where…" Her mouth formed a hard straight line. "I won't live in that house and RJ's money helped start the store. I don't want to be reminded of him. I just want to get away and start over."

"If that's what you want, I won't hold you to the lease. But give yourself some time to think about it. You've made it through the most difficult time at the store and now you're about to reap the benefits. The restaurant was full tonight, things are picking up."

"No," she said and shook her head. "No. The house and the store will be up for sale as soon as the lawyer sorts out all the ownership questions. I just wanted you to know you're going to have to find a new tenant." She walked away.

I turned off the air conditioning and rolled down all the windows.

I crossed the inland waters and headed up Tamiami. Traffic

was sparse and I hit every green light, increasing the sense of wellbeing that the blissful weather had already delivered.

The man on the gate checked his clipboard. "Sorry, ma'am, your name isn't here. I can't let you in unless one of the owners calls and puts your name on the list."

I called Sheila.

"I really don't think I want to talk about RJ anymore," she told me.

"Oh, I think you'll want to hear what I have to say. It'll give you a heads-up before the police arrive."

"Put the guard on your phone," Sheila responded.

I handed over my cell and the guard listened and said, "Yes, ma'am. She's on her way." He winked at me.

Sheila met me at the door. She didn't look well, was tired and disheveled, and the welcome wasn't as warm or as happy as the last time I'd stepped over her threshold. Inside the house was as cold as her welcome, in fact it was like stepping into a walk-in freezer, air conditioned to the point of discomfort.

Silently, she led the way out to the room overlooking the natural lands at the back. Lights were on in the family room, making it impossible to see anything happening outside in the eagles' nest, but Sheila hadn't drawn the curtains against the night. It gave me the creeps to see that big black expanse and know anyone could be out there looking in, although what they'd be doing in the middle of a swamp even I couldn't imagine.

Sheila flopped down on the couch, one leg curled up under her and waited. I sat on the arm of the couch across from her and studied her. Her whole angry defensive attitude answered my questions before I'd even asked them. "Ray John told the Cagels that he met a woman living here who he'd arrested for prostitution when he was a deputy sheriff."

If looks could kill, my life had just ended. "That's what he had over you," I guessed. She glared at me with real malice. "Don't panic yet," I said. "I'm the only one who has guessed your secret. Ray John didn't give any names."

"I was just a stupid kid."

"Are you still stupid, stupid enough to kill Ray John?"

"That would be really dumb, wouldn't it?"

I'd played enough golf against her to know she was a risk-taker. Sheila never took the easy shot, the safe shot, she always went for the Hail Mary, trying to give herself an edge. Always pushing, she tried to make you play beyond your game, forcing you to make mistakes. There was never a laidback friendly game of golf when Sheila was around, not even in non-tournament situations. She'd made a few enemies at the Royal Palms with her aggressive play, so she had more than enough guts to kill someone. "Ray John recognized you from back then and was holding it over you, using it to control you, making you do what he wanted."

Her jaw hardened. I was betting she was trying to decide if she would be better telling me to go to hell and toughing it out or pleading innocence and throwing herself on my mercy. She made her decision. She decided I was a soft touch. "I had just turned twenty. I got myself in a bad situation with some very bad people. They had a hold over me, took away all my choices."

"Is there a record of your arrest?"

She hesitated, not trusting me but afraid to blow me off. I

was betting Sheila didn't trust too many people and that enlisting my help seemed like a better option than having me run to the cops with my story. "Yes," she finally said. "But not under the name I use now." She eyed me carefully, assessing me and how much risk I was to her. "So, unless I'm arrested and booked, I'm going to deny ever knowing RJ except as head of security for the Preserves. All right with you?"

"It'll probably work until they take your fingerprints."

"Are you going to tell?"

"No skin off my nose if you tell the police or don't."

She let her breath out in a long whoosh of relief and said, "I wish I could get away from here."

"But not right now, it would be a mistake. You'd call attention to yourself. Just keep your head down and don't lose your nerve." I smiled at her. "Pretend it's all tied up on the eighteenth and you've got a twenty-foot putt to win. I've seen you make that, so I know you can do this."

She gave me a faint smile. "Suppose you won't want anything to do with me now."

"Who says? What makes you think I'm that judgmental?"

"I'd do anything if I could just undo the past."

"Wouldn't we all?"

"But I really have done some things I wish I could change."

"Do you have a gun?" The question popped out of my mouth without registering in my brain. If it had gone through any form of filter before it reached my mouth I wouldn't have said it.

I'd just worn out my welcome. She stiffened and all signs of weakness and vulnerability disappeared. "Why are you asking?"

"In case the police check for registered firearms for every-one in the Preserves."

"No," she said and crossed her arms. "I don't have a gun."

"Oh, I see, it isn't registered, is it, because you'd have to give fingerprints? You probably stole it off an old boyfriend. What kind of a gun is it?"

"I didn't say I had one."

"You didn't need to, your reaction answered for you."

She grimaced.

"If it isn't the same caliber as the one that killed Ray John, you're off the hook."

"I've got a 9mm Glock. What caliber was the gun that killed RJ?"

"I have no idea." I was wondering if it was the same size as the Beretta. Did the size of a gun represent the size of the cal-iber? Was a Glock something you could stick in a bag without anyone noticing? "How big is a Glock?"

She uncoiled herself without speaking and left the room. While she was gone I went to the window and searched the near dark for whatever horrors it might hold. I don't much like the dark anymore. Life has thinned out my courage. I heard Sheila's footsteps and turned to see her enter the room, hold-ing a gun out in front of her with both hands. She was pointing it at the floor but with her legs spread in a shooter's position. Her eyes told me her intent.

"Don't," I pleaded.

CHAPTER 50

Crazy fear. Was she really going to kill me? I wasn't sure. All I knew was the dull grey piece of metal with the black hole in the center, rising to find me, looked like death. I locked my eyes to hers.

She smiled an evil smile. "Am I scaring you, Sherri?"

"Yes, now put the damn thing down."

"I'm not pointing it at you, well not where it will do you any harm. I thought you wanted to see it."

"Put it down, Sheila, before there's an accident."

She smiled again, "Oh, if I shoot you, it won't be an accident."

I waited for her to decide if she was going to kill me, afraid to say anything in case it was the wrong thing, afraid to push her over some edge that only she could see.

"Everything I worked for could be lost. I don't deserve this. I've tried so hard."

My eyes went back to the circle of death, the small back hole about to eat its way through me. Was it my imagination or was the barrel of the gun coming still higher?

"You're the only one that knows about me," she hissed.

I watched the dull metal barrel rise from my ankles to my knees and now to my waist.

"Killing me won't solve anything."

"You're the only one who knows. I could put you out in that marsh there and leave you to nature."

"The guard knows I'm here. So does my staff. I told them where I was going. If you kill me, Styles will see you get the death penalty. We still have one in Florida, you know." I wasn't sure if that was still true.

The gun wavered a little. She took a different tack now. "I didn't say I was going to kill you. Where did you get that idea?"

"You gave a real good impression of it. Now put that damn thing down."

"I'm just showing you the gun like you asked. You did ask for it, Sherri." It was back to my knees. "I thought you were interested in my little friend. It's a semi-automatic with ten rounds in it and it weighs about…" she thought for a minute, "say, half a pound of butter and its barrel is six inches long. Is that what you wanted to know, Sherri?"

All I wanted to know was if I was going to get out of there alive.

"I don't want to lose everything," Sheila said in a hypnotic singsong voice. "For the first time in my life I have someone who truly loves me, who wants to take care of me. And he's rich. That's always nice, isn't it? You know how nice rich is, don't you, Sherri?"

"I'm leaving now." I said it but it took a little time for my legs to get the message and start to walk.

Slowly with sweat creeping down my sides, I stepped towards her. One step and then stop, and then I repeated the crazy hesitation waltz of fear, like a bridesmaid going towards her execution. My whole being was focused on the Glock. If the muzzle came up even a fraction of an inch I was ready to dive under the nearest piece of furniture. Another step. I fixed on those eyes locked on me, hoping to see what she planned soon enough to give me an edge. Her eyes were hard, never blinking, never telling her thoughts. I glided on. When I was two feet in front of her I stopped again.

She was trying to decide. I could see it in her eyes. We stared into each other's souls while she made up her mind. Her eyes flicked away and her hands slowly dropped. The muzzle of the gun pointed at the floor.

I started walking again, passing her without a word. Goosebumps ran up and down my arms. The hairs on the back of my head were standing out like little antennae, my skin was prickling, alive and taking in sensory data. Everything was suddenly clear and sharp. I could smell the potpourri in a blue-and-white Chinese bowl on the table; the clicking of my heels on the hardwood echoed like the sound of a gunshot to my head. From outside came the barking of a dog and the sound of a man's voice calling. I wanted to be out there, alive and safe with sane people, people who were normal and good, because I'd just seen evil in those green eyes. I'd seen death.

I waited for the sound of the blast as I walked slowly towards the front door. Did you hear the explosion or would the bullet hit ahead of the sound?

"Don't tell anyone or I'll come find you," she screamed behind me.

At the door now I fumbled for a second with the lock, my mind unable to grapple with the simple act of turning the bolt.

The lock gave up its secret and opened the door and I stepped outside. A light over the door flicked on and the warmth of the night wrapped around me like comforting arms after the icy chill of the air-conditioned house.

Joy bubbled up in me, the possibility of life filling me with hope. "Don't run," I told myself. "Don't run." I still wasn't convinced that I was free.

Surely she wouldn't shoot me out here where everyone could hear and someone might see? But who knew what the bitch would do and who was there to see in the dark and empty street. No, I wasn't safe yet. I had my keys out before I reached the pickup, jerking open the door and locking it behind me as though that would keep me safe from bullets, as if the windows weren't still down, allowing anyone to reach in and grab me. My hands were shaking, the key not fitting into the ignition with my palsied rumba. Finally, more by accident than trying, the miracle worked and the truck started.

Sheila came out on the step, watching me, but there was no sign of the gun in the overhead light. Maybe she wouldn't kill me. I backed away from the house. I was safe. Please god, let it be true. And please don't let her come after me. I checked Sheila's house again, expecting to see the garage door go up. It wasn't Sheila who came after me.

I peeled out of there, going too fast for a residential street. The security guard who stopped me before I hit the first inter-section must have thought so too. In fact he must have been parked in the shadows in front of Sheila's house.

CHAPTER 51

The red light on the roof of his SUV went on and a siren made a woof woof sound. I debated ignoring him. He wasn't like the real police, was he? Common sense kicked in and I pulled over to the curb and watched him get out of his car, taking his time strolling up to the pickup, checking it out as he came. I turned on the overhead light in the cab, wanting anyone looking out their window to see what went down. But there was no one to see. The houses, with mature and lush plantings, were set too far back from the empty street for the owners, locked inside watching reruns, to hear or see anything. The security guy and I were all alone.

He leaned an arm in my window, a pale hairy arm. "This is a residential area, ma'am. There are children playing here and the speed limit is thirty miles an hour."

His faded red hair was only slightly thinning; the freckles on his face hadn't turned into age spots or pre-cancerous lesions, but his body had run well ahead of him into ugliness. His belly sagged over his belt and his shirt was way too tight. His name tag said Mark Cummings. He was the guy who found Ray John's body.

Anger triumphed fear and words spewed out that were better left unsaid. "I was just visiting your friend, Sheila, your little playmate." Without ever being word-checked by my brain, the words flew out of my mouth like a bird released from a cage. "You remember, the wild party girl Ray John introduced you to." I hadn't even begun to think about this on a conscious level, it was just that wild imagination of mine taking a huge leap. Ray John liked power. While Sheila might not appeal to him, a little old for Ray John's taste, he wouldn't be above humiliating her by shopping her around. He probably used her to pay favors and debts and keep a hold on the old men he came up against in the Preserves. If you can't batter the enemy, find a way of blackmailing them, that's the way Ray John would work. And farming out Sheila to Mark Cummings would make sure he stayed away from the rec hall when Ray John was entertaining; it would keep Mr. Cummings happy and doing Ray John's bidding. It would also keep Mark Cummings from reporting Ray John's involvement with underage girls.

Cummings stepped back from the window of the pickup. "I don't know what you're talking about."

"Right, you stick to that story. Were you into little girls too or did Ray John keep them for himself?"

He moved, fast and violently.

I jerked sideways, away from his hands.

Knuckles white, he gripped the door with both hands, his jaw working back and forth as he fought for control.

A terrible thought overtook my imagination. Maybe Sheila had called him and he had been coming to help her move my dead body. I put the truck in drive and I straight-legged the gas. Not for a second did I worry about running over him, I just wanted to get away.

I looked in the rearview and saw him running for his car. Stupid, stupid, stupid…pissing off yet another person with a gun. I'd just had one scary person drop off the radar in the shape of Ray John and now I'd gained two more. One day soon my mouth would be the death of me.

I took the first right, wanting to be out of sight quickly and then turned sharply left, watching to see if he was following me.

I zigged through the twisting roads, checking my rearview mirror over and over. Twice I was sure I saw Mark Cummings behind me. My hands tightened on the steering wheel, remembering being rammed by Ray John. Twice the vehicles following me turned into driveways as sweat slid down the sides of my body.

The Preserves is confusing to drive in at the best of times and these were far from the best of times. I was too intent on searching for Mark Cummings and cursing out Sheila to concentrate on my driving and it was only when I made the same weird turn for the third time that I realized I was going in circles. I stopped at the intersection, trying to decide where I was and how to get away. A tall black wrought-iron carriage light spread a soft glow over the road in front of me. The street sign said Turkey Trot. I went left instead of right and this time I came to a bridge over the stream and then to the lake. I followed this street around to the clubhouse and by the time I reached it I'd slipped from anger to melt down. I was shaking. I was a danger to myself and everyone on the road. I pulled in behind the clubhouse and parked, a foolish thing to do. I never for a moment thought that if I wanted to avoid Mark Cummings the one place I shouldn't be was at the community center for the Preserves, the place where Ray John had been murdered and where Cummings would come sooner or later. But I wasn't thinking about him coming to the office. I wasn't thinking, period.

The overhead light I'd turned on when Mark Cummings stopped me was still shining; the light made me feel comforted and safe as I collapsed on the steering wheel, trying to breathe through the panic.

The joy in being alive lasted all of a minute and a half. Miguel was right — from now on I was going to mind my own business. I'd messed up big-time by getting involved. Lacey wasn't one bit better off because of anything I'd done; maybe she was even in worse trouble. I vowed right then and there never again to own a gun. They kept ending up in the wrong hands.

But no amount of self-censure could make me believe I deserved what Sheila had done and nothing would ever make me believe she wasn't considering killing me. The only thing that saved my ass was that she didn't want to get caught and she knew she couldn't get away with it. If she had thought she could kill me and make the body disappear, I was dead. I still might be if she could talk Cummings into helping her. Instead of following me, what if he had gone into talk to Sheila? What if she had talked him into helping her to get rid of me? Underneath that beautiful exterior, sophisticated and urban, was a cold calculating creature.

"Hello," a voice said.

CHAPTER 52

I raised my head to see the bride of Chucky. I gave a startled chicken sound. The Kewpie doll from the Royal Palms had turned into some kind of horrible caricature from *The Rocky Horror Picture Show*. "Dammit Janet, you're too old to catch the bouquet," flashed through my mind. Didn't this woman have a mirror? Not even Thia could make this outfit work. The skirt and jacket were black and made out of what looked like material for jogging suits sewn inside out, the seams ragged and curling. I would have thought she'd made a horrible mistake and put it on the wrong way out if it hadn't been studded with silver grommets outlining where a bra would be on a normal-sized person.

"Hi, Sherri."

"It's you," I said, meaning, "it's you, Anita, and not the bride of Chucky."

Anita Charters leaned in towards me and asked, "You okay?"

"Almost," I said and tried to smile, glad to see someone who didn't want to kill me. She might look like a walking garbage bag but at least she was harmless.

"You have a distinctive license plate," she said.

What in hell was she talking about?

"You really don't look well." She moved back from the truck and opened the door. "Come with me, you need a drink."

She said the magic words — a drink. I'd follow her anywhere for a drink. I turned off the overhead to save my battery and grabbed the keys and my bag.

At first I couldn't understand where she was going; she didn't go out of the parking lot or walk around the clubhouse to the path along the lake but headed for the barrier wall around the compound. The wall was faced with cedars. Anita trotted for them at a suicidal speed, determined to smash herself against the concrete, but at the last second slipping between two column-like cedars in the row that fronted the barrier. She disappeared behind the greenery. It was a crazy place to find booze but the promise of a drink was all I needed to follow her.

Between the stucco wall blocking off the street and the thick hedge of cedars was a four-foot-wide grass path. The lights from the back of the recreation center hardly penetrated here, but from what I could see in the dim light it looked as if it was a corridor for utilities. Unconcerned about the lack of illumination, Anita was off, a marathoner in clogs. I figured she must need a drink even more than I did.

We only went about a hundred yards before the path ended in a six-foot wooden gate set in the hedge. Anita opened the gate and went in.

Like an errant child sent for a time-out, the backyard of the house hunkered down in a corner, a triangle up against the eight-foot-high stucco wall in the corner of the compound. Diffused light glowed through a curtained window from the golden stucco house. Totally separate from the other houses, heavy foliage planted up the sides dwarfed the house, and a strange secret garden surrounded an algae-dark kidney-shaped pool built for little people.

The need for alcohol had led me to many a strange place but this one was the strangest of all, eerie even. Anita sped around the flagged edged of the pool towards the back door with me on her heels. She wasn't getting away from me — I so wanted that drink. A motion detector light came on as we approached the back of the house.

The back door was unlocked. "Come in," Anita ordered. She marched into the dim interior without waiting to see if I would follow; not even civility was going to stand between her and the booze. I glanced around the backyard, suddenly wary and trying to decide if I would follow her or go back. What was freaking me out? Maybe it was just the leftover fear from Sheila and her pal. But they couldn't find me here — here I was safe.

The overhead light switched off, plunging the backyard into blackness. Could I find the path back in the dark? How easy would it be to find the gap between the two cedars? It was then I realized what a mistake I'd made stopping at the rec hall. If I went back now who was going to be waiting for me? I shivered and went in.

Tiny wall sconces lit the hall, throwing tall eerie shadows onto the ceilings and casting barely enough light to see. Anita had disappeared but I could hear her. I went down the dark corridor to the front of the house. The room I entered smelt musty and disused, like a load of wet laundry forgotten in a washing machine for days, but what the hell, it came with a drink.

The twilight had already slipped into full night when I had left Sheila's. Although the street lights were on, the plantings seemed to have grown up over the windows of Anita's house, barring any light from the outside. Or maybe no light standards were placed in front of this forgotten house. Either way, no light shone in the windows. Anita switched on a table lamp. Its glow was swallowed by the heavy dark furniture that sat on nearly black hardwood floors. My eyes settled on a silver bar cart. That was all I was interested in.

"Sit," she ordered.

I sat. I would have sworn Anita Charters was a silly ineffectual woman incapable of giving anyone orders but she was doing a pretty good job of sorting me out.

She went to the bar cart, opened the ice bucket and frowned. "I'll get ice." She clumped out, not an ounce of grace in her. Watching her go I realized for the first time that she was bowlegged. I sank back on the cut-velvet sofa and closed my eyes, grateful to be safe. From an adrenalin high, I was sinking into an exhausted funk. A drink was just what I needed and within minutes I had a very hearty Scotch in my hand.

"The police came to see me," Anita told me.

I sipped my Scotch so not interested in her problems.

"Someone told them I had a gun."

"You did, you told them you had a gun."

"What? I did not."

"Well, you pretty much announced it in the Sunset. There're no secrets in bars."

She worked that one around for a while as I made inroads on my Scotch.

"Why were you at Sheila's?" she asked. She waved a hand. "Oh, don't waste time trying to deny it. I was playing bridge. Janie's husband came in and said he saw you at Sheila Dressal's."

"Who is Janie?" One of us wasn't making sense. I took a nice bracing glug of the Scotch. Who the shit cared what the crazy woman was talking about as long as the ice didn't melt in my drink? I hate watered-down Scotch.

Anita had also lost interest in this Janie person. "R.J. Leenders was a pig. He deserved to die."

"Oh yeah, we can all agree on that. Is this Glenlivet?"

"Yes."

"Thought so," I said, proud of my palate, but then the smoky taste of ten-year-old Scotch is pretty distinctive.

"He deserved it," Anita said again.

Hadn't I already agreed with her on this point? I rolled the glass between my hands and tried to decide if I was going to call the police and have Sheila charged with threatening me. It was going to be my word against hers, but should she be allowed to get away with it? She might kill someone the next time. But the cops couldn't arrest you for what you might do, or we'd all be in jail.

I rubbed my forehead. I was starting to feel a little wasted but then it had been that kind of a night. "Where's Thia now?" I don't know why I asked this question but it seemed important.

Anita's head shot up and her jaw jutted out. She said, "Never mind. You forget about Thia. She's going to New York. She's going to have a career, going to be famous. Thia has it all."

And Anita didn't, a duck giving birth to a swan.

"When's she going to New York?"

"As fast as I can get her there." Anita was trying to protect her daughter, wanted to get her out of Florida before some nasty truths came out. How much did Anita know about Thia and Ray John? Or did she have another reason for wanting Thia away? Would she cover for her daughter if she knew she was a murderer?

If I committed a murder, would Ruth Ann cover for me? I already knew Tully would. Maybe that was just how things were with parents. And if Anita was trying so hard to protect Thia, did that mean she knew Thia had killed Ray John? Shit, I didn't want to know. Miguel was right, I should just mind my own business and let the rest of the world do the same. Look where it had almost gotten me with Sheila.

She pointed at me with her highball. "I bet that Sheila was the one mouthing off about me having a gun. She was in the Sunset last night."

"Look, all the cops had to do was run your name through the gun registration. They could find out for themselves if you had a gun. They're probably running a check on everyone in the Preserves."

She thought about it and then drank about half her drink, "Maybe, but Sheila has always been jealous of me."

I managed to keep my thoughts on that to myself.

"Or that Mark Cummings told them. He likely killed RJ. He drove in right after that girl left," Anita said and emptied her glass.

CHAPTER 53

That alarm bell, which had started ringing earlier, far off and distant, now was clanging like I'd stuck my head in the belfry. "You seem to know a lot about it."

She got to her feet and headed to the bar cart. "Everyone does, that's all they talk about out here. The Preserves," she snorted, "more like purgatory."

"People are scared."

She threw ice cubes at her glass. "You bet they are." Her tone was angry and aggressive, not frightened. At least one person in the compound had it together.

"Are people scared about what's going to come out or are they scared because they've got a murderer in their midst?"

"Who the shit cares?" she replied. The weepy woman from the Royal Palms had evaporated.

I tried a new gambit. "Ray John had a hold over a lot of people."

"Not me." She plopped back against the overstuffed cushions, knees spread and heading in opposite directions, clogs dropping off her feet to the floor. "No way I'd let that piece of shit beat me."

"Ray John," I looked for tactful words, "well, he was playing a big part in Thia's life."

"Ray John is dead. Things will get back to normal. People will forget. Ray John Leenders can't hurt anyone now. He was a bastard. Do you know where he was shot?" She made a gun of her hand and pointed to three places as she said, "He was shot in the head, the heart and the crotch, but on him they were all the same organ." She laughed, a nasty depraved sound.

And I laughed. Don't know why it seemed funny but it did. Control seemed to be slipping away. The room was strangely out of kilter. After yeoman amounts of practice, and at great expense to my liver, it seemed I was losing my ability to handle alcohol. I was so sleepy I could barely keep my eyes open. Perhaps it was the combination of near death and the joy of escape, mixed with the adrenalin rush and booze, but a heavy blanket of tiredness was swamping me. I stretched out my arm to put the glass on the table. I misjudged where the table was and it tilted dangerously before I shoved it further onto the ebony surface using both hands. I wasn't well. "Have to go." I struggled out of the depths of the couch, almost made it to my feet and fell back.

"You haven't finished your drink yet, barely touched it." Anita's voice wasn't friendly.

"Air...need to go." I made it to my feet this time.

"You don't look so well. Just stretch out where you are until you feel better."

"Saturday...busiest day." I was walking slowly, dragging my feet through molasses. What was wrong with me? "Short-staffed." I headed for the front door and not back out the way I came in.

From behind me I felt a hand clamp on my shoulder, fingers

digging in, Anita holding me back with her cruel and painful claws.

"You know, don't you?"

"Don't know." The head shake to go with the words threw me off balance. "Don't know."

"You were there that night. I thought it was a young girl but it was you. I saw your license plate as you were leaving, RIF RAF, and you saw me coming through the hedge, didn't you?"

"No, no, wasn't there."

"I made a mistake at the Sunset when I told you RJ was shot three times."

Bingo, the thing I'd forgotten and wanted to ask Styles — how many times was Ray John shot?

"The cops haven't told anyone that piece of news, have they? And I shouldn't have told you about my gun."

"Did you use it to shoot Ray John?" Stupid question. Wrong, wrong, wrong thing to say. Why did I want to know?

"Didn't have to, RJ's was right there on the desk, just waiting for me." She smiled at me. "Good of him to provide the weapon. No one will ever connect it with me." She smiled again. "And I went out to shoot my own gun so any powder residue could be explained. Smart of me, wasn't it?"

I backed away from her, my hand scrambling for the door, hunting for the knob, but she grabbed me by the front of my blouse.

"You aren't going anywhere," she said and shook me.

What was wrong with me? I couldn't defend myself, couldn't make my arms work enough to push her away.

"He called me an ugly old skank. He shouldn't have done that."

"What did you give me?" was what I tried to say but my tongue was too large and it came out all garbled. My body, growing heavy and no longer obeying, slumped. Only Anita's grip on my shirt held me up.

"You are such a nosey bitch," Anita told me. A noise came from outside the front door…she stopped and looked at the door, her eyes widening as she heard the key.

The front door opened and I heard footsteps. I couldn't make my body cooperate enough to turn my head and see what was happening.

Thia walked around us.

"What are you doing home?" Anita demanded, still gripping my shirt.

Thia looked from me to her mother and said, "What's up?"

"Why are you here? You weren't supposed to come home," Anita screamed. "Go away, you can't be here."

I thrust my weight backwards towards the open door. The force of my momentum ripped my shirt from Anita's grip and threw her off balance. Thia caught my arm as I stumbled. She held me upright.

Anita recovered quickly, reaching out for me but Thia used her right arm to hold her mother off.

"You don't look too good, Sherri. How much did you drink?" Thia asked me.

"Few sips, don't understand." I had to get out of there. I twisted my body, pushing forward with my weight, intent on getting out the door.

"What did you give her, Mom?" It was hard to tell if Thia's hand on my arm was helping or holding me back. "Have you been in my room?"

I threw myself forward and bumped up hard against the edge of the open door, rolled off it and out onto the step.

I could hear them arguing behind me. I didn't look back. I tried to run but it was more of a stagger.

CHAPTER 54

I wobbled down the flagstone path, not running as much as I was trying to keep going forward and stay on my feet. The uneven walkway curved left to the drive where the small sports car sat, still running with the door open. Could I beat them to the car, close the door and drive away?

Momentum and a misstep sent me stumbling across the flagstones and onto the grass away from the car. Control was gone. I couldn't go back to the vehicle. I hurtled forward across the front lawn. Escape was all.

Somewhere in the night I heard laughter and a voice calling goodnight. Safe, a haven, that's what I needed. I stumbled towards the voices, over the curb and onto the street. Arms windmilling, I fought to stay upright.

"Wait, wait," Anita called behind me.

Across the street a man and a woman were getting into a Jaguar.

"Help," I croaked, stumbling towards them. "Help." My arms flapped.

The man turned. "Sherri?" He started towards me.

I focused on staying upright, intent on the man in front of me and I fell into his arms as the world went dark.

My eyes opened to see beautiful brown eyes in an equally beautiful brown face. "How are you feeling?" the nurse asked.

"Bad." I closed my eyes and left the world again.

The next time I opened my eyes, Dr. Travis said, "Welcome back."

"You were there," I said.

"Yes," he answered. "I was there."

"Thank you."

He smiled. "You're welcome." I looked down. He was holding my hand. How strange was that? In the nearly ten years I'd been married to Jimmy he had never been more than polite. I'd practically done cartwheels to get Jimmy's parents to like me but it had never happened. Now he was holding my hand and as I watched he covered both of our hands with his other one as if I might escape. Very strange. I closed my eyes.

Styles' voice called me back. "What the hell happened?"

I ignored him and slid my head to my right on the pillow and looked at Dr. Travis. "What was in that drink?" My mouth was thick and wooly.

"We think it was Rohypnol." He saw my confusion and tried again, "Flunitrazepam."

"A roofie," Styles put in.

"Good god," I wailed. "Date-raped by the bride of Chucky."

"What?" Styles said. "Try and make sense." He was annoyed with me. Well, he better get used to it because there was a whole lot more to come. His annoyance would soon know no bounds.

"How?" I asked.

This question Styles seemed to understand. "The mother and

daughter are denying any knowledge of what happened to you. The mother said she found you in the parking lot, said you were sick so she brought you home. Said you'd been at some other woman's house and it must have been put in a drink there."

"I didn't have anything to drink there. Anita slipped it into the Scotch she gave me."

"Why?"

"Because she made a mistake when she told me Ray John had been shot three times." Carefully, I turned my head to face him. "I forgot to tell you."

His jaw clenched. "The gun registered to her wasn't a twenty-five. She didn't use her own gun to shoot Leenders."

"Well, it was Anita that gave me the roofie. She probably got the drug from Thia, who got it from Ray John. That would be my guess. Lots of weird stuff was going on out there. I don't think I'd ever have gotten out of that house alive if Thia hadn't come home."

"I need details," Styles said.

"Need to sleep."

"No, Sherri," Dr. Travis said, shaking my shoulder gently. "You must try and stay awake. It will be better. Talk to the detective, it will help you stay awake."

"Okay." I licked my lips with a tongue like a slab of liver.

"Here…" Dr. Travis let go of my hand and slipped an arm under my shoulders, lifting me off the bed. "You need to drink as much as you can." He brought a glass to my lips.

Not even my lips would behave. Nothing was working and the glass was at the wrong angle. More water spilled out the sides of my mouth than ran down my throat.

"Sorry," Dr. Travis said. "I should have gotten you a straw. Go get a straw," he said to Styles.

Styles trotted off just as he was told.

"Wow," I said in disbelief. "He listened to you. He never listens to me, must be all that medical training."

He laughed and laid me gently back against the pillows. He went to the small bathroom and came back with a towel and started dabbing lightly at my face and damp chest. "I've got you all wet."

Had the planet spun upside-down while I was asleep? "Like the converters we had as kids," I told him.

He looked confused. "What?"

"Toy man that turned into a car."

Dr. Travis said, "I don't understand."

I shook my head. "Neither do I." Dr. Travis was a robot who had converted into a human. Maybe it would last, but I doubted if he could change a lifetime of ice. I'd best not give in to this nice side of him, keep myself in check until I saw if this was an aberration. "I was surprised to see you there…and grateful," I told him.

"Bernice and I were just coming out of John and Judy Wood's after having dinner with them. I was so surprised to see you stumbling towards us with that horrible woman coming after you." He put the towel on the night table. "She was going to kill you, wasn't she?"

"Yes," I answered, the reality of it only now sinking in.

Styles came back with the straw and put it in the glass. This time Dr. Travis used a button to raise the bed. Styles held out the glass and I sipped from it. I was pretty sure I could do all this for myself but I was enjoying the novelty of being fussed over. Besides, it was giving me some time to sort through things.

"Enough," Styles said and plopped the glass back on the night table. "Talk."

Dr. Travis answered for me. "Take it easy. She's still woozy."

"All right," I mumbled. "This was what happened. Lacey told me about Ray John meeting a woman in the Preserves he had once arrested for prostitution when he was in the sheriff's department. Lacey didn't know her name but it was easy enough to figure out who it was. It was Sheila Dressal."

"What?" Dr. Travis gasped. "She's engaged to a guy I play golf with."

Styles wasn't distracted. In a cold and angry voice he asked, "Why didn't you just call me and tell me?"

"I didn't want to just destroy her life," I said. "She was starting over. I saw her the day after Ray John died. I knew she was celebrating his death, definitely relieved that he was dead, but I didn't think she killed him."

Styles snorted with disgust. "You're equipped to judge?"

"Yeah, you're right, but like I said, I couldn't just drop her in it, could I?"

"No," Dr. Travis said and patted my hand, which he was holding again. When had that happened? "Being you, you wouldn't want to hurt her."

Okay, this was just too weird. "What?" I slid sideways on the pillow to look up at him. "Who are you?"

"You still should have called," Styles said.

"I was stopped for speeding by Mark Cummings." I told him what I figured had been happening in the Preserves. "And then I got lost and Anita captured me. When she took that shortcut home behind the recreation hall she saw the license plate on the truck. Like Mark Cummings, she saw it the night Ray John was murdered and remembered."

"Stupid plate," Styles said.

"It was Anita who killed Ray John Leenders." My brain took a right turn. "Was he shot three times — in the head, the heart and the crotch?"

"How did you know that, it wasn't released to the public?"

"Anita told me. She enjoyed telling me. She didn't think I was ever going to get out of that house. And I wouldn't have gotten out if Thia hadn't have come home unexpectedly."

Styles didn't need to hear any more. "Is there anything else I should know before I go down the hall and tell her she's under arrest?"

"Down the hall? What is she doing in here?"

Styles raised his eyes to Dr. Travis.

I turned to look at the man holding my hand. "It was Bernice," he said. "She saw that woman chasing you and took a swing at her with her bag. Dropped her like a sack of potatoes right onto the curb. She wasn't unconscious but she did seem confused so I thought it was best that she come to the hospital in case of concussion."

"And in case of a lawsuit," I put in.

"That too," Dr. Travis said, but he wasn't looking too nervous. Actually, he was looking quite pleased. "Bernice always was a fine athlete with a wicked backhand."

I started to laugh but it was too painful. I put my hands up to my head where the guys with hammers were.

"Take it easy," Dr. Travis cautioned me before turning to Styles. "I think she's had enough for now, don't you?"

Styles went on a bit about getting a statement from me and then left the room without a goodbye, plenty pissed off with me. I didn't care. My head hurt and my stomach wasn't feeling too good either. I just wanted to sleep.

That wasn't going to happen. There was a racket in the hall and Tully burst into the room with a nurse on his heels.

"It's all right, nurse," Dr. Travis said and rose from the bed where he'd been sitting. "This is the patient's father." He held out his hand and shook hands with Tully. "She's going to be fine, a little hungover but that's all. She can go home whenever she's ready. I'll go and talk to her real doctor and get it cleared." He turned back to me. "And you," he leaned over and pecked me on the forehead, "try to stay out of trouble. Bernice may not be there to rescue you the next time."

Tully patted Dr. Travis on the back. "Thanks, and thank Bernice for me."

"Sure," Dr. Travis replied and left the room.

"Well, beam me up, Scotty. I've seen it all," I said. "What are you doing here?"

"Bernice called me and told me you were in the hospital. I've been waiting forever to get in. They said the doctor and a cop were in here and I should wait until they were done. Couldn't wait any longer. How you doin', little girl?"

"Like the doctor said, fine except for a hangover but we both know they won't kill you."

"Are you ready to go home?"

I threw back the covers. "Call in the dogs and piss on the fire," I said. "Let's get the hell out of here."

CHAPTER 55

Four days later, nervous and dreading what was about to take place, I silently rode the elevator at the Tradewinds with Tully and Uncle Ziggy.

Clay waited at the open door to the apartment as we got off the elevator. Tully stepped forward and held out his hand to Clay. "Good to see you again, son."

"You two know each other?"

"Yup," Tully said. "I used to hunt with his pa."

Nothing ever stays tidy in my life; nothing is ever what it seems. Humiliating to know how unaware and confused I really am. While I thought I was keeping the compartments of my life locked well away from each other, they'd been doing their own thing.

"Two old crackers like Bill Adams and me, course we knew each other. Sorry to hear of his death, son, he was a good man."

"Thank you, sir, five years and I still miss him."

I turned to Uncle Ziggy. "And you and Clay are partners on your property?"

"Seems like," he said. His skin was red and shiny but his smile was big and happy. "Clay and I are real close."

I'd never really had any control over anything, not Ray John, not Sheila…and sure as hell not Anita. She told Styles she walked in and found the gun on the table and shot Ray John in a moment of madness over what he'd done to her little girl. She thought it was Ray John's gun, and with luck it would stay that way.

But Anita denied trying to kill me, wasn't telling anyone her plans for me. My first words to her when I looked up at her from the steering wheel had been, "It's you." She thought I was saying, "It was you who killed Ray John," when what I had meant was "It's you, Anita, and not the bride of Chucky."

I think she decided right there to kill me. Go figure, a little misunderstanding that nearly got me killed when I hadn't a clue she'd shot Ray John. But there was no way Styles could prove she meant to do anything but drug me.

"Are you going to keep us standing here all day while you catch flies with that open mouth?" Tully asked.

Clay reached out and took a small night bag from Tully's hand. "Come this way. I'll show you Ziggy's room."

Halfway across the living room, I called to Clay. "I don't know why you're smiling. Mrs. Whiting called this morning to say she could no longer work here."

"Good," Clay said. "That woman drove me crazy."

The End

ACKNOWLEDGMENTS

I would like to thank Maureen Rowell for her generous support of Artspring with her purchase of a character naming.

I hope Peter says it's brilliant.